ALEX CAGE
CLEAN FAST-PACED ACTION THRILLERS

JOIN THE READER'S LIST

Get the latest releases and exclusive giveaways - sign up to the Alex Cage Reader List:

www.AlexCage.com/signup

ALSO BY ALEX CAGE

Orlando Black Series

Carolina Dance

Bayside Boom

Family Famous (Novella)

Bet on Black

Leroy Silver Series

Contracts & Bullets

Aloha & Bullets

Politics Thieves & Bullets

Get the latest releases and exclusive giveaways, sign up to the Alex Cage Reader List.

www.AlexCage.com/signup

BAYSIDE BOOM

AN ORLANDO BLACK NOVEL

ALEX CAGE

There are thousands of words in this book, and yet that's not enough to express all the ways she encourages me. So I'll keep it short:

To my wife, Devette.

BAYSIDE BOOM

KEEPING IN TOUCH with family has become difficult in the modern world. Despite the technological leaps and the many avenues of long-distance contact, people are still very much disconnected from each other. Such were the thoughts Orlando Black contemplated as he sat on a bench facing the Alcatraz Shoal. The water was still and the sky was clear. The busy sound of a large crowd and many enticing aromas drifted from the various restaurants and food stands behind him. The day was sunny, quiet, and cool and Black felt comfortable in his boots, jeans, T-shirt, and light coat. He removed his cell phone from his pocket and looked at the screen before poking at it and holding it to his ear. After a few rings, a female's voice eased on the line.

"Hello?"

"How are you?" Black asked.

"Wow. Well, if it isn't the winner of this year's Worst Brother Award."

"I won again this year?"

"You seem to win every year." The voice chuckled. "Where are you?"

"Fisherman's Wharf."

"What? You're in San Francisco?"

"Yep. I thought I'd drop by and surprise my little sister."

"Aw, how sweet. Maybe you don't deserve that award after all. But I'm actually not in town."

"Oh really? Where are you?"

"I'm in Chicago right now."

"Chicago?"

"You know I've been bouncing around for work since the whole military thing. I don't think the Corps would take me back."

"Well, you did break your C.O.'s jaw."

"That sexist pig had it coming. It can be so hard for women in the Marines."

"So what are you doing in Chicago?"

"I have a private security gig I'm working."

"Be careful with those companies."

"Oh, now you want to put on your big bro pants and protect me?"

"I'm serious."

"Chill out."

"Olivia Jane Black, I mean it!"

"Okay, okay, I'll be careful, and you know I don't like it when you use my full name like that."

"That's all I'm asking. There's no need to put yourself in harm's way, especially when you don't need the money."

"I can take care of myself."

Black nodded. "Yep, I know."

"Hey, have you been to see Mom and Dad?"

"No, not yet."

"Make sure you visit them."

"We'll see," he shrugged.

Olivia sighed. "Look, I know they're not blood, but I feel they're my mom and dad. Go see them, okay?"

"We'll see," Black repeated.

Multiple voices on the other end of the line filled his ear.

"I have to go," Olivia said. "I have a meeting. Love you, bye."

"Hey, be careful," Black said, but the call ended before he could finish speaking. "You too, little sis," he muttered to himself.

He sat on the bench for a while and enjoyed the view. After some time, the food smells made his stomach growl. *I better get something to eat*, he thought, patting his stomach.

He stood up from the bench and walked across the wooden pier and up a sidewalk, where he joined throngs of pedestrians. The streets were filled with food carts, balloon artists, musicians, and painters. Just about all types of performance entertainment were present. Black fought through the crowd and crossed the street, where he ran into an entirely different group of people. They were marching around the deck of Pier 39, thrusting large signs into the air. He read a few of the signs. One read, *I can have as many kids as I want*. Another, *In memory of the brave in New York*, and yet another, *Say NO to P.L. 324!* He stopped walking, curious. A young lady from the group approached him.

With her fingertips, she brushed her fine blond hair behind her ear and smiled. "Hi, sir, are you here to march with us?"

"What?"

The young lady extended a flier. "We're here to stop the public law 324 that the president is trying to pass."

Black looked down at the flier. In large font stood the number 324 with a circle around it and a line crossing through it. Below the circle was written, *Kids are precious*, and under that there was a description that compared a president he hadn't voted for nor cared about to a donkey. There was also today's date, a time frame, and the location of Fisherman's Wharf. Black looked at the girl and was about to speak, but a guy who looked to be in his early twenties stepped up and put his arms around the young lady, kissing her on the cheek.

"What's up, babe, who's this?" he asked.

"This is a gentleman who I believe wants to march with us," she said, smiling and raising her eyebrows.

"Oh, so you're here for the protest?"

Black shook his head. "I don't even know what you're protesting."

"324," the guy said.

Black stared at him.

"Basically the government is saying if we have more than five children we have to pay a population tax. Crazy, right?"

"We should be able to have as many kids as we want," the young lady added.

"So are you guys planning on having six kids?" Black asked.

"No," they said in sync.

"Do you have any kids?"

"No," they said again.

Black said nothing.

"But we have rights," the girl said.

"Yeah, it's just wrong, dude. And we're not going to let what the government did in New York scare us," the guy said.

Black squinted as the couple was pulled away by the crowd, marching down the street and chanting in protest.

He shrugged and walked off across the pier. As he entered a restaurant, he noticed a camera above the door. Inside were many empty tables, a couple of waiters, and a bartender. The ceiling fan squeaked and the smell of seafood and alcohol stuffed the place. Black creaked across the wooden floor towards the bar. He sat on a stool and lifted a menu from the counter. The bartender was cleaning a glass. He wore a white button-down shirt with the sleeves rolled up to his forearms. There was a black apron across his waist above his black slacks. He finished washing the glass and draped the cloth he used to dry it over his shoulder before looking over at Black.

"So, what can I start you off with?" he asked.

"I'll start with a water," Black said.

"You got it." The bartender grabbed a glass, filled it with water, and slid it in front of Black. "It's a madhouse out there, huh?"

Black began looking through the menu. "The West Coast is usually a madhouse when it comes to political issues," he said.

"Well, the East Coast has been chaotic as of late too," the bartender said, craning over and wiping the countertop.

Black looked at him.

The bartender stood straight, looking at Black. "Oh, you haven't been watching the news?" he asked.

"I've been on the road a lot."

The bartender grabbed the remote and turned on the TV, which hung suspended over the bar.

Black looked as the screen flicked on, displaying some news broadcast. A pretty news anchor was speaking. Imposed next to her face was a rectangular box showing footage of New York City, near Times Square. There was a lot of smoke and people. Emergency responders were everywhere. Black's sharp eyes quickly picked out *324* and *bombing* in the headline at the bottom of the screen.

"It's still unclear how the peaceful protest of two days ago turned into a chaotic and gruesome scene," the reporter said.

Black sighed and shook his head before turning his attention back to the menu.

"Pretty unfortunate," the bartender said.

"Yes, it is."

"Some believe the government had something to do with it."

"So I heard."

"What do you make of it?"

Black looked at the bartender. "Make of what? The bombing or the law?"

"Well, both I guess."

"I don't know, but I don't think the government is behind the bombing."

"What makes you say that?"

"If government officials want something to happen, they create laws, which is what they're doing in this case. It's business to them. Whoever is behind the bombing feels a personal attachment to what they believe the law stands for. This person feels victimized. They probably feel that if the law were in place they would've never been a victim."

The bartender nodded.

"As for the law itself, I don't think I care either way. I don't have any kids nor do I plan on having any."

"Personally I'm for it. I don't care what all these rights activists are saying. If you're collecting a check from the government and you have more than three kids, you should get snipped."

"Snipped?"

"Man, you really haven't been watching the news. If you get government assistance and you have more than three kids, 324 says you have to get snipped or tied to continue receiving assistance."

"I heard it was five kids."

"That's for everyone, assistance or not. If you have more than five kids you have to pay some type of tax."

Black quietly looked at the menu.

The bartender began washing glasses. "It makes sense to me," he said. "I believe it'll help with many of the issues we face in this country. I was reading somewhere that something like ninety percent of criminals come from a fatherless home."

The bartender continued talking while Black stared up at the TV, watching scenes from the tragic event.

•   •   •

FORTY MINUTES LATER Black was back outside. The group of protesters had nearly doubled in size. He shook his head. *What do they believe they're going to accomplish?* He began to thread through the noisy crowd. Then something caught his eye. One of the protesters, a slender guy, was wearing a dark coat, cap, and shades. In one of his hands was a sign that read, *NO 324!* and in his other a small duffel bag. He eased his way through the people, blending in. He stopped and carefully looked around before gently dropping the duffel bag to the wooden deck of the pier. He then walked away quickly. Black walked after the guy, but then he heard his commanding officer's voice from back in his military days: *If they drop it to the ground, chances are it can make a kaboom sound.* He looked at the duffel bag and spotted some wiring through the zipper slit. Squatting, he unzipped the bag. His eyes slightly widened, his mouth gaped open, and he felt drops of sweat blooming around his neck. Inside the bag was a home-made bomb. Small, but big enough to cause some damage.

Black snatched the bag, pushing and shoving through the crowd. "Out of the way! Move! Get out of the way!" He ran to the edge of the pier and lobbed the bag over the waves with all his might. His body draped over the railing as he watched the bag sink into the water. As it dropped just below the surface there was an ear-rocking boom. He dove face down on the deck as the whole pier shook, people ran and screamed, and the smell of the ocean water swept through the crowd. Black lay drenched on the wooden planks with the taste of saltwater in his mouth. He watched the rushing feet of people, the fins of fish flapping on the deck around him. Then his eyes fell on the back of the guy with the cap. He was power-walking away from the pier, peeking over his shoulder every two seconds.

Black grimaced and gritted his teeth. He jumped to his feet and went after the guy.

When the guy looked over his shoulder and saw Black's

approach, his fast walk turned into an all-out sprint. He raced through the frantic crowd, slapping and elbowing a path.

Black chased him onto the street. The sound of tires screeching rang heavy in the air—the man was nearly hit by a car. Black continued after him as he turned onto a road with a steep downward slope. The guy looked back, lost his footing, and tumbled for a couple steps, losing his hat and exposing his sandy blond hair in the process, but lurched back to his feet. Black carefully shuffled downhill behind him. Cutting through an alley, one and then the other crossed another street and ran into another crowd of people. Black ducked in between people, maintaining a visual on the man but keeping invisible to him. The man stopped and scanned over both shoulders before slowly jogging towards a trolley bus. He entered the packed trolley and stood near the exit, staring out at the surrounding herd of pedestrians.

Black sprinted after the departing trolley, hopped onto the back bumper, and remained hidden from its passengers in a squatting position. The trolley crept down the road for a few minutes before stopping. The man stepped off and slowly looked around, seemingly concluding that he was in the clear. Black jumped from behind the trolley and rushed him. Noticing him with alarm, the guy pushed a woman in the crowd towards his pursuer.

Catching her and moving her to the side with a, "Excuse me, ma'am," Black continued chasing after his suspect.

The pursuit continued through the mass around the trolley and up an inclined street. They raced, approaching a couple of construction workers tending to the sidewalk. The sandy-haired man forced his way through the workers, while Black skipped off a nearby wall, avoiding the workers entirely.

"Hey! Watch where you're going!" one of the workers shouted as the pair bolted by.

The distance between them shrank. The guy was running

out of gas, and Black was right on his tail. They shot past a hotel and a restaurant, where the aromas of freshly baked bread, wine, and pasta and the sound of table talk mixed in the air.

Enough of this! Black grabbed one of the chairs from the restaurant patio and slung it with great force. The chair smacked against the guy's back. Toppling to his belly, he skidded across the pavement. Sirens wailed close by.

Black lifted the man by the back of his shirt and threw him against the wall of the narrow alley next to the restaurant. "Where are you going so fast?" he said with his forearm to the guy's throat, wedging him against the wall.

Out of breath, the man gasped, "Get off me!" He struggled free and raised his fist.

Black shrugged fearlessly. "Really?"

The man swung at him but missed, and the next second, Black's fist connected with his gut. The guy hunched over and something fell from his pocket, hitting the ground.

Black ripped the guy's sunglasses off and was taken aback as he met a pair of blue eyes. "What? You… you're pretty young."

The young man staggered backwards and then ran down the alleyway. Black knelt and picked up the device that had fallen from his pocket, putting it in his own. He looked on as the young guy disappeared around the corner. He took a step after him, but thought better of it as rolling sirens invaded the area. Flashing red and blue lights passed by as Black ducked out of the alley and walked in the direction of his car.

CHAPTER
TWO

"WHAT IS THAT?" Lead Agent Jake Toben asked, leaning over a seated man and pointing at a spot on the screen.

The man operating the computer looked over his shoulder at Toben. "It's not the best footage, and it's hard to make out with all of the smoke and chaos."

"That's why I have you here, computer whiz Agent Boyar. We need to make sense of the footage we have."

"I'm hardly a computer whiz," Boyar replied, pushing his glasses up the bridge of his nose. "Why are we spending so many resources on this anyways, when it happened on the other side of the country? Shouldn't the local New York agencies handle this?"

"You're not being a team player, Agent Boyar. An attack on one part of the nation is an attack on us as a whole. That's probably the biggest threat to this country," Toben said, patting Boyar on the back.

"What is?"

"That we don't walk in agreement. We don't work together like we should."

Boyar shook his head. "Or it could be that you're afraid the director will do away with our unit, and you want to justify our existence by butting into someone else's territory."

"You're so negative. You should try being more positive."

"I'm just saying, the unit is small, there's only three of us, and the director doesn't seem to like you very much."

Toben sighed, looking down at Boyar then back at the computer screen. "Hey, hey, zoom in there," he said, pointing again. Boyar zoomed in on a person wearing a dark coat, cap, and shades.

"Huh…"

"What is it?" Boyar asked.

"That's a female."

"It's hard to make out, but I'd say yes. A redhead. Her hair is tied into a knot under the cap."

"Right."

"So what?"

"She seems pretty calm considering all the chaos happening around her."

Boyar shrugged.

The office door swung open. Inside stepped an athletic brunette, wearing a dark pantsuit with a DHS jacket.

"Hey, you two," she said, smiling, "I have some news."

"Agent Chapp, what do you have?" Toben asked.

"H—Hi, Ashley," Boyar said with an eager smile.

She innocently winked at Boyar. "Hi, Victor," she said before facing Toben. "There was an attack near Fisherman's Wharf just an hour ago. It's very similar to the attack that took place in New York."

Wrinkles crossed Boyar's forehead. "So there was a bomb?"

"Yes. It's all over the news now," Ashley said.

Boyar stood from his chair, grabbed the remote, and turned on the TV.

"Wait… There was a protest today, the same as in New York," Toben said.

"Exactly," Ashley replied.

"Casualties?"

"Apparently none."

"Really?"

The news broadcast displayed on the TV showed a reporter questioning one of the protesters on the pier of Fisherman's Wharf.

"So can you describe what you saw here today, sir?" the reporter asked.

The man cleared his throat, "Well, we were all out here protesting peacefully, then out of nowhere there was a loud boom. Water was everywhere and people were running and screaming all over the place…"

Toben shook his head. "Something is not adding up. We need to get down there now," he said.

"Sure thing, I'll drive," Ashley offered.

"Okay," Toben said, throwing on his DHS jacket.

"I'll go get the car."

Boyar watched as Ashley left the office, Toben noticed wryly.

"That's not going to happen, and since you two are in the same unit, it *shouldn't* happen," he said.

"What are you talking about?"

"You know what I'm talking about."

Boyar chuckled, shaking his head.

"Look, Boyar, I need you to stay back here just in case Agent Chapp and I need some information."

Boyar threw his hand at Toben. "Yeah, yeah, I got it," he said, turning back to his computer.

"Thank you," Toben said, walking to the door. "Oh by the way," he called to Boyar, who looked back at him. "We're no longer butting into someone else's territory now that there's a potentially connected incident in our backyard. See, think positive. We're all in this together," Toben continued, smiling.

Boyar shook his head at his computer.

Toben exited the office and walked in the direction of the elevators.

"Agent Toben," a voice called.

He turned and was met by a middle-aged woman. She had caramel-colored hair and wore a white blouse with a long grey skirt.

"Director Hanten, how can I help you?"

"Where are you off to?"

"Going to follow up on a lead I have."

Hanten raised an eyebrow. "Oh really, what lead is that?" she inquired.

Toben hunched his shoulders. "Just came across my desk. I'll let you know more when I find out more about it."

Hanten nodded. "I'll hold you to that. Good day, Jake," she said.

"Good day, Barbra," Toben said as he entered the elevator, glaring at Hanten's back as the doors closed. "Ahh, evil," he sighed, poking the first-floor button.

As the elevator jerked into motion, Toben's phone rang. Lifting it from his pocket, he stared at it briefly before ignoring the call and replacing it in his pocket. The elevator stopped on the first floor and he made his way through the lobby, out to the front of the building, and into the car with Ashley.

"Ready, boss?" she said, biting her bottom lip.

"Let's go," he replied softly, with a smile on his face.

Ashley put the car in gear and cruised down the road, driving a few blocks before turning into an empty parking lot. She threw the car in park, killed the engine, unbuckled her seatbelt, and jumped around Toben's neck, kissing his face.

"I couldn't wait to get you alone," she said.

Toben's phone rang again, vibrating between them. "Hold on, one sec," he said, pulling the phone out of his pocket. He ignored the call once more.

Ashley rolled her eyes and exhaled. "So is that her?"

"Yes."

"I thought you were going to tell her about us."

"It's not that easy."

"What do you mean?"

"We do have a kid together."

"Oh here we go again. Jake, we had this conversation before. You need to decide what it is you want."

Toben grabbed Ashley's hand. "Look, this is a very complicated situation. You knew that getting into it. Situations like this take time. Plus, with us being in the same unit and Hanten putting our team under a microscope—"

Ashley pulled her hand back. "I get it. Let's just keep it professional," she interrupted. She buckled her seatbelt and fired up the engine.

"Ashley, wait—"

"Just call me Agent Chapp, please. So where to, Agent Toben? Fisherman's Wharf, right?"

Toben dropped his head, nodding slightly. "Yes," he sighed.

THE DRIVE TO Fisherman's Wharf was short and quiet. Neither Toben nor Ashley said another word during the ride. The area was swarming with law enforcement and emergency responders. The two parked on the street, slid from the car, ducked under the caution tape, and walked towards the pier. A local San Francisco police officer approached them, stopping them by raising his open palm to chest height.

"I'm sorry, but you're not allowed past this point," he said.

Ashley removed her badge, flipping it open. "I'm Agent Ashley Chapp and this is Agent Jake Toben. We're with the Department of Homeland Security," she asserted.

"Oh. Well, in that case, welcome to the party."

"Can you fill us in on what happened here?" Toben asked.

"Sure, follow me," the officer responded.

As they followed the officer onto the deck, Toben's phone rang. "You two go ahead. I have to take this," he said, pulling it out of his pocket for the third time.

Ashley rolled her eyes and followed behind the officer.

"Hi, honey," Toben said into the phone.

"Hi," a woman's voice answered. "I called you twice and didn't get you."

"Yeah, I know. I'm busy with this case."

"Well, Matt is in trouble again at school."

"Again? What did he do this time?"

"The principal mentioned something about skipping school. I was so mad I tuned some of it out. He wants us to meet him at the school."

"Aaah… sweetie, do you think you can handle the meeting yourself? I'm on this case."

"Of course you are."

"What does that mean?"

"It means your family takes a back seat to your job." She raised her voice.

"Wait, Kristi, now that's not fair. I work matters of national security."

"You say that every time."

"That's because there are a lot of threats to national security."

"I think it's because of parents like you that there are so many threats to the nation. I'll be fine going on my own… again. Enjoy the rest of your day." Kristi hung up.

"Kristi, Kristi… ah boy." Toben exhaled, placing his phone in his pocket and creaking over the pier's deck to Ashley and the officer.

"Are we good?" the officer asked Toben as he approached.

Ashley looked at Toben, eyebrows raised in anticipation of his answer.

"Yes," he answered, nodding.

"Well, good," the officer replied. "Okay, as I was starting to tell Agent Chapp here, witnesses saw two men. One was a slender white man. He was wearing a cap and sunglasses. The other was a black man with an athletic physique. From what we gather, the white man dropped a small bag on the deck and the black man picked it up and tossed it into the water over there."

"That's it?" Ashley inquired.

The officer shrugged. "The good news is no one was hurt."

Toben looked around the pier and noticed a security camera outside of a restaurant. He looked at Ashley. "The eye in the sky may be able to provide more information," he said, throwing his head in the direction of the restaurant.

The two thanked the officer for his assistance and walked over to the restaurant. Inside was quiet—no customers, and apparently no one working. The employees were standing around talking and looking out the restaurant windows at all the activity. They stared hard at Toben and Ashley as they entered.

"Is there a manager here?" Toben asked the hypnotized employees.

All of them, mainly young adults, looked at the pair with bewilderment. Eventually one of them pointed towards the bar, where a bartender was wiping the counter.

"Thank you," Toben said sarcastically.

"Talk about customer service," Ashley followed up, as they walked towards the bar.

"Excuse us, sir," Toben greeted the bartender. "Are you the manager here?"

The bartender stopped wiping and looked up. "Yes, I am."

Toben flashed his badge. "I'm Agent Toben, and this is Agent Chapp. We're with the Department of Homeland Security."

"Nice to meet the two of you. How can I help you?"

"The camera outside, does it work?"

"Yes, sir, it does."

"Was it recording during the… incident?" Ashley asked.

"Yes, ma'am, it was."

"Great, can we see it?"

"Sure. Follow me."

He led them through a dark hall to the back of the restaurant. There was a small six-by-six room, lit only by the glow of computer monitors. It smelled of heated electronics and dust.

"Here we are," the manager said, stepping inside the room and moving behind a desk with a mouse and keyboard.

"Can you roll the footage taken just before the explosion?" Ashley asked.

"Sure thing," he said, typing on the keyboard then moving the mouse.

The footage popped up on the monitor showing law enforcement walking around and then, with a click of the mouse, the figures moved backwards in fast motion as static raced across the screen.

"Did you notice anyone or anything unusual before the explosion?" Ashley asked as the footage rolled back.

"No, we've been pretty quiet. The last customer we had was some guy, but he left just before the chaos."

"Some guy? What did he look like?" Toben inquired.

"I don't know… he looked to be in good shape, about your complexion, dark jeans, plain shirt, light coat, seemed normal, but smart—"

"What do you mean, smart?" Ashley interrupted.

"Well, we had a discussion about that law 324 and the bombing in New York. Apparently, he didn't know anything about it before today."

"And?"

"For someone who just heard about it today, he seemed to

know a lot about the psychology behind the bomber. Like, what would make him tick."

Ashley's forehead wrinkled above squinted eyes.

"Hold right there," Toben requested.

"Here?" the bartender asked, pausing the video.

"No. Go up a couple frames."

He clicked the video up a few frames. "That's him. That's the guy I was talking about."

"Are you sure?"

"Yes."

"I see you have a printer. Can you print that frame out?" Ashley asked.

"Yes, I can."

"We will need a copy of all the footage from today too," Toben said.

"I can do that too," the bartender replied.

The printer powered up, zipping and jerking for a few moments before the manager removed the printed image from the tray and handed it to Toben.

"Here you go. I'll start copying the footage to a file."

"Thank you," Toben said before snapping a picture of the image and typing away on his phone. He then threw his head towards the doorway, gesturing for Ashley to follow him. The two stepped outside of the room. Ashley folded her arms with her head slightly tilted and her lip line arching downward.

"I just sent the image to the team email addresses," Toben said. "Call Boyar and have him run a search for this guy. I'll wait for the copy of the footage."

"Sure thing, boss," Ashley pouted, walking to the front of the restaurant.

Toben shook his head and sighed, looking down and focusing on the image. "Who are you and where are you?" he whispered.

CHAPTER
THREE

BLACK WAS DRIVING in the financial district. He was on Kearny Street, one of the busiest streets in the entire city. Running the length of the street on both sides were shops and restaurants. There were many people hiking up the vibrant sidewalks, in and out of the various stores and eateries. The sound of traffic and music outside enveloped the car. *I don't remember it being this busy the last time I was here*, Black thought to himself.

After a few more minutes on the road, he veered into the driveway of a large hotel, a concrete structure rising about thirty stories high. Above the front entrance was a walkway that crossed over Kearny Street, leading to a park in Chinatown. Black parked under the walkway in front of the hotel entrance. He grabbed a billfold from the glove compartment and exited his black Viper GTS, passing through the automatic doors into the lobby. His clothes were still a little wet from the incident at the pier. He squeaked across the hotel's lobby floor towards the front desk clerk. He had a few eyes on him, and those who walked by kept at a safe distance. The receptionist welcomed him with squinted eyes followed by a forced smile.

"G—good afternoon, sir," he said.

Black nodded. "Good afternoon."

"How may I—" the clerk started before crinkling his nose, seemingly overtaken by an unpleasant smell.

Black noticed, looking down at his shirt and sniffing. He looked at the clerk. "Ocean water," he explained briefly, hunching his shoulders.

"Oh, I see," the man softly replied, raising his eyebrows. "How may I help you?"

"I'd like a room."

"Okay, do you have a reservation with us?"

"I don't."

"Okay." The clerk exhaled, moving the computer mouse and staring at the screen. "I'll have to see what we have available, sir," he said slowly.

As the receptionist typed away, Black turned and looked around the lobby. He had already found his ETWs on the first floor. He knew where the exits were. He knew there were no threats. He noticed many objects that could be used as weapons.

The man regained his attention with a, "Sir, we have a room available."

Black turned to face him.

"It's a king-size suite."

"That'll work."

"How many nights will you be staying?"

"Just two."

"Which credit card will you be using today?"

"I won't."

The clerk narrowed his eyes and poked his lip. "Well, how will you be paying?" he asked.

"Cash."

"I see. Well, there will be a slight additional fee per night."

"That's fine."

The clerk handed Black some forms to fill out. He then

provided key cards and details regarding parking and different amenities at the hotel and the surrounding area. Black paid for the room and thanked the clerk before walking back outside. After parking his car, he grabbed his travel sack from the trunk and took the elevator up to his room. He found it neatly organized and smelling like fresh linen and pine-infused surface cleaner. There were the usual suspects of a hotel room: a bed, a couple of small dressers, a TV, a small desk, a small fridge, and a bathroom. He walked to the bed, tossing his travel sack on it. The contents of his pockets he emptied onto the small desk before entering the bathroom and taking a steam shower.

He came out of the shower wearing a towel and sat down on the bed. On the nearby desk he noticed the small device left behind by the young man he had pursued. He went to pick up the device and sat back down on the bed. He held the device in one hand to inspect it, flipping it around and tilting it from side to side. It was a small clear plastic tube. Inside it were some wires and a couple of tiny circuit boards. On one end, a wire about one inch in length was sticking out of the tube and on the other end was a red button. Black knew exactly what the tube was: It was a remote detonator for the improvised explosive device the guy had dropped at the pier. He exhaled, lying back on the bed.

"ORLANDO BLACK," BOYAR announced as Toben and Ashley entered the office.

"What was that?" Toben asked.

"The picture of the guy you sent. His name is Orlando Black. His file says he served in the military as a captain. Was in a few Special Forces units and received a number of commendations. The guy is a hero." Boyar turned back towards his computer. "Something strange, though," he added.

Ashley walked over to her desk and sat.

Toben walked up behind Boyar, arching and looking over his shoulder. "Strange how?" he asked.

"The time he served after leaving Delta Force and before leaving the government is locked."

Toben pinched his chin thoughtfully. "Hmm."

"Maybe the government had him in something top secret."

Toben nodded. "Based on what you found out about him, do you think he'd have any trouble making an IED bomb?"

Boyar chuckled. "This guy? No trouble at all."

Toben stood straight and exhaled in thought.

"Oh yeah. The director wants to see you. Looks like this incident spiked the interest of another agency."

"Yeah, I'm sure the FBI is all over this."

"Probably, but that's not who the director has in her office."

"Who's in there?"

"The DIA."

Toben's eyebrow raised and one corner of his mouth followed in a smirk. "What are they doing here?"

Boyar hunched his shoulders.

"I'll go see her. While I'm doing that, look over this footage." Toben handed Boyar a CD.

"Also, Kristi called a couple times," Boyar said.

"Yeah… I need to talk with her too."

Ashley, staring at her computer, let out a sigh.

"You okay, Ashley?" Boyar asked.

Toben looked at her, dropping his head slightly before leaving the office. He walked to the door of Director Hanten's office and knocked.

"Come in," Hanten's voice called.

Toben stepped into the room, closing the door behind him. In Hanten's office was a coffee table. On one side of the table was a sofa, and on the opposite side, two chairs. On the sofa sat Hanten and in one of the chairs, a man. He was wearing a suit and had his legs crossed. He had a head full of dark hair and a clean-shaven medium-tanned face. He had beady eyes and dimples. Not cute, inviting dimples, but the rigid, cold kind.

"Agent Toben. This is Special Agent Karl Stokes with the DIA," Hanten said, gesturing in the direction of the man.

Stokes stood and reached out to Toben. They shook hands.

"Nice to meet you," Stokes said.

"Same here," Toben replied. His forehead wrinkled as his hands moved to his hips. "DIA. Don't you guys handle more of the foreign intelligence gathering?"

"Well, this is a special circumstance," Hanten jumped in.

"Yes. I'm with a special unit of the DIA. We handle more of the… *domestic affairs*," Stokes said.

Toben said nothing.

Stokes sat down, crossing his legs again.

"So, Agent Toben. You said you'll fill me in on that lead you were following," Hanten said.

"Oh, well, I don't have much to share right now," Toben said softly.

"Okay then. I want your team to assist Agent Stokes and his team on an investigation."

Toben cleared his throat. "What investigation is that?"

"There was a bombing attempt earlier today at Fisherman's Wharf," Stokes said. "Did you hear about it?"

Toben shrugged. "Yeah, I heard about it."

Hanten scowled. "We already know that's where you were earlier."

"So why ask?" Toben asked, looking at Stokes.

Stokes hunched his shoulders.

"It doesn't matter," Hanten continued. "Just share what your team knows with Agent Stokes' team."

Stokes exhaled, standing from his chair and buttoning his

blazer. "No need. We already have what you have," he said, walking towards the door.

"Which is?" Toben called after him.

"Everything. We'll find this Orlando Black. We'll be in touch."

"Wait—" Toben started, but Stokes had already exited the office. Toben turned to Hanten. "We don't even know if Black is our guy."

The director stood, sighing. "I guess we'll know soon enough." She pointed to the door. "That's all for now, Agent Toben."

He eyed her and then shook his head before walking out.

OUTSIDE OF THE hotel, Black was lingering, wavering on which direction to walk. There was a lot on his mind, and staring at the four walls of his room wasn't helping. He wondered how a kid so young had gotten involved in a bombing attempt and how he had been able to get his hands on the materials for an explosive device.

He was about to cross Kearny Street, but something caught his eye. It was a white Honda Accord parked in the hotel's driveway. A very popular car, so it wasn't that which concerned him; it was the people in it. Black glanced in the direction of the car a few times, pretending to make sure no traffic was coming down the street while inconspicuously observing the Honda's occupants. They were two men. Both wore shades and had their lips set in stern, straight lines. The one behind the wheel had a messy crew cut with dirty blond hair sprinkled around his face. The guy in the passenger seat had a smooth face and a textured Caesar cut. His hair was a silky black. He looked Asian.

Black shrugged it off. He didn't sense an immediate threat, so he crossed the street and, after a time, arrived at a park in Chinatown. A walkway led him under a structure with a pagoda roof and a concrete floor. There were a number of benches, light poles, and small trees throughout the surrounding park, and moving amongst them were pigeons and a number of people. Most of the people were older and of Asian descent and were practicing what Black immediately identified as tai chi. Most were pretty good. He could tell they had been doing it for a long time.

Black looked around, hunching his shoulders. *Well, I guess I can get my practice in here.*

He began to go into his own tai chi practice with comfortable, slow, calm, graceful movements. Black was near the end of his form when he felt the eyes of someone on his back. He made note of it but continued to finish his form.

He stood still with his eyes closed for a moment, allowing the energy from his exercise to sink down. "Are you going to stand there and just look at me for the rest of the evening?" he asked, turning around to face his observer.

The man watching Black was an older Chinese gentleman. He was dressed in a traditional Chinese suit. His top was white, his pants black, his socks white, and his shoes black. He had grey hair with streaks of black, and there were wrinkles on his face and hands.

"No, young man. I just think you are extraordinarily skilled," he said. His English was very good.

"Thank you, sir. Nice pajamas, by the way," Black said.

The man chuckled, walking towards Black. He had great posture, but there was a slight limp in his step.

He extended his hand. "My name is Tip Jin."

Black shook it. "I'm Orlando Black."

"Good to meet you, Orlando Black."

"Likewise."

"Where did you learn that form?"

"I picked it up in Asia."

Jin nodded. "Do you have time for a friendly spar?"

Black's head lightly tilted back, his eyebrows raised and

his mouth slightly opened. "I don't know…" he said, considering the old man.

"Ahh, don't worry about me, I'll be okay."

"Okay, sure."

"Great. Over here," Jin said, pointing to an area at the center of the park.

The two men walked across the concrete towards the open area. Pigeons evaded them, making their *coo roo-c'too-coo* calls as they flew out of the way.

"Is this good?" Jin asked.

Black nodded.

Individuals in the park began to circle around the two in anticipation. A breeze blew through the park, carrying with it the smell of stir fry, oak, and car exhaust, as well as echoing chatter.

"Who's this man?"

"Master Jin is about to spar with someone."

"Come see."

"I saw this guy practicing, he's pretty good."

"Jin is one of the best fighters in the world, though."

"Sifu Jin is fighting again?"

Jin declared, "The one who makes direct contact first wins."

Black nodded and closed his eyes. When he opened them, he fell into a deep stance, fluently circling his guard hands in front of him.

Jin dropped into a stance as well, slowing waving his arms. He made a move first, rapidly lunging at Black.

Black's eyes widened instantly. Jin's fist approached him fast—faster than any opponent's he had seen in a long time. He was able to evade the jab, barely. Jin's fist missed his face by less than an inch.

Black swung to his opponent's side and shuffled backwards before gaining his footing and reestablishing his stance.

The crowd continued to chatter.

"Did you see that?"

"Wow!"

"No one ever eludes Master Jin's first attack."

Jin relaxed, nodding his head. "Very good," he said, smiling at Black.

Black exhaled. This old man is fast. I better be careful or he's going to show me up.

Jin returned to his fighting position. He sprang at Black with a front kick.

Black side-stepped Jin's leg and made a move to double-palm push him, but Jin had already spun to his other side.

Black's nose crinkled and his teeth gritted. *How did he—?*

The two circled around each other clockwise, attacking and parrying. Neither made direct contact. After a few seconds, they pushed off one another, both sliding back into a fighting stance.

Black squinted.

Jin cracked a smile.

The two calmly stared at each other before closing their eyes. Their breathing was quiet and slow. In that moment, the sound of the crowd and the traffic on the streets died down. The breeze of the wind and the aroma of food disappeared. The men raced towards each other even as they opened their eyes.

Jin waved his arms up and down in a diagonal path.

Black circled his arms, one clockwise and the other counter-clockwise.

They were quick. It was like watching two cars on a collision path. Some people from the crowd closed their eyes, shrinking away in anticipation of the impact. But there was no impact. The two men stopped face to face, perfectly in sync. Both their breathing deepened.

Black had the edge of his hand touching the side of Jin's neck.

"Looks like you got me, young man," Jin said.

Black looked down briefly. "Looks like you got me too."

Jin's hand was speared at his gut.

The opponents stepped back from each other, and the crowd began to clap and chitchat.

"I was right, you have extraordinary skills. Thank you for the opportunity to spar," Jin said, cuffing his fist and raising it towards Black.

Black slightly bowed. "The pleasure was mine, Master Jin."

Jin stepped closer to Black again. "You're very good, but there's something I noticed," he said.

Black's eyebrow rose.

"You probably already know this, but I sensed you expending much energy to hold back anger. If your anger was less kindled, you would've easily beaten me."

Black nodded, considering Jin's words.

"But like I said, you're very aware of your movements, so I'm sure you already know that... Well, that was fun. Maybe we can do it again sometime."

"I'd like that."

"Enjoy your day, Mr. Black."

"You do the same."

Tip Jin walked off, stopped near a tree, and began to practice his forms.

Black strolled out of the park and soon arrived at the intersection of Kearny and Washington Streets. He looked to his left to observe oncoming traffic and noticed the same white Honda he had seen earlier, but this time parked on Kearny near the curb.

Are these guys following me?

He crossed Kearny, continuing east on Washington. Traffic was only one way on Washington, heading west. No eastbound vehicle could enter. *This will give me a chance to lose these guys, and if I see them again, I'll know for sure they're following me. Seeing the car only once could be nothing to worry about. Twice, not likely to be nothing—and three times, definitely not.* Black continued up the sidewalk on Washington. The street was narrow like an alleyway at first, but after a while it opened up. He saw a number of small establishments and caught a glimpse of the Transamerica Pyramid on his left as he passed by. After another couple blocks, he ducked into a sandwich shop. He figured it would be a good time to fill up, especially since he hadn't eaten anything since he had left the pier, and that was around brunch time. He placed his order and sat down, taking his time with his food.

After finishing his meal, Black used the restroom then stepped out of the restaurant. The sun was setting and darkness was rapidly coating the sky. Parked across the street was the white Honda. *Yep, they're following me.* He hiked back towards the hotel, but not down Washington Street. It would have made it too easy for the white car to follow behind him. He would have been an easy target. Not a smart move. But heading south and then turning west onto a street with east-flowing traffic, that would be a smart move. And that's what Black did. The street brought him to the front left side of the hotel, and he quickly entered. He pretended to use a computer in the main lobby, which allowed him to covertly observe the front driveway of the hotel from his peripheral. A few moments passed before the Honda slowly crept towards the main doors. The car stopped for a few seconds and then pulled away, disappearing onto the road.

Black walked to the desk clerk. This time it was a young lady.

"Hello, sir. You need something?" she asked, smiling.

Black smiled back. "Yes, I have a friend staying here. If I give you his name would you be able to tell me what room he's in?" he asked.

The young lady's eyebrows slightly arched downward and the corners of her mouth pulled back, exposing her teeth.

An apologetic expression. "I'm sorry, sir, but we don't give out that information. It's for the security of our guests."

"What if I'm law enforcement?"

"Even so—you'd need a special warrant."

Black nodded. "I understand. Thank you."

He took the elevator up to his room and confirmed that everything was as he had left it. He gave some thought to who it could be that was following him. A long list of enemies ran through his mind. He soon shrugged it off and decided to turn in, figuring he would check out early the next morning and leave town.

CHAPTER
FOUR

TOBEN ARRIVED HOME a little later than usual that evening. He whipped his car into the driveway of his two-story suburban home and parked next to his wife's minivan. Looking at the house, he released a deep exhale before slowly exiting the car and going inside. The lingering aroma of dinner met him at the door.

Toben smiled. "Kristi?" he called, shutting and locking the door behind him. He walked towards the kitchen, turning into the living room. "Krist—," he started, but stopped short when he saw her sitting on the couch, in the darkness, palming her forehead.

Toben quickly walked over, sat next to her, and put his arm around her. "What's wrong?"

Kristi sniffled. She rubbed the back of her hand across her nose and looked at him. Her eyes were red. "Nothing, just another day for me," she said, hunching her shoulders.

Toben took his finger and settled a curl of black hair behind her ear, then used the back of his hand to caress her cheek. Her brown skin was smooth, though wet from her tears.

Kristi turned her face away from his hand.

"There's something wrong," Toben said, looking around the house. "And where is Matt?"

Kristi faced Toben and sucked her teeth before releasing a deep sigh. "I told you he had issues at school again today."

Toben's eyes narrowed and his mouth slightly gaped open. "I—I thought you met with the principal."

"I did."

"Wasn't Matt there?"

"Yes, Jake!" Kristi raised her voice. "If you were there, you would know this."

"Well, where is he?"

Kristi looked away and chuckled, shaking her head.

"Well?" Toben asked again.

"I don't know. On the way home from meeting the principal, he jumped out of the car and ran."

"What? Wh—Where did he go?"

"I don't know."

"What do you—"

Kristi stood from the couch. "I mean I don't know!"

Toben carefully stood up with his palms facing her, patting the air. "It's okay. Calm down."

"Don't tell me to calm down," Kristi responded, placing one hand on her hip and the other to her forehead. She walked into the kitchen.

Toben followed.

"I made some food. I wasn't sure when either of you would get home."

"I'll talk with him, okay?"

Kristi shook her head, "Yeah. I've heard that before. We need you here."

"Look, you know—"

"You work matters of national security. Yeah, I know, Jake, I hear it all the time."

Toben's next inhale was more audible. He exhaled slowly.

Kristi folded her arms and looked down at the floor, then

back at Toben. "And do you have something you need to tell me?"

"I told you I'll talk to Matt," Toben sighed.

"That's not what I'm talking about," Kristi hinted.

Toben stood quiet for a moment. "I... I... don't—," he stammered, struggling for words.

Kristi was about to say something, but the hum of a motor drifted in from out front. "That must be Matt," she said instead.

"I'll talk to him," Toben said, walking to the front door. He opened the door to see a blue Chevy Impala parked in front of his house. He walked down the steps and across the yard. The faint sound of music and the smell of weed met him halfway. In the driver seat was a young white male with sandy blond hair. He glanced at Toben briefly with big blue eyes.

Toben walked to the front of the car and stood over the hood. The car's headlights drew a large shadow behind him. Motionless, he stared through the windshield. Matt was in the passenger seat. He glanced at Toben with his eyes bulging and mouth gaping. He rubbed the top of his low-faded hair then dropped his head before turning to the driver and whispering something. Toben stayed where he was with arms folded, eyes squinted, and lips slightly puckered.

The music volume lowered. Matt looked at his father once again before opening the car door, throwing on his backpack, and climbing out. Toben tracked his son's steps as he stepped up the curb. The blue car pulled off.

Matt walked past Toben and towards the house.

"Matt!" Toben called after him.

Without even a turn of the head, Matt went up to the front door.

"Don't walk away from me when I'm calling you, boy!" Toben dashed after him, grabbing his arm and shutting the door behind them. "Didn't you hear me?"

Matt shrugged his father's grip from his arm. "Get off me!"

Toben grabbed his collar. "Who do you think you're talking to?!" he fumed.

"What's going on?" Kristi yelled from down the hall.

Toben released his grip and the boy pulled away.

"Who was that in the car?" Toben asked.

"No one."

"What happened?" Kristi asked, entering the foyer area.

Matt filled his cheeks, then exhaled heavily.

"Your son here was out smoking weed and—" Toben started.

"Matt, where have you been?" Kristi interrupted.

He didn't answer, just looked at her.

"I made dinner, so let's just eat, okay?" she implored.

"I'm not hungry!" he barked, then adjusted his backpack and raced up the stairs.

"Get back down here!" Toben demanded.

Kristi's gaze fell to the floor and she began to sob.

Toben walked and put his arms around her. "It'll be o—"

She threw his arms away from her. "Ju—just don't," she said, shaking her head and walking down the hall.

Toben took a step after her but his phone rang. He sighed, reaching into his pocket and lifting his phone. "Toben," he answered.

"Good evening, Agent Toben," a familiar voice replied.

"Who's this?"

"It's Special Agent Karl Stokes from the DIA."

"How did you get my number?"

Stokes chuckled. "Really?"

"How can I help you, Agent Stokes?"

"You can't."

Toben clenched his teeth and shook his head but made no reply.

"Are you home, Agent Toben?"

"As a matter of fact, I am. Do you need something?"

"I just wanted to inform you we found your guy," Stokes continued.

"Who, Black?"

"Yep."

"Wait. Like I was trying to tell you earlier, we're not sure if he's our guy."

"We'll know soon enough. He was there on the scene, right? So we can at least get some information from him."

"I guess we can question him."

"Don't worry, Agent Toben, we'll bring him in tomorrow. Enjoy the rest of your evening," Stokes said and ended the call.

"Prick," Toben grunted.

He opened the front door and paused to look over his shoulder up the stairway and then down the hall before walking outside. Entering his car, he poked at his phone and held it to his ear. The phone rang until a voice messaging prompt started. He immediately hung up and dialed another number. It rang three times before someone answered.

"Hello?"

"Boyar, it's Toben, did I wake you?"

"Are you kidding me? It's still early."

"Good, how about grabbing a drink with me?"

"Okay. The usual spot?"

"The usual spot," Toben echoed.

THE USUAL SPOT was a popular sports bar Toben frequented. He immediately spotted Boyar at the bar, sitting with a drink in his hand and staring down at the bar top. The music, the chatter, and the smell of chicken wings were a barrage on the senses. Toben eased through the crowd to Boyar, patting him on his shoulder. He looked up and nodded as his partner found a seat next to him.

"Weird day today, huh?" Boyar said, throwing back his bottle.

Toben sighed. "Yeah, tell me about it," he said. "I'll have my usual," he instructed the bartender.

The bartender nodded, turning towards the drink counter.

"Agent Stokes called me tonight," Toben said, facing Boyar.

"Oh, the DIA guy. What did he want?"

"Just to inform me they found Black and don't need our help with anything."

Boyar chuckled, shaking his head. "Well, at least it's not our problem to deal with. After what I read about the guy, I don't want to be the one going after him."

"Yeah, but we don't even know if he's our guy."

"Well, he was there, so he may have some information."

"That's the same thing Stokes said."

Boyar shrugged.

The bartender slid a foaming glass across the bar to Toben. "There you go, Jake."

Toben nodded in thanks.

The bartender walked to the opposite end of the bar to serve two men who had just walked in.

"So, how's Kristi?" Boyar asked.

Toben sat quiet for a moment. "She... she's okay," he said, turning up his glass.

"Good. What about Matt? I haven't seen him in a while."

"He's being a young adult."

"Oh. That's one of the reasons I haven't settled down yet."

"What, kids?"

"Exactly."

Toben chuckled. "I figured you'd want a house full of them."

"Nah. That can be pretty expensive, especially if this new law passes."

"Just pulling your chain."

Toben's phone vibrated in his pocket. He removed it, checking the incoming number. He jumped from his seat. "I have to take this," he said.

Boyar threw his hand up in acknowledgment.

Toben stepped outside to answer the call. "Hi."

"Hi," a female's voice replied softly. "Where are you?"

"I'm out having a drink with Victor."

"Do you have time to talk—in person?"

"Sure. I can be over in about fifteen minutes."

Toben ended the call and hurried back to Boyar. On his way, he noticed the two men at the opposite end of the bar watching him. They attempted to disguise their efforts by quickly looking away. He didn't recognize them, so he just shrugged it off.

Boyar looked over his shoulder as Toben approached. "Is everything okay?"

"Yeah—yeah, sorry, but I have to go," he answered, reaching for his wallet.

Boyar waved him off. "Don't worry about it. You paid last time, I got it."

Toben nodded. "Thanks, I'll see you tomorrow," he said, threading his way to the door.

TWELVE MINUTES LATER, Toben parked in front of a three-story concrete building. It was a condo development that rested on the corner of intersecting streets. The neighborhood was flat, which made it easier to see down the streets, in contrast to the more hilly areas nearby. He exited the car, scanned the area, and walked up the sidewalk. Arriving at the front door of a particular condo, he knocked twice.

The sound of someone moving inside rolled against the door. A few moments later, it was unlocked and cracked open.

"You made it," Ashley said with a forced smile.

"I did."

She opened the door further, moving aside as Toben entered. She closed and locked the door, taking a moment before facing him.

"Look, Jake—"

"Ashley, I—" Toben spoke at the same time.

They both fell silent, creating a cloud of hush in the room.

Ashley broke the silence. "Let's sit down," she suggested, pointing to her left.

The two walked across the hardwood floor past the stairs and into the living room, Ashley leading the way and Toben following. There was a sofa facing a wall that had a flat-screen TV mounted on it. In front of the sofa was a coffee table and on either side were cushioned chairs. They looked comfortable but contemporary. There were a few pictures on the wall and coffee table of Ashley with some older woman whom Toben knew as her mother. Ashley sat on the sofa and Toben on the chair to her left. Once again, they both began to speak at the same time.

Ashley raised her palm to her lover. "I'll go first," she instructed.

He nodded in agreement.

"Jake... I—I can't do this anymore. We can't do this anymore. What are we doing?"

Toben's lips split apart.

"We work together, and you have a wife and son, for crying out loud. I can't expect you to leave your family," Ashley continued. She stood, shaking her head, "This is not the woman I am."

Toben looked towards the floor. He exhaled then stood, grabbing her hand.

Ashley softly pulled her hand away and slightly turned her face.

Toben grabbed her hand again, moving in closer and

pressing his forehead against hers. "You're right," he whispered. "You're right and I'm so sorry."

"It's not all on you."

"Yeah, but I'm the married one."

"And I knew you were married."

"Yeah."

Ashley pushed Toben's chest gently, creating some distance between them. "We just can't do this anymore, okay? Someone is bound to get hurt."

Toben, tight-lipped, nodded. "Yeah… you're right—you're right."

The two stood in silence for a few moments.

"Well, I guess I better be heading home," Toben said, walking to the door. "I have a feeling tomorrow will be a long day."

Ashley frowned. "What makes you say that?"

Toben turned to face her, holding the doorknob. "Ahh… I received a call tonight from that DIA agent, Stokes. He said they found Black and will bring him in for questioning tomorrow."

"That's a good thing, right?"

"Maybe. It's just strange that he's putting so much emphasis on this guy, when there was another *suspect* on the scene."

"He may not know about the other guy."

Toben shook his head. "I don't know… I'm positive his team has all the information we have and maybe even more."

"Well, at least we can get some information from this Orlando Black, and Boyar is continuing to collect camera footage from the surrounding businesses. So we'll have more information to help us get to the bottom of this."

"Yep. Provided Hanten lets us continue to work the case."

Ashley tilted her head, smiling. "It'll be okay."

"Okay. Well, good night," Toben said, opening the door and stepping out.

"Good night. See you tomorrow, boss," Ashley replied.

Toben made it to the sidewalk before turning to her and cracking a smile.

She smiled back, slowly closing the door.

He pivoted and started towards his car, noticing a flash of light to his right as he did so. A white Honda was parked across the street. Another flash of light glinted from the car, then another. Toben's eyes narrowed. He took a deep breath, placed his hand on his issued .40 Smith & Wesson, and paced straight towards the Honda. As he approached, the headlights flickered on and the car screeched past him. He stood in the middle of the street, lightly panting as the car hung a sharp left at the intersection.

BLACK SPRANG FROM bed early the next morning. He stood stretching and yawning for a moment before falling to the floor and performing his push-ups. Next were sit-ups, followed by some deep stretching and form practice, and breathing exercises to conclude. He stepped into the bathroom and hovered over the sink, shirtless. The warm water felt good on his face. He watched his reflection in the mirror while taking a washcloth to his body. After getting fully dressed, he strapped his dual knife holsters around his ankles and loaded his pockets with his belongings that rested on the small desk. Picking up the detonator device, he contemplated tossing it into the trash. But he figured the better play would be to mail it to the authorities on his way out of town.

He grabbed his travel sack and walked to the door, making one last sweep of the room before heading downstairs. At the desk was the same receptionist who had checked him in the day before.

"Good morning, sir," the clerk said.

Black nodded. "Morning. I'm checking out," he said, placing the room key cards on the counter.

"Okay," the young guy noted, sliding the cards closer to

himself. He inspected one of them before turning his attention to the computer screen and typing. "Hmm… it says you were booked for two nights—yeah, I remember, I was the one who booked it. Is everything okay with the room?"

"Everything is fine. I just won't be staying as long as I thought."

"I see. I'll get you on your way, sir."

"Thank you."

Eight minutes later Black was in the parking garage starting up his car. He drove out of the garage, turning left onto Washington Street. The early morning darkness still covered the sky. The streets had zero foot traffic. There were no vehicles on the roads, with the exception of a few parked cars. He drove past the intersection for Kearny Street and into Chinatown. In his rearview mirror he saw the bright reflection of headlights behind him. He flipped on his indicator to make a right turn. As he veered right the car behind him indicated the same and followed. A couple minutes later he indicated he was turning left and the car again followed suit. Black got a good look in the side mirror as the car angled after him. It looked like the same white Honda Accord he had seen the day before.

At the next intersection, he flicked the signal indicator for a right turn. The car trailing him did the same. But Black didn't turn right; he turned left at the last second. The car followed behind him anyway. A few intersections later, he signaled for a left turn but made a right. The driver behind him did the same.

Black sighed. "Great," he grumbled.

He eased off the gas, bringing his car to a cruise. His pursuer slowed as well. He approached a stop sign, revving the Viper's engine before shooting past the sign and making a left turn, then another, then a right. He ran through a red light while the car behind him made every attempt to keep up. Black floored it until he had a straight shot to the Golden Gate

Bridge. The bridge, like most of the city, was empty that time of the morning. Black accelerated across it until the headlights of the car following him disappeared. He rode the far right lane, the lane closest to the bridge's sidewalk. He squeezed the brakes. His car slowed, jerking forward while the tires mildly screeched to a halt.

He threw the car in park and waited. The sun lifted over the horizon. The smell of ocean water seeped through his car while the breeze softly knocked against it. He tapped his fingers on the steering wheel, watching his mirror, noticing the headlights of the pursuing car rapidly approaching. As the car neared, it slowed and came to a stop about a car's length behind the Viper.

Black exhaled. "Well, I guess I better introduce myself," he said quietly, exiting the car and leaving the engine running.

He walked towards the other car, peering past the bright headlights that glared in his face. He saw two figures in the front seats. When the headlights were killed and the four-way emergency blinkers came to life, Black was able to make out the figures. The same two guys from yesterday. The men sat still, giving their target a hard stare. Black leaned against the trunk of his car with folded arms, staring back even harder. The men looked at each other, the one in the driver seat said something, and the other shrugged. The two exited the car. From the passenger side stepped out the silky black-haired man and from the driver side the man with the messy blond hair. Both men had their hands close to their hips, touching the butt of their firearms. They walked to the front of their car and faced Black.

Black stood up from the trunk of his car, carefully unfolding his arms. "How can I help you two?"

"We're the SFPD," the guy with the slick hair said.

The guy with the messy blond hair looked at him silently.

"Do you have any proof of that?" Black asked.

The blond man stepped forward, opening his light coat

slightly and exposing his badge clipped to his belt. "Is that proof enough for you?" he said.

Black shook his head. "So you are cops. Just not very good ones."

"What are you trying to say?" the slick-haired guy said.

"I'm saying you two may not be good for your jobs. I already know you're not good at your jobs. If you were, I would've been stopped for at least one of the multiple traffic laws I broke. Since I wasn't, I ask myself, are these two good for their jobs?"

"We saw those traffic violations. That's why we pulled you over."

Black raised an eyebrow. "You didn't stop me, buddy. I stopped on my own, remember?"

The guy didn't reply, looking down towards the pavement.

The other looked at his partner, briefly closing his eyes and shaking his head. He then looked at Black. "We're on a… special assignment. We believe you may have some information that can help us on our case."

"And what case is that?"

"There was an attempted bombing yesterday."

Black nodded.

"We received information that suggested you might've been there."

"I was."

"Okay, good, good. Did you see anything?"

"Yeah, a lot of people running scared."

"Did you come in contact with the suspect?"

Black rolled his eyes up to the left, retracting his lips. "Hmm," he gestured, shaking his head and then hunching his shoulders. "I don't know. It's possible."

"Did you see him drop anything?"

Black stood quiet, poking his lips out.

"We know at some point you were in possession of the bomb," the slick-haired man chimed in.

How did the local PD get so much information so quickly? Black pondered. "Oh, you mean the bag I threw over the pier, thus saving a lot of people's lives."

"Yes. Thank you for that; it was very brave," the other guy said. "Did you get a good look at the suspect?"

Black said nothing.

"I'm sure he did. He remembers. Enough of this!" the slick-haired man said, reaching behind his back.

The blond man raised his palm to his partner. "Wait!"

Black rushed him, ramming him into the slick-haired guy and against the car. A gun dropped to the pavement. Black delivered a punch, connecting with the eye of the blond-haired guy and following through by hitting the other square in the nose.

Both fell to the pavement.

Black picked up the gun, aiming it at the two men as he removed their side pieces, SIG Sauer P226s, and then throwing these off the bridge.

The men squirmed around in pain. Black patted them down and found no other weapons on either. He then removed their wallets and stepped back, keeping the gun aimed at them. The two men slowly sat up, leaning their backs against the front of the Honda.

Black inspected the wallets, memorizing the information on the licenses. He tossed the first wallet at the feet of the man with the messy hair. "Nick Reeves." He did the same for guy with the slick hair. "Kevin Guo. So, which one of you wants to tell me what's going on?"

Both men were silent.

"Well, don't you both speak at once," Black said, waving the gun between the two. He observed scratched alloy on the slide and breech of the firearm—a Glock 19. *Would you look at that*? "So no one wants to answer that question. How about you tell me instead why a cop would need a gun with the serial number filed off. You have your standard issued guns— or you *had*, rather. What, were you planning on killing me?"

"Aw… if it came to that," Reeves said.

"It sounds like a good idea now," Guo added.

"You two are beginning to try my patience. Like I said, you're not good at your jobs and considering how shady you are, you don't deserve to be cops. I have ways of making you answer, and using them won't bother me one bit. You two are not real cops."

A few cars passed by on the other side of the bridge. The breeze which stirred the men's hair carried with it the sound of approaching oncoming traffic. Black listened and heard the faint sound of sirens. He looked down the bridge and spotted the flash of red and blue lights.

He looked down at the two pieces of scum sitting on the pavement.

Reeves grinned, throwing his head in the direction of the sirens. "Good luck telling them that," he mocked.

Black's eyebrows lowered, his eyes narrowed, and he exhaled, glaring at Reeves.

Reeves' eyes widened. He looked away briefly, quieted.

Black smiled. "I'll see you two later."

The sound of the sirens drew closer and the red and blue lights reflected off the Honda. Black swiftly turned and entered his car, lay the gun on the passenger seat, shut the door, and threw the car into drive. The Viper's tires spun against the road, launching the car forward like an arrow from a bow. It was a straight shot down the bridge. No traffic ahead of him. By the time he reached the final gear, he had fully crossed the bridge, leaving the flashing lights and echoing sirens far behind. He continued on the road, turning into a right curve, and then a left, and again a right. On either side of him were grassy hills. He zoomed through a tunnel, meeting the morning light on the other side. A sign welcomed him to Sausalito, along with a view looking over a mountainside suburb and out to Richardson Bay.

He continued on the road, checking his rearview mirrors every few minutes to make sure he wasn't being followed. About fifteen minutes passed and he was turning right onto Interstate 580. The highway became a bridge. He drove across a large body of water for five minutes before reaching land and heading south. The morning traffic began to crowd the roads, bringing with it the sound of horns, the smell of exhaust, and a feeling of annoyance. Black found a parking lot in the northwest portion of Oakland. He looked around. There was not one piece of litter in the parking lot, every car looked shiny and new, and the buildings looked modern. Farther up the street, graffiti was on the buildings, trash rolled across the pavement, and people were standing on the corners.

Black shook his head. He put his car in park and moved the gun from the seat into the glove compartment before reclining in his own seat. "Looks like another fine mess you got yourself into, Black," he sighed. A few moments passed and his stomach growled. He looked across the street and saw a small restaurant nestled between a bookstore and an ice cream shop. He stepped out of the car and crossed the busy street, entering the restaurant. Inside to Black's right, people were lined up at a register placing their to-go orders and moving on with the business of their day. Running the register was a woman. Her attention was split between the customers and the kitchen. She would take an order and then yell to someone in the kitchen, greeting every customer with a smile.

A young waiter approached Black. "Good morning, sir. How many will be dining this morning?" He looked to be nineteen or twenty, wore a belt with his shirt tucked in, sported a faded haircut, and was well spoken.

"Good morning. Just one," Black answered.

"Okay, follow me, sir," the young man said, grabbing a menu and leading Black to the other side of the restaurant, which had far less activity. There were a few booths and tables, all unoccupied.

"Will this work for you, sir?" the young waiter asked, gesturing at a booth.

"This will work just fine," Black said, sliding into the seat.

The server laid the menu on the tabletop. "What can I start you off with to drink?"

"I'll have a glass of water and a cup of coffee, black."

"Okay, take some time to look over the menu and I'll be back with your drinks and take your order then."

"Thank you."

Black opened the menu and after a couple minutes of looking, knew exactly what he wanted. He folded the menu, laying it on the table in thought. "Think, think, think, think," he whispered to himself. A moment later the server approached again, setting the water and coffee on the table.

"Sir, have you had a chance to look over the menu?"

"Yes."

"I forgot to mention, but we also have vegan options if that's better for you," the young man said, producing a small notepad and pen.

"No, that definitely won't be necessary. I'll have your three-egg scramble, bacon, grits, and rye toast."

The young man jotted it down. "Okay, I'll get this in for you." He picked up the menu and walked towards the kitchen.

Black sat quietly sipping his coffee in thought and watching the morning crowd slowly die down. The waiter returned with his food. He cleared his plate and continued thinking.

Moments later the woman who was running the register eased up to his table. She placed one hand on her hip and ran the other across the wrinkles on her face and up through her grey hair, rubbing her forehead.

"Are you all done, son?" she asked.

Black nodded. "Yes, ma'am."

"How was everything?" she asked, grabbing his empty plate from the table.

"Delicious."

"Good."

"Are you the owner, ma'am?"

"Yes. Me and my husband. He's in the back now."

"You guys had quite the crowd this morning."

"It's like that just about every morning. But with the help of a couple hired cooks and servers, we manage. Also my grandson, whom you've met, helps out too."

"Seems like a good kid."

A smile arched on the woman's face. "Yep. He was raised right," she proclaimed proudly.

At that, a group of young men entered the restaurant. The first guy was short, black, and sported a low-fade haircut. The second was a chubby white guy with brown hair, and the last was a tall black guy with a short afro. As they entered, clamor and misbehavior followed them from the other side of the tracks.

"Ah… unlike this unruly bunch," the lady remarked, walking back towards the register.

"Hey, Mrs. G. What's up?" the short guy giggled as she walked by. The other two in the group whispered to one another before laughing loudly.

"Good morning, young men," she responded without looking their way.

The server who had taken Black's order came from the kitchen and walked towards Black's table.

The chubby guy eyed him, pointing in his direction. "Who's he supposed to be—Urkel?" he blurted, fist-bumping the tall guy as the third jeered.

The waiter placed the check in front of Black. "How was everything, sir?"

"It was great."

"Good," the young man smiled and started towards the register.

"Hey, kid," Black called.

The server pivoted.

"Don't let those knuckleheads get to you. They're just jealous. Keep up the good work."

The young waiter shrugged. "I know," he replied, continuing to the register.

Black grinned, impressed with the kid's confidence. He watched the group of hoodlums as they ordered their food and paraded out of the restaurant. Something caught his eye as they did. All three had their pants sagging, but as the tall guy exited, the back of his shirt lifted and exposed the butt of a gun. Black was certain it was a Glock 19, the same type of gun he had taken from the cop on the bridge.

"Whattaya know," Black whispered, laying cash on the table and following the noisy trio outside. He kept his distance and trailed them two blocks up the street. The young men crossed a street and posted up on a graffitied wall near the curb. Black took cover behind a corner on the other side of the street. The group ate their food, joked and laughed, and slap-boxed. It all looked like fun and games until a gold sedan pulled up. The tall guy stood at the curb while the chubby one walked to the far end of the wall and grabbed something from inside a small crack in the wall. The short guy followed him, looking out as his partner removed a small bag. The chubby guy then walked to the gold sedan and craned in towards the driver before stepping back on the curb. The gold car pulled off. The guy looked around, easing a wad of cash into his pocket.

Black stepped from behind the corner and paced across the street.

CHAPTER
SIX

THE TALL GUY was leaning against the wall. His two friends were walking toward the opposite end of the block.

Black approached him. "So, whatcha got for me?" he asked, rubbing his hands together.

"Excuse me," the guy shrugged, looking Black up and down. "Do I know you?"

"No. I'd say you know me just as much as you know the person who was driving that gold car."

The guy looked away, chuckling while twisting a piece of hair from his afro, before turning his attention to Black again. "I don't know you, man. You better bounce before something bad happen to you," he said.

"I just wanna know whatcha have."

The young man pushed from off the wall and stepped closer to Black. "Yo, are you deaf? I said, kick rocks," he demanded, pointing to the other side of the street.

At that time his two buddies started making their way over.

"Yo, Jay, what's up?" the chubby white guy called as they approached.

"Nothing. Just somebody don't listen too well, that's all."

"Well, put 'em in check," the short guy boasted.

The two guys approached Black on his left as he faced Jay.

Black threw his head in their direction. "Who are these guys?"

"Those my boys. That mean they got my back."

Black pursed his lips, nodding sarcastically.

The chubby guy looked at Black's feet, slowly raising his gaze up to his face. "Yo, you buying something?"

Jay briefly moved his sights to his chubby white friend. "We don't know him," shaking his head in disapproval.

The short guy stepped forward, circling to Black's front, stopping between him and Jay. "Oh, he's here to buy. I say let him buy," he said, staring up at Black.

"He could be a cop, dummy," Jay said.

The short guy looked over his shoulder at Jay then back at Black. "Hey, you a cop?"

"Do I look like a cop?"

The young man was quiet for a moment. "What are you looking to buy?"

Jay sucked his teeth and shook his head.

"We have the rock, the flour, and if you really want to go on a trip, the water," the short guy continued.

Black shook his head. "I don't want any of those," he said. "I want a gun."

The group stood silent for a second before bursting into laughter.

"My man, yo, you in the wrong place."

"That's what I'm saying. We don't know him."

"You want a gat? Get gone, bro. We don't sell guns," the short guy laughed, waving Black away. "That's like trynna get a car at a grocery store."

Black didn't move or say anything.

"Make tracks," the guy said again.

"I just want to know where I could buy a gun."

"Yo, son, this guy might be a cop," the chubby one said.

Jay's eyebrows dropped and wrinkles formed around his nose. "You wanna gun, I got one for you," he shouted, pushing his short friend aside and raising his Glock at Black.

Black caught his wrist and quickly bent it, taking control of the gun. His other hand crushed into his attacker's stomach.

Jay hunched over, coughing painfully.

Black used the same hand he punched him with to push his head back.

The young man stumbled back. His afro hit the wall, followed by the rest of his body as he slid down onto his butt on the sidewalk.

The short guy launched at Black.

Black delivered a side kick to his chest, sending him flying into the hands of the third guy.

The chubby guy caught his friend and fell to the pavement, back first. Grunts and the sound of fabric against concrete scratched through the air.

Black haphazardly aimed the gun at the two guys laying over each other on the pavement. "Do either of you have a gun?" he asked.

They shook their heads simultaneously.

"Well, Big Boi, I suggest you get out of here. And take Vanilla Ice with you."

The two staggered to their feet and raced up the sidewalk.

"Let's get out of here!"

"Yo, move it, son!"

Black shook his head, directing his attention back to Jay, who was sitting against the wall. "'Your boys.' 'Got your back,'" he mocked, inspecting the gun.

The serial number was filed off, just like the other gun.

Jay shook his head. "Aw… whatever, man. You won't get away with this."

Black looked at Jay, raising the gun about chest height. "This is a dirty gun. Where did you get it?"

"Did you hear me? You won't get away—"

"Shut your mouth! I wasted enough time with you. So you're going to tell me what I want to know or I'll make you," Black glared at him.

The young man was quiet, but he nodded.

"Where did you get this gun, kid?"

"I—I don't know her name."

"You got it from a female?"

"That's what I said."

"What does she look like?"

"I don't know. Nice body, long red hair, and she spoke with some type of accent."

"Okay. And where can I find her?"

A beige car slowly crept up the street.

Jay sighed. His eyes followed the car as it drove off. "I met her at one of those units out at Pier 40. It was near that joint where people sail—The Spinning Sails or whatever. Look, that's all I know, okay? Now can you leave? You're costing me money."

"How did you hear about her?"

"Around," Jay groaned annoyingly.

"Around where?"

The young man shook his head. "You ask too many questions, what do you care? There's a few people around the way that use her for... for supplies."

"What do you mean, supplies?"

"Guns, drugs, fake IDs—"

"Explosives?" Black interrupted.

Jay shrugged. "I guess."

Black briefly looked up to the sky in thought. "Jay, is it? You need to stay off the streets, especially for the next couple days."

Jay lifted himself from the concrete. "Look, I never met my father, but I know for sure you're not him."

"If you never met him, how can you be so sure?"

Jay cast a stern gaze on Black. "What did you say?"

"Stay off the streets."

"Pfft," Jay gestured, looking away and shrugging his hand at Black.

"Let's try this a different way. If I see you out here again, you and I are going to go another round."

Jay said nothing.

"I'm taking this with me," Black said, waving the gun before tucking it in the back of his pants. He then crossed the street and made the two-block hike back to his car. There he carefully placed the gun in the glove compartment, positioning it so he could easily distinguish it from the other gun. He then drove out of the parking lot and took off down the street.

LATER THAT MORNING, Toben exited his own car and walked towards the DHS building. The late morning sun beamed warmth from a clear sky, contrasting with the cool wind. He crossed paths with a few passersby on his way to the front entrance of the building.

A security guard greeted him. "Good morning, Agent Toben."

"Good morning," Toben replied.

Before entering the building, he noticed a couple of familiar faces across the street. One was Stokes. He was bent over talking to a guy sitting at the wheel of a green pickup truck. The man had blond hair. Toben remembered seeing him at the sports bar just the night before, but now he had a black eye.

The two exchanged words briefly. Then Stokes stood, pointed his finger at the guy, and dismissed him with a wave before turning away.

The guy in the green pickup rolled up the window and pulled off.

"Hmm," Toben huffed, walking into the building.

A few minutes later, he was in his team's office. Boyar had headphones on as he sat typing away at his keyboard. Toben walked towards him. Boyar noticed his approach and slid the headphones down onto his neck.

"You're in a little late," he commented.

Toben's eyebrows lifted briefly. "Yeah... I had a long night," he said.

"Is everything okay?"

"Yeah, yeah. Has Agent Stokes been up here?"

"No, I haven't seen him yet."

"Good. Is Agent Chapp in?" Toben asked, looking around the office.

"Yes. She is."

"Where is she?"

"Oh. She mentioned she was going down to the range to blow off some steam," Boyar answered, leaning back in his seat and adjusting his glasses.

"That actually sounds like a good idea. I think I may join her for a bit."

"Okay. But wait—before you go, let me show you something I found from yesterday."

Boyar leaned forward, jabbing a key on the keyboard. He then grabbed his mouse, whisking it around and performing a number of clicks. An image appeared on his screen. "Here it is."

It was a picture of two men in the middle of a street, apparently crossing. One of the men had his hand on the hood of a car. The other was trailing behind him at a close distance.

"What is it?" Toben asked, looking over Boyar's shoulder.

"This guy here should look familiar," Boyar said pointing at the trailing guy.

"Yeah. That's our guy, Black."

"Yep. It's hard to make out, but he's wearing the same clothes as in the other footage."

"Who is he chasing?"

"I don't know yet, but here's a better picture of him," Boyar said, clicking the mouse.

An image of a white male appeared on the screen. He was wearing a dark coat, a cap, and shades.

Toben's eyes shone. "It's a bit blurry, but he seems to fit the description the eyewitnesses gave of the guy who dropped the bag with the bomb."

Boyar nodded.

"So this is proof that Black wasn't alone." Toben cuffed his chin. "Who else knows about this?" he asked.

"Just you and me now."

"Let's keep it that way. Tell me the moment you ID the other guy."

"Sure thing," Boyar replied.

Toben stared at the image for a moment.

Boyar noticed. "What's the matter? You know him?" he asked jokingly.

"I'm not sure."

"Huh?"

Toben jolted his head, breaking his glare. "I'm going down to the range. I'll let Agent Chapp know. Remember, this stays within this unit."

"Okay."

Toben exited the office and took the elevator to the lowest level. He stepped out of the elevator into a short dark hallway leading to a small, dimly lit foyer. The sound of faint gunfire zapped his ears as he walked to the check-in counter.

"Good morning," Toben said.

A gentleman sitting on the other side of the counter looked up. "Good morning. Now where did I put it...?" he mused, scanning his desk and scratching his snow-colored hair.

Toben stood quietly, waiting.

"Ahh, here it is."

The older man slid a clipboard with a sign-in sheet under the thick glass that divided him from Toben.

Toben signed the form, removed his gun, and passed it all into the man's wrinkled hands.

"Thank you," the older gentleman said, browsing the paperwork. "So what will you be practicing with today?"

"Just the Smith & Wesson."

"Okay." The man looked down at his desk briefly. "You'll be at lane six. I'll buzz you in."

With that, a humming noise followed by a click echoed from a door on Toben's right. He entered the range and was hit by the scent of gunpowder. He looked down the fifteen-lane firing range and spotted Ashley. She was in lane five. Under the earmuffs, her hair was tied in a knot. She was in shooting position, looking down range through her safety goggles. She fired three rounds before Toben made it past her, entering his own lane and inspecting the gun that rested on the table in his booth. Once he heard Ashley's gun slap her table, he peeked around the lane divider.

"Good morning."

Ashley faced him. "Good morning, Agent Toben," she replied, completely removing her earmuffs and laying them on the table.

The two were silent for a few seconds as Ashley removed her goggles and placed them on the table next to the earmuffs. She then held a button located on the left partition of her booth. The overhead monorail made a zipping noise and her target began to reel in from the far wall.

"I wanted to let you know Boyar has footage of the other suspect at Fisherman's Wharf," Toben said.

"Really?"

"Yep. And he matches the description the eyewitnesses gave."

Ashley nodded.

"For now, I want this to stay between us," Toben continued.

"Keeping secrets? That's something we're good at."

"I mean between the three of us in the unit," Toben said, stepping into his booth and removing the paper target from the overhead monorail clip.

Ashley shrugged and followed him. "Has Agent Boyar identified this guy yet?"

Toben shook his head. "Not yet," he replied, looking over the paper target.

"I'm curious. Why do you want to keep this a secret?"

Toben sighed, clipped the target back overhead, and turned back to Ashley. "Something is off."

She smiled. "Maybe you're a little paranoid. You have a lot going on."

"I'm not kidding, Ash—last night when I left your place there was a car outside. I'm almost certain someone was surveilling me."

Ashley tilted her head and squinted her eyes. "You're serious?"

Toben nodded. "That's why I want you to be careful," he said, turning to the table and reaching for his safety glasses.

"I will, but we need to get these suspects in custody so we can get some answers."

Toben put on the glasses and grabbed the earmuffs. "Well, supposedly, Stokes will be bringing Black in sometime this morning. But I saw him outside earlier, and he looked empty handed."

"I know he didn't think catching a guy like Black would be easy."

"A lot of unanswered questions."

"There are. I'm heading back up to see if Boyar needs help with anything."

"Okay, I'll be up in a little. But remember, be careful."

Ashley half nodded before turning in the direction of the door.

"And Ash, about last night—I just…"

"Jake, we have work to do," Ashley cut him off and paced away.

The door buzzed, she opened it, and stepped through. Toben watched until the door slammed shut. He exhaled, turning his attention to his target. After throwing on his earmuffs, he pressed the button that operated the overhead target retrieval system. The monorail thumped then whined the paper target down range, stopping slightly beyond the halfway mark. Toben picked up the gun and inserted the magazine. He stepped closer to the firing line, orienting himself as best he could with the target line. He lifted the gun, aligning the rear and front sights with the target. He shot a round. There was a short pause before he squeezed the trigger and fired another round. Then another. And then another.

Toben lowered the gun and peered down range. "Not my best work," he muttered to himself, pressing the retrieval button. The paper target whizzed back to him and the door buzzed open as he laid the gun on the table. Footsteps approached. He turned.

"Oh, you. Good morning," he said indifferently.

"Morning, Agent Toben. Your subordinate told me you came down here," Stokes said.

"How can I help you, Agent Stokes?"

"Just wanted to check and see if your team has come across any new information."

"Anything we know I'm sure you already know." Toben looked over Stokes' shoulder. "Where's Black?" he asked sarcastically.

"My people ran into a—a bit of a snag."

Toben placed his hands on his hips, chest poking out. "Oh

really? And who are your people? They're agents, right? What are their names?"

Stokes chuckled, stepping closer. "Sorry, Agent Toben, but that's above your pay grade. Sensitive information. I'm sure your director wouldn't want to hear about one of her people jeopardizing this investigation."

Toben lifted his chin in the air and said, "Hmm. I'm sure she wouldn't want to hear about you using resources to surveil her people. Or that a 'special agent' with the DIA is not equipped to handle a man like Black. Maybe you've been behind a desk for too long."

Stokes smiled, turning his attention to Toben's paper target. "May I?" he asked, pointing at it.

Toben shrugged. "Be my guest."

Stokes stepped to the target, examining it, while the other folded his arms, quietly watching.

The paper had the bull's-eye at the center and five concentric scoring rings radiating outward from it. Toben had shot four rounds. There were four bullet holes to the left of the center, all between the third and fourth rings.

Stokes looked back at Toben. His nose crinkled and his lips curled as if he had smelled something bad. He hunched his shoulders. "Um... pretty precise, but not very accurate. Better than what I thought it would be, though," he said, pressing the button and sending the target back down range.

Toben took in a deep breath and let it out sharply. His eyes glowered and his lips curved down, but he said nothing.

The target stopped near the end of the range, a couple feet away from the bullet trap. Stokes lifted the gun from the table, disregarding the safety goggles and earmuffs. He then aimed down range, firing four rounds in quick succession. When the last bullet was fired, he sat the gun on the table and jabbed the button. The target began to float back to the front. He turned to Toben. "There's some training that's so rigorous it's impossible to forget, no matter how long you've been behind a desk. It'll be a matter of time before I personally go after Black myself. Let me know everything your team finds. It'll be a shame if your wife finds out where you spend your nights when you're not at home," he finished, quickly walking towards the door.

Toben watched him with wide eyes. Slightly shaking his head, he placed his attention back on the target. There were four new bullet holes, all located between the first and second scoring rings—two to the left of the bull's-eye and two to the right.

Toben's eyes grew even bigger and his jaw dropped. "Who are you really, Agent Stokes?" he asked himself.

At that question his phone rang. His wife's number jumped on the display. Toben dashed to the door and was buzzed into the foyer area.

He tapped the answer button. "Hi, Kristi. Is everything okay?"

"No, it's Matt," Kristi said. "He's not at school, again! The principal says he may have to expel him. I'm so tired I just don't—"

"Hey, hey—don't worry. I'll find him and take care of it."

"Jake I—I—"

"Don't worry. Just try to relax and wait by the phone for my call."

"O—okay. I love you."

"I love you too. Wait for my call."

Toben ended the call, raced to the counter, collected his gun from the range master, and hurried upstairs to his unit's office. Boyar was sitting at his own computer and Ashley was looking over his shoulder. Both looked at Toben as he hurried through the door, jogged to his own desk, and typed madly on the keyboard. His screen lit up and he dragged the mouse to an icon, clicked, and an application opened.

Ashley stared at him.

Boyar swiveled his chair in Toben's direction. "Is everything okay?" he asked.

Toben didn't answer. He typed into a field marked "tracking ID." A map came up featuring an orange dot near the Mission Bay area.

Ashley and Boyar looked at each other and shrugged. The two then made their way to Toben's desk.

"That's the new tracking app," Boyar commented.

Toben softly nodded with his eyes glued to the screen.

Ashley stood quietly with her arms folded.

"So… who are you tracking, boss?" Boyar continued.

Toben sighed. "Matt."

Ashley unfolded her arms. "What's wrong with Matt?"

"He's been skipping school," Toben answered, shaking his head.

"Uh-oh…" Ashley breathed, folding her arms again and taking a small step back from the desk.

Boyar pointed at the screen. "He's heading north towards the South Park area. He's moving fast—must be in a car. Where did you put the tracker?"

"In his backpack. He must be in the car with that kid I saw him with last night—uh… I have to go get him."

As Toben stood from his desk, Hanten entered the office.

"Good morning, everyone," she said. "Agent Toben. The DIA has come across some new information. We have intel that suggests that a meeting of significance to this case may take place sometime later today. I need you to come to my office for a briefing."

"Wh—what meeting?" Toben replied.

"Like I said. There's possibly going to be a meeting today and we have reason to believe Milo Petrak will be there," Hanten clarified.

"Milo Petrak?" Boyar echoed.

"The arms dealer, Milo Petrak? Who we can never seem to build a case against?" Ashley followed.

"That's the one," their boss confirmed.

Toben's eyes narrowed and his shoulders rose. "Why? What does Petrak have to do with this?"

"Stokes seems to think he may be behind the bomb."

"I thought Stokes believed Black was behind the bombing."

"It's possible that Petrak could've supplied Black the materials for the bomb."

Toben nodded. "Okay. I'll be there. Just need to make a quick run first."

"Where to?" Hanten inquired.

"Just a family emergency."

"Did someone die?"

"No. Not yet, at least."

"Okay, well, you can make your *run* afterward."

"But it's concerning my son. You know how it is."

Hanten's eyes dropped to the floor briefly, she flattened her lips, and she stared at Toben for an awkward moment. "I don't know how it is, Agent Toben. I'm too busy worrying about this country's security to be a parent or overly concerned about my own household. I have a whole country of households to worry about. And so do you. I'll see you in my office," she concluded, walking out.

"Whoa," Boyar said, walking over to his desk and sitting.

"I wonder what that's about." Ashley said.

"Agent Boyar, anything on the ID of our new guy?" Toben asked, stepping to his own desk, ripping a piece of paper from a small notepad, and lifting a pen.

"Nothing yet."

Toben began to write. His two partners looked at one another and continued to watch as he stood and walked over to Boyar with the paper in hand.

"I need a favor. Can you continue to track Matt's location?"

"Um… sure," Boyar replied, grabbing the piece of paper and turning to face his computer screen.

Toben turned to Ashley.

"Agent Chapp, I need a favor from you too. Is it possible… you could… um… go get Matt and bring him here?"

Ashley threw a hand on her hip, her head tilted, and her eyebrows raised. "Excuse me?"

"I was wondering if you would go get—"

"No, I heard you. But I'm not a babysitter."

Boyar turned and chuckled. Toben gave him a look that said *mind your business*. His laughter disappeared as he once again faced his computer.

Toben carefully placed a hand on Ashley's shoulder, walking her a few steps away from Boyar. "Look, I have this meeting with Hanten," he spoke softly. "I think Matt may do something stupid and get himself in trouble."

"Sounds like a family issue. Why can't his mom go get him?" Ashley said in a quiet tone.

Toben exhaled. "I need someone who's good at tracking people. You know, who can follow someone without being seen if needed."

Ashley laughed, looking at the floor briefly and shaking her head. "Argh… Okay, but you're going to owe me."

Toben palmed his hands together. "Thank you," he said, making a pivot toward the door.

"Before you go," Ashley said, stepping closer to him. "Don't ask me to do anything like this again." And she walked off towards her desk.

Toben stood quiet, staring at her back for a few seconds before walking out of the office.

CHAPTER
SEVEN

THE AIR WAS cool under a bright sun. Black sat parked at Pier 40, looking across the four-lane street, beyond the pedestrians, the passing vehicles, and cable car toward the building of The Spinning Sails. He opened the glove compartment and removed his lock pick kit and the gun he took from the kid, Jay. He got out of the car, keeping an eye out as he tucked the gun in the back of his pants and placed the lock pick kit in his pocket. He cut across the busy street and through a parking lot to the front of The Spinning Sails. To his right was a harbor filled with small sailboats. To his left, a white commercial dock building. The building had multiple storage units extending about fifty yards into the bay.

"Hmm," Black exhaled, walking into The Spinning Sails.

Inside was quiet but cluttered. Black walked around looking at the different sailing pictures, Jet Skis, life jackets, and other water recreation items for sale.

It wasn't long before one of the workers approached him. "Can I help you find something, sir?" an ivory-toned blue-haired girl asked, smiling.

Black faced her with a smile of his own. "Nope, just browsing."

Her smile grew. "Okay. Just to let you know, we're running some specials on our sails and Jet Skis rentals this week. If you want more information on it, I can give you the breakdown."

"That won't be necessary."

"Okay, sir. Let me know if you need anything," the girl said, turning away.

"You know, I do have a question," Black said as she was pivoting.

The girl faced him again. "What's that?"

Black pointed his thumb to his left. "Those storage units. Do you guys rent them out?"

The young lady shook her head in the negative. "Oh, no, sir. You'll have to go to the office next door if you're interested in renting a unit."

Black nodded. "Thank you. And—I like your hair."

Her dimples cratered her cheeks as she tried to conceal her smile.

Black left The Spinning Sails and walked up the sidewalk and into the white commercial building. To his right was a counter with a computer monitor, mouse, and keyboard resting on it. Directly ahead was a door, and to his left were a few sitting chairs. It was completely empty and silent.

"Really?" Black muttered to himself, looking behind the counter. There was no one working the front and he didn't see any indication that anyone would be coming, either. He turned and left the building. As he was about to cross the street, something caught his eye—a blue Impala parked in the lot of The Spinning Sails. From the passenger side stood a teenager whom Black had never seen, a kid with light brown skin and a low-fade cut. From the driver side exited the same blond-haired blue-eyed guy Black had chased the day before. He was wearing a new pair of shades and a cocky look.

The kid with the low fade lifted a backpack from the car and threw it over his shoulder. The other guy waved at him and said something that Black couldn't make out, due to the distance and the noise of passing vehicles. The one with the backpack then shrugged and set it back inside the car. The two made their way to the sidewalk, heading towards the white building. Black turned around, looking innocently in the opposite direction as the two approached. They strolled up the sidewalk and into the building, using the same entrance that he had used just a few minutes before. A moment later they stepped out again. The blond guy looked around and hunched his shoulders before shaking his head in a disappointed fashion. Black watched from his peripheral while pretending to admire the view of the harbor. The two stood looking around for a couple of seconds before the blond guy pulled his phone from his pocket and held it to an ear. He spoke into it while raising his free hand in the air. It was a gesture of *where are you?* Then he stood still a beat, listening. After a few seconds, he nodded and put the phone back in his pocket. He spoke to his buddy while gesturing further up the sidewalk. The two continued in that direction.

Black tailed them, dodging other pedestrians and taking in the sight of the Dwight D. Eisenhower Highway bridge about a half mile before him. The young men walked for a few minutes before making a right at the corner of the old Maritime Recreation Center. Black looked around the corner, watching, as they climbed over a wrought iron gate and dropped with a thump onto the shabby wooden deck beyond it. The two then continued through the opening of a chain link fence. The one with the low fade was looking to his left over the water at a docked naval vessel. The other was pointing at the side wall of the old Recreation building located to their right. The wall was in need of a new coat of paint. There were a number of metal roll-up doors down its length. The two continued creaking across the deck towards the end of the building.

Hopping over the gate was easy for Black. He zipped

through the chain link fence and carefully crouched down at a corner wall next to some wooden crates where the shadows provided shade and cover. Pressing his palms against the chill damp wall, he peeked and saw the two guys stopping near the end of the building. They stood at one of the metal doors, looking around as if they were expecting someone. Within seconds, the faint droning of a motor approached from the bay. It was a Jet Ski. Operating the Jet Ski was a woman wearing dark sunglasses with red hair tied into a knot. The two guys turned their attention towards her as the Jet Ski bounced over the waves. They exchanged a few words that Black couldn't make out. He quietly climbed on top of the crates and pulled himself up to the roof of the building, which was warm from the sun. He inhaled the stench of tar as he bellied across the roof towards the two young men. Soon he was above them—not directly, but about three yards away. Black quietly rolled to his side and peeped over the ledge.

The woman turned off the Jet Ski, jumped onto the dock, and tied it off. She reached to the back of her head, removing a clip, letting her hair down, and whipped it in a circular motion before running her fingers back through it.

"You're right, she's hot. She looks older," the young man with the low fade whispered.

"Yeah, she's in her mid-twenties, but don't be fooled by her looks. She can be real feisty. I think it's a redhead thing," the other whispered back.

The woman squeaked across the deck towards them. She used her index finger to push her shades up her nose. "You made it," she said.

Her accent. It's Czech, Black said to himself.

"Yeah. Where'd you go? I thought you'd be at the front office," the blond guy said. "There's no one working the front."

"So? Not like I'm expecting a lot of customers or anything," the woman said before looking at his buddy.

The blond guy smiled. "Johana, don't you think your dad would get upset if you're not working?"

The woman glared at him. "Don't use my name in front of company. Who's this?" she asked, nodding at the guy with the low fade.

"This is Matt—the one I was telling you about. He's cool."

Johana looked Matt up and down. "So, Matty. You look way too young to be a cop. But how do I know you're not wearing a wire?"

"What?" Matt said.

"C'mon. I told you he was cool," the other young man said.

Johana stepped up to his face. "You mean like you said you could handle the protest at Fisherman's Wharf yesterday?"

The guy said nothing, looking away and shaking his head.

Johana walked over to Matt. "Lift up your shirt," she said, removing her shades.

"Huh? Why?"

"Do it!" Johana demanded with stern eyes and flexed jaw muscles.

Matt glanced at his buddy. The blond guy hunched his shoulders. Matt sighed, lifting his shirt. Johana browsed over him front to back. She patted his pants legs and checked his pockets before taking a step back.

"Well, I guess you're clean, Matty," she said, giving him a wink.

"I told you," the other guy said.

Johana rolled her eyes. "So do you know what it is we do here?" she asked Matt.

"Kinda."

"Kinda?" Johana repeated briefly, glancing at the blond.

He returned with a shrug that said, *what do you want me to do about it?*

"Let me ask you something, Matty," Johana continued. "Are you an only child?"

"Yep."

"Are your mom and dad still married?"

"Yeah."

"Okay. Do they love each other?"

"I'd say they do."

"Do you think they love you?"

Matt hesitated before answering, "I'd say so."

"Hmm."

"Hmm what?"

"Must be nice to have the perfect family."

"Wait, you got—"

"Dad goes to work and Mom stays home. At dinner everyone sits around the table smiling and happy."

Matt raised his palms to Johana. "No, you mu—"

"Taco Tuesdays, Friday family nights, Dad and Mom so in love, and you're their straight-A, bow tie-wearing, pride of life, little Matty. I bet y—"

"You don't know the first thing about me!" Matt shouted, interrupting. "My dad is hardly ever home, and I can't remember the last time I saw my mom smile!"

Johana eyes widened, but she was quiet.

Who are these kid's parents? Black thought.

"And straight-A?" Matt continued, laughing nervously. "I'm close to being kicked out of school. I don't like my life. I don't want to go to school, and I definitely don't want to go home."

"Okay, okay, calm down, Toben," the blond guy said.

Johana patted Matt on his shoulder. "Sorry about that, Matty, I didn't mean to excite you."

Matt exhaled.

"We know what you're going through," Johana said, pointing between herself and the other guy repeatedly. "Let me show you something," she said, waving for them to follow her to one of the roll-up doors.

The sound of keys clinking, a lock snapping, and then metal grinding rang in Black's ear.

"I have a lot of toys, Matty."

The three disappeared into the storage unit.

Black slowly pushed himself up with his elbows. He heard the wooden deck squeak and immediately he dropped back to his belly. He looked over the edge and noticed a brunette with an athletic build making her way towards the recently opened storage unit. Her hand rested on her holstered firearm.

She was twenty feet away from the unit. Then fifteen. Then twelve. Black heard whispers of concern waft from the unit. The brunette made it about ten feet from the unit before Johana slipped out.

"Hold it right there, DHS!" the brunette yelled, one hand still resting on her gun and the other hand thrust at Johana, palm forward.

Johana threw her arms up. Her eyes were fixed on the other woman in jaw-dropping bewilderment.

"Matt?" the woman called.

Matt and his buddy stumbled out, the latter with raised arms. "A—Ashley?" Matt stuttered. "What?—what are you doing here?"

"I should be asking you that. Who are you two?"

"They're just my friends."

Ashley took her hand off her gun.

Johana and the blond guy relaxed, lowering their arms.

"Friends, huh? Why are you not in school?"

"What are you, my mom?"

"Absolutely not."

"Then don't act like it."

"Shut up. Your father sent me for you. Let's go."

"I don't care. I'm not going anywhere."

Ashley's eyes narrowed and her lip poked out. Matt sheepishly stared at her face. He stood quiet, looking away briefly.

"This is going to go one of two ways. Either you come with me with both your feet on the ground or I drag you out of here by your feet. Your choice."

I like her, Black thought to himself.

Matt looked at his two 'friends.' "Man, I tell you," he huffed, walking past Ashley, barely missing her shoulder.

Ashley watched him as he passed before turning her attention to the others. "Who are you two?"

"I'm just a friend—" the guy quickly said.

"I work here—" Johana said at the same time.

Ashley directed her next question at the young man. "Shouldn't you be in school too?"

"No. I graduated a couple years ago."

Ashley took a step in the direction of the storage unit. "What's in there?"

Johana scooted closer to the unit, blocking her path. "This is private property. We take our clients' privacy serious, so you can't go in there."

"Huh. Who did you say you are?"

"I work here. My father owns the place."

"And who is your father?"

"Do you have a warrant?"

"Not yet."

"Are you charging us with anything?"

"Not yet," Ashley repeated.

"Well, I have some work to do. If you don't mind leaving, I would like to get back to it," Johana said with a smile, throwing her hand out towards the front of the building.

Ashley shared her gaze between the two of them. "I'll see you around," she said, turning and following Matt to the front. They watched until she and Matt disappeared around the corner of the building.

The young guy with the blond hair dropped his head and exhaled. "Phew! Good thing she didn't go into the storage unit."

Johana looked at him with a grin on her face. "Yeah. Good thing for her," she said while lifting a gun from behind her back.

Black immediately noted that it was identical to the other two unmarked guns he had taken possession of.

"Whoa. Were you actually going to use that on her?" the young guy asked.

"If it came down to it," Johana replied, aiming the gun at him.

"Wait—wha—what are you doing?"

"Ahh great," Black whispered to himself.

"I thought you said he was cool," Johana raised her tone.

The kid stumbled back and lifted his hands in an attempt to shield himself from the gun. "I—I thought he was," he stuttered.

"Then why was the Department of Homeland Security here looking for him?"

"His dad works for them."

"Oooh, that's just brilliant, genius!" Johana fumed, pushing the gun's muzzle closer to the young man's face.

The guy dropped to the wooden deck butt first. His hands remained in a shielding position. "Please!" he cried out in shuddering fear.

I better help him, Black thought, using the ledge to carefully lift his body.

"How do you think they found him?" Johana demanded.

No, she's not going to kill him. She's smarter than that, Black *relaxed at the thought.*

The guy didn't answer.

"Hey, I asked you a question."

"I—don't—I—don't know."

Johana huffed. "Look at you. Get up," she said, tucking the gun in her backside.

The guy slowly lifted himself to his feet. Johana stepped within kissing distance of him and used the back of her hand to brush off his shirt before resting that hand on his shoulder.

"I'm sorry," she apologized. "I just don't want anything to throw a wrench in what we have planned. I tell you what. How about you go out of town this time and I'll head down state. How about it? It's Florida, the weather should be nice."

The young man wiped her hand from his shoulder. "I already checked, there's going to be some rain."

Johana sighed. "I think you should go anyway. The heat is heavy here and we can't afford another—"

"What? Another mistake like at Fisherman's Wharf? Look, I told you some guy got in the way."

"I know, I know. I just think you should let me handle things here because the state of California is on high alert, like how New York is right now. That's all."

"Yeah… maybe we should just hold off for a—"

"What?" Johana raised her voice.

"It—It's just… we're doing this to help kids, but I saw how kids got hurt in New York and I can't get some of the images out my head. And you have guns and bombs. I just can't…"

Johana paused and inhaled a labored breath. "There are always some that suffer for the greater good. Plus, we've come too far to quit now. You're in too deep."

The young man said nothing just dropped his head.

"I tell you what. After you come back from Florida, that's it."

"You mean we're done?"

"Yep."

"Ahh. Fine, I'll go, but that's it for me."

"Good. Wait here a minute," Johana said, stepping into the unit. There were a few thumps followed by the sound of a drawer bumping open and then sliding closed. She came out with some documents in hand. "I thought you would agree, so I've already got the IDs and plane ticket ready for you." She gave the guy the documents. "This should be easy. It'll be nearly impossible to track it back to us," she concluded, walking back towards the unit.

"I know. I just need the *sauce*."

Johana closed and locked the roll-up door. "Right. I have it stashed up front, in the back. C'mon," she said, leading the guy across the deck towards the front of the building.

Black slowly pushed himself up from the roof. He watched as Johana opened the swinging door to the metal gate and the two disappeared around the corner of the building. He climbed over the ledge, hanging by his arms for a couple of seconds before softly dropping to the deck. He looked towards the front of the building again to make sure no one was coming. Removing his lock pick, he walked to the storage unit that Johana had closed and locked moments before. He went to work and had the door open within seconds.

The unit was spacious and reeked of a gaseous-metallic odor. There were a number of tools scattered about, and parts that appeared to belong to some type of small boat or Jet Ski. On the right side of the room was a surfboard rack holding two boards. Under the rack was a toy remote control boat. Directly in front of Black was a workbench. There were pieces of blank paper scattered around it, a couple of pencils, some electric wire, a couple TV remotes, and a few short PVC pipes. On the upper left corner of the table was a small bucket filled with screws, nuts, bolts, nails, and other small metal pieces of the like. He noticed a large sheet of plywood resting against the wall to his left. He removed the plywood from that wall and settled it on the perpendicular facing wall, thus exposing a large toolbox with multiple sliding drawers.

Black started with the bottom drawer, which was the

largest. He slid it open and immediately was hit with a strong smell. Inside were a couple of bottles of hydrogen peroxide and some all-purpose cleaning solution. Black closed the drawer and opened the one above it. There were nothing but tools inside it.

He reached for the top and final drawer. Giving it a tug, he felt resistance. It was locked. He removed his lock pick and fiddled with the lock for a moment before it clicked open. Inside was a cardboard box with the flaps slightly open. On the outside of the box was a label showing a shipping address, but no sender. Black committed the address to memory and began to open the box. A smile grew across his face. Inside the box he found exactly what he thought he would: an unmarked Glock 19 just like the others he had seen. He closed the box, leaving the gun inside. Under the box were a few documents. The first was a flier—the same flier the protesters at Fisherman's Wharf tried to give him the day before. The second was a small map of a popular theme park located south of L.A. called Fantastic Galaxy. The last document was a flier just like the first, except the location given was Times Square in New York. Black closed the drawer and replaced the plywood. As he finished, he paused at a noise echoing behind him. It was the slide of a gun clicking into place.

CHAPTER
EIGHT

BLACK RAISED HIS hands, exhaling sharply.

"You have ten seconds to convince me not to pull this trigger," a woman's voice informed him.

Black looked over his shoulder. Johana had her gun trained on him. "You shouldn't point a gun at someone unless you're ready to shoot them," he said.

"Eight!" Johana counted.

"I'm here on business."

"Seven!"

"I'm a client of yours."

"Five!"

"The guns we bought from you are faulty!"

"Fou—" Johanna stopped counting.

"Let me show you. I'm going to lift up my shirt." At that Black carefully grabbed a fist full of his shirt near the back collar, pulling upward. He felt the shirt lifting over the butt of the gun. "See. That is one of your guns, right?"

Johana said nothing.

Black kept his hands up as he turned to face her.

"Turn around!"

Black turned back around and heard the woman stepping

closer to him. He felt the back of his shirt being lifted and the pressure from her hand against the gun tucked into his pants. Before she could grab it, he spun around, seizing her gun with one hand while pushing her shoulder with his other hand. The two of them whirled a semi-circle. The force was enough to rip Johana's grip from her gun. Black, holding Johana's gun, went to aim it at her but she kicked it from his hand and sent it smacking onto the deck outside. He reached for the gun tucked in the back of his pants. Just as he swung it to his front, Johana struck his hand, flinging the gun into the surfboard rack. Black jabbed that same hand at Johana, palm up. Johana stepped back nimbly, eyes narrowed, nose crinkled, and fist balled.

"Hmm. Someone's had a few lessons, I see," Black commented.

"Oh, there's a lot more to see," Johana scoffed, charging at him. She threw two punches and followed up with a kick.

Black blocked all three attacks with one hand before pressing the palm of that same hand into Johana's ribcage. The push sent her staggering back into the workbench. Nuts and bolts spilled from the bucket, dinging against the floor. Sheets of paper flew in the air as pencils and PVC pipes rolled from the bench and bounced on the floor.

She regained her footing, fist raised and intensity wrinkling her face. She raced towards Black, leaping in the air, delivering one kick and then another before descending back to the floor.

Black shuffled backwards onto the deck, slapping away his attacker's kicks. In the process, his back foot smashed through one of the planks of the deck. He quickly removed his foot and glanced into the hole he had just created. He noticed a PVC pipe attached under the plank. It was the same size as the ones on the workbench inside the unit. He didn't have much time to think about it, though—his opponent continued her assault, delivering a near perfectly timed round kick at him. Black caught her kicking leg, quickly sweeping her other.

Johana hit the deck back first. Her gun was resting on the deck just a couple feet above her head. She released a loud gasp before rolling to her front and impulsively pouncing towards it.

Black noticed but was too far away to beat her to it.

Johana snatched the gun and aimed it at Black.

He quickly took cover behind a wall of another unit as two bullets chipped at the corner. He reached down and removed a knife from his ankle holster. Peeking around the corner, he saw Johana untying the rope for the Jet Ski from the support pole. Black stepped from behind the wall.

Johana noticed and fired another round, nearly hitting him as he ducked back behind the wall.

He attempted to step out again, but saw Johana sitting on the Jet Ski with her gun pointed in his direction. This time three rounds boomed from the gun, knocking chunks from the corner wall as Black retreated. The rev of the Jet Ski turning over shortly followed. Once again Black raced from behind the wall. He dashed down the deck as Johana rode into the open waters. He stopped at the end of the deck, watching her back as she bounced over the waves. Then something strange happened. She stopped. She was about twenty yards out as she removed what appeared to be a remote from her pocket.

Black watched with squinted eye and pursed lips. A second later, his eyes widened. "Oh you psych—" he yelled, sprinting back up the deck. He passed the open storage unit before he heard the first blast. It sounded like it came directly from the unit. It was a loud *POW* followed by an even louder crack. The wooden deck shook. Black's heart hammered against his chest and a long high-pitched tone buzzed in his ears. The deck rattled under another explosion and small fragments of wood flicked against his back. He bellowed a grunt in an attempt to increase his pace as the hairs on his arms and around his neck raised in anticipation of another explosion. He raced through the chain link fence and, out of instinct, jumped. Floating through the air, he cleared the wrought iron gate. He looked down to his feet and saw wood erupting, spatters of water in air, and smoked debris clouding the area. He felt the shock across his back as he landed on the concrete sidewalk. The cloud of smoke waved across the street. Pedestrians gasped and screamed. A few drivers shrieked their cars to a stop. Others continued to drive past, some laying on their horns. Black coughed and fanned the smoke from his face. "Ahhh," he exhaled, rocking forward to his feet.

He peered through the smoke and debris, making out a silhouette of Johana as she jetted across the water. Brushing the dirt and dust from his clothes, he jogged towards his car.

TOBEN PUSHED OPEN the door to his unit's office. The door absorbed the force of his aggravation, swinging open wide enough for at least three people to enter before closing again.

"Okay, I'll see you then," Toben said into his cell phone before dropping it into his pocket.

Boyar was sitting at his own desk, headphones on, eyes glued to the screen. Ashley was at her desk, looking Toben's way as he entered. At Toben's desk sat Matt. He was pressing and swiping at his cell phone.

Toben nodded to Ashley in thanks. He quickly paced over to Matt, snatched the phone out of his hand, and placed it on the desk.

"Hey—"

"What were you thinking?!" Toben fumed. "Are you trying to get kicked out of school?"

Matt stood. "Why not? I don't want to go there anyways," he said with a sour look on his face.

Toben's chest puffed, his nose crinkled, and his breath became short. "You're walking on some very thin ice, boy," he said, glaring at Matt.

Matt said nothing, looking into his father's eyes with pouting lips.

Toben looked around his desk before looking Matt up and down. "Where's your backpack?" he asked, raising both hands, palms up.

Matt hunched his shoulders. "I—um…" He struggled for words.

Toben fluttered his hands, briefly closing his eyes and shaking his head. "You know what? Just go to the back," he said, pointing at a room in the back of the office. "I'll deal with you in a minute."

Matt rolled his eyes before grabbing his cell phone, walking to the room in the back, and closing the door.

Toben stepped to Ashley's desk. "Thank you."

Ashley looked up, slight smile. "No problem. But like I said, you're going to owe me one."

"Who was it you said you found him with?"

"Like I told you over the phone, some so-called 'friends.' There was a blond kid and a redhead. She had a smart mouth."

Toben nodded. "I think that's the same young man I saw him with last night, but the redhead is new to me."

Ashley shrugged.

"I'll ask Matt about it," Toben concluded, turning towards Boyar. "Agent Boyar. Anything on that guy Black was chasing in the footage?"

Boyar removed his headphones and faced Toben. "What?"

"Anything on that guy yet?" Toben repeated.

"Oh, um—nothing yet. And it's going to take more time than I thought, actually," Boyar answered.

Toben walked toward him. "What do you mean?"

"The FR tech isn't finding a match," Boyar said, shaking his head.

"Our facial recognition technology is state of the art."

"Yeah, it's not the technology. It's the image. The quality is not great. I sent it upstairs to the graphic artists. They'll be able to pull better quality from it."

"What's the ETA?"

"With everything that's going on, it could be a day or so…" Boyar sighed.

"What? That's too long?"

Boyar hunched his shoulders.

Toben shook his head. "Okay, just stay on them," he said, patting Boyar on the shoulder and walking into the back room.

It was about ten by eleven feet in size. There was a white board on the wall opposite the door. On the left wall hung a flat-screen. In the middle of the room stood a circular table with four chairs around it. Matt was sitting in the chair closest to the white board. He looked up briefly as his father entered before burying his head back into his mobile phone.

"Boy, put that phone down," Toben demanded, closing the door behind him.

"Pfft," Matt huffed, turning his face away from his father.

Toben walked to his side and stood over him. "Let me tell you what's going to happen. Your mother is coming to pick you up and take you back to school—"

Matt, sitting, looked up at Toben then looked away. "I'll just leave again," he grumbled.

Toben slammed his hand on the table.

The boy jumped in his chair and looked up at his father, shocked.

"Your mother is going to pick you up and take you back to school. You're going to apologize to her for making her cry, and when you get to school, you're going to go apologize to the principal. Then you're going to get all the assignments you missed and apologize to your teachers. After school you're going straight home to do your assignments," Toben said with a stern voice.

Matt sat quietly, face in a pout.

"Am I clear?" Toben continued.

"Ye—Yes."

"Yes what?"

"Yes, sir."

Toben walked to the door. Reaching for the handle, he turned back towards Matt. "That kid you were with, the one driving the blue Impala—"

"Last night?" Matt interrupted.

"Yeah, the one you were smoking weed with. What's his name?"

"I call him Ty," Matt answered with a puzzled look on his face.

Toben stared at his son, expecting more.

"Dad, seriously. I only know him as Ty," Matt repeated.

Toben exhaled, nodding and turning back towards the door.

"Hey, Dad. Don't you think you should apologize too?"

Toben faced Matt again. "What?"

"Mom. Shouldn't *you* apologize to her? You've made her cry too, a lot of times. A lot of nights I've heard her."

Toben stood quiet for a beat, eyes dropped. "Be ready when your mom comes to pick you up," he said, opening the door. He stepped out of the room, pulled the door shut, and walked to Ashley's desk. "Thanks again."

"Don't mention it."

Toben lingered for a moment.

"How's the brief going?" Ashley inquired.

"Ah, okay, I guess. Basically, I'll just be tagging along."

"So Stokes' team will be taking the lead, I'm guessing."

"No, it's actually the FBI's operation, believe it or not.

Come to think of it, I haven't met anyone from Stokes' team yet."

"Hmm," Ashley gestured, drumming her fingers on her desk.

"Yeah… exactly my thoughts. I better get back to Hanten's office. The Petrak meet is tonight and Stokes is on his way back here to finalize on the briefing," Toben said, looking back at the room where Matt was. "Hey, can you—"

"Yes, I'll keep an eye on Matt until Kristi gets here," Ashley cut in, smiling.

Toben returned a smile and walked out of the office. Near the elevators he came upon someone's back as they faced the far wall. It was Stokes, talking quietly into his cell phone.

"What do you mean he's nowhere to be found?" Stokes muttered. "Just find—" he listened for a couple seconds. "I don't care. Don't call me until you find him," Stokes concluded, dropping the phone to his side and turning around. "Oh… Agent Toben. It's not polite to sneak up on people," he said, surprised.

"I wasn't sneaking. Just heading to the director's office," Toben replied. He nodded at Stokes' phone. "Your people having trouble?"

Stokes placed the phone in his pocket, grinning. "Nothing for you to worry about. I guess we better get this briefing over with. After you," he said, throwing his head in the direction of Hanten's office.

"No—no, I insist," Toben said, extending his hand towards the office in invitation.

Stokes gave Toben a rigid stare before cutting his eyes, tugging at the collars of his blazer, and walking to Hanten's door.

Stokes entered the office first. Toben followed.

Hanten was sitting on the sofa looking at documents spread over the coffee table. She looked up. "Have a seat, you two."

The two sat across from her.

"Agent Stokes, have you talked to the FBI?"

"Yep. The informant confirmed that Petrak is meeting a buyer tonight. The FBI's lead on this operation has his team ready to go."

"I still don't understand how running a sting operation on Petrak gets us any closer to who's behind the bombings," Toben said.

Hanten looked at him with pursed lips.

Stokes reached into his inside blazer pocket, removed a document with a picture clipped to it, and laid it on the coffee table. "Petrak may be supplying the explosives to Black."

"You mean to whoever's behind the bombing?" Toben clarified.

"Yeah, that's what I mean," Stokes replied, pointing at the picture. "This is what they call 'sauce.' It's a new explosive agent. Very advanced. Undetectable to any explosive trace detectors or bomb-sniffing dogs. This is what we believe Petrak is in possession of."

In the picture was a small tube with a clear liquid substance inside it.

"Yes, we know about this stuff," Toben said. "It's clear, scentless, tasteless, and it can maintain its form under extreme temperature changes. And when mixed with something as simple as soda, it causes a large explosion. But sauce is not as new as you would think. There were variants of it used during Desert Storm."

"We have intel proving that sauce was used in the bombing in New York," Hanten said.

Stokes nodded.

"Right, but at Fisherman's Wharf it was a simple battery-charged IED."

Hanten shrugged. "Okay, could be separate bombers."

Toben huffed. "Both attempts happened at protests against the new law 324. That can't be a coincidence."

Hanten and Stokes remained quiet.

"And both were a bit sloppy," Toben continued. "Especially at Fisherman's Wharf. Petrak is careful. That's why it's been so hard for us to build a case against him. I don't believe he'll be involved with people this sloppy—just not his style. And from what I read about Black, these bombings don't match his profile, not even close. We're missing something," Toben concluded.

The office became silent.

Hanten broke the silence. "Be that as it may, Petrak is still dealing tonight and I want you two to be there. You should probably head over to FBI HQ and get fully briefed on the specifics of the operation tonight."

Toben's phone rang. He pulled it from his pocket and saw his wife's number on the screen. He looked at Hanten. "Sorry."

"No, you should take that," she said.

"Are you sure?" Toben asked, confused.

She nodded yes.

Toben stepped out of the office, answering the phone. "Hi, sweetheart."

"Hi. I'm downstairs," Kristi said.

"Already? That was quick. I'm on my way down."

"Oh, wait—Ashley's down here."

"Okay."

"She's waving me over. Yeah... she's going to escort me up."

"Okay, I'll see you up here," Toben ended the call. He walked back into his office and noticed that Boyar was still seated at his desk, headphones on. Toben continued to the back room.

Inside the room Matt jumped at the sound of the door opening. He looked at his father expectantly, phone in hand.

"Get ready to go. Your mother's here."

Matt stood and stuffed his phone in his pocket. He started for the door, but Toben lifted his arm, blocking the way.

"Remember what I told you to do."

Matt stared at his father's face in silence and he stared back, waiting for a confirmation.

Matt slowly nodded. "Yes, sir."

Toben moved his arm and followed Matt out of the room.

Ashley was just about to sit down at her desk. "She's waiting near the elevators," she informed Toben.

"Thanks," he replied.

Matt walked out of the office first and Toben trailed. The echo of idle chit-chat flowed down the hall. Toben saw his wife near the elevators, but she wasn't alone. Stokes was there with her.

Toben picked up his pace, passing by Matt to reach Kristi and Stokes first. The two were smiling in conversation.

"What's going on here?" Toben asked.

"Hi, honey," Kristi responded.

"Nothing. Just telling your wife how nice it is to work with you."

Toben squinted his eyes. His lips parted, but he said nothing.

Kristi noticed Matt approaching and raced over to him.

Toben and Stokes locked eyes.

"I was so worried about you. You can't do that again. Do you hear me?" Kristi's voice resounded.

"I know. I—I'm sorry," Matt replied.

Kristi released a long sigh before giving Matt a hug. "Let's go," she said, walking with him to the elevator and pressing at the console.

Toben moved his gaze from Stokes to his wife and son. "I'll be down in a second," he said.

Kristi acknowledged him with a forced smile. The elevator doors dinged open and then thumped closed again after she and Matt entered.

Toben turned his attention to Stokes. "What were you talking to my wife about? Why were you even speaking to her?"

"Nothing. Just small talk."

"Stay away from my wife," Toben demanded.

"What? Afraid I'll tell her about your extracurricular activities?"

Toben stepped up to Stokes. He was inches away from his face, glaring at him.

Stokes returned a smirk that challenged, *What are you going to do about it?*

Toben relaxed and took a small step back.

Stokes kept his eyes on him. "Hmph. Well now," he said, walking around Toben. "I have to use the restroom. Then I'm going to grab a bite and head over to FBI HQ. See you there, Agent Toben."

Toben watched, upset, until Stokes disappeared from view.

CHAPTER
NINE

BLACK'S PAST TWO hours had consisted of stopping for gas, driving and parking strategically to make sure he wasn't tailed, and contemplating his next move. His tank was full, no one was following him, and he was cruising through downtown South San Francisco. The town was small, clean, and a little busy. There were a number of people strolling the sidewalks. There were many cars, some parked, but most flowing on the roads.

He made a left and drove another quarter of a mile before he reached his destination. It was an orange-hued brick building at the top of a small hill. There were four white pillars standing before the building's front entrance, and concrete steps leading up the hill to it. Black parked on the street in front of the building and hiked up the hill to the side entrance.

The first thing he noticed as he entered were short bookshelves, about chest height. There was a bathroom, a play area for kids, and a front counter. Black spotted what he was looking for and began to walk towards it. On the other side of the building was an area with a few long tables. Resting on top of the tables were computers. There was practically no one in the area. Out of about sixteen computers, only two were being used. As Black approached the computer desk, he was intercepted by a middle-aged black woman.

"Good afternoon, sir," the lady said with a slight smile, using her index finger to push her glasses up. "Can I help you find something?"

Black smiled. "No, just wanted to use the computer for a little while. Looking things up on a cell phone can be annoying."

Her smile grew. "It *can* be annoying. Well, if you need anything, anything at all… just let me know."

"Thank you."

The lady walked away, looking back at Black a few times before walking into a room behind the front counter.

Black sat at the computer. He shook the mouse and was welcomed by a screen that read *Grand Avenue Library*. He opened up a browser and typed in the web address of a search engine. The first name he searched was *Matt Toben*. The top search result was the only relevant one, but it led him to a social media site that listed the profiles of many Matt Tobens. *None of these look like the kid I saw at the pier*, Black thought to himself as he looked through the profile pictures. He tried a second search: *Ashley DHS*. He got way too many results to wade through and knew his search wasn't specific enough. He thought for a second before typing in a third search for *Ashley Toben DHS*. This time he found something useful. One of the top search results linked him to a website for the Department of Homeland Security, West Coast division. The top of the page read *Customs and Border Protection Support* and *Threat Prevention Unit* was listed beneath it.

There were pictures and names of three people on the page, along with a paragraph of information about each. The first was a black man with light brown skin. He was clean-shaven and sported a small fro and a smile on his face. Next to his picture was the name Jake Toben and the title "Lead Agent." Black read his information. *Seems like a stand-up guy,* Black thought. The following picture was someone that Black had seen before—the brunette from the old pier. She stared at the camera with numb eyes and a hard smile. The name Ashley Chapp displayed next to her picture.

"Someone didn't care for picture day," Black whispered to himself.

The final picture was of a fair-skinned man with dark brown hair dressed into a classic fringe. He had glasses over his dazed eyes and his mouth was slightly open as if the camera caught him by surprise. Victor Boyar was his name.

Black reclined, folding his arms, looking intently at the screen. "Oh yeah. I almost forgot about her," he mumbled, leaning towards the screen. He typed the name *Johana* and got nothing but some wiki and dictionary sites providing the origin and history of the name. The next couple searches were of the two cops he left on the Golden Gate Bridge, Nick Reeves and Kevin Guo. He didn't find much more about either of them that he didn't already know. One thing that stuck out was that Guo had a social media profile and on his page was a picture of him, Reeves, and one more guy whom Black had never seen before. The man had dark hair, an aquiline nose, and strong dimples. The three looked to be at some bar or casual social event.

Black relaxed into his thoughts, tapping his fingers against the desk, trying to connect all the dots. *Still too many unanswered questions.* Leaning forward again, he typed the shipping address he had seen on the box inside the storage unit. A link to a navigation site displayed. Black clicked it and was taken to a site that provided step-by-step directions and a map of the location. It was in Treasure Island. Black memorized the directions, closed the browser window, and restarted the computer. He stood from the table and walked to the same door he had entered.

"Have a good day, sir," the librarian beamed, leaning over the counter and waving at him.

Black stopped, returned a smile, and continued out the door. He slid in his car and took 101 North to I-80 East. The highway ran into the Oakland Bay Bridge. The bridge was occupied by late afternoon traffic, but the sights were stunning. On the right was a breathtaking view across San Francisco Bay. On the left was a remarkable scene consisting of a large body of water, the ferry ports, and mountains. It was a beautiful portrait framed in steel trusses. He continued across the bridge, thumping over the bridge joints every few seconds.

When he reached Yerba Buena Isle, he took the exit for Treasure Island. He followed the road around the outside of the small isles. After a mile and a half of driving, he was invited into Treasure Island by some palm trees and a marina side by side with the Treasure Island Administration Building. He made a right at the next street past the Administration Building and drove a couple hundred feet before he heard his mental GPS system tell him he had reached his destination.

It was a large warehouse structure sitting behind the Administration Building. Unlike the latter, however, there was no name or sign revealing the identity or purpose of this building. It was surrounded by tall barbed wire fencing and there was a security hut at the front driveway. Black made a right turn off the road and slowly approached the security hut. Immediately a guard exited it and extended his arm, signaling for Black to stop. The guard was wearing a black cap, a black shirt, and camo fatigue pants. He carried an AR-15 in his hand and a firearm on his hip. Black also noticed that he was wearing an earpiece. Stepping to the driver's side door, the guard motioned for Black to roll down his window.

"How can I help you, sir?" the guard asked.

"Is this where I go to apply for the government position?" Black played it off.

The guard shook his head. "No. You may want to try this building," he said, pointing at the Administration Building. "Or the building here across the street," he continued, throwing his thumb in the direction of the road.

"Oh. So this isn't a government facility?"

"No, sir. This building is privately owned. Now if you go down—"

"What is it you guys do here?"

The guard shortened his stance, sighed heavily, and said, "We process and package seafood here, sir."

Black nodded at the man's rifle. "You guys must be packaging sharks with that kind of firepower," he remarked.

The guard hunched his shoulder and cocked his head. "You never know," he said, shaking his head.

"You're right. You don't." Black responded, turning his attention to the windshield and pointing. "So, I go down here—"

"Yeah—yeah, so you go down and make a U at the circle roundabout," the guard interrupted, rushing his words.

Black nodded, confirming he understood.

The guard stepped back from the car, pressing the small push-to-talk unit clipped to his shirt. "We have one turning around," he said before releasing the unit.

Black rolled up his window and continued down the long driveway. He wanted to go to the end of the driveway and get a peek of the other side of the building but didn't want to raise suspicion. He made a U-turn at the roundabout and noticed that the front entrance to the warehouse was behind a sliding gate. Through the metal diamond links of the gate, he spotted an armed guard. He was standing, holding his rifle, watching Black as he completed his circuit in the roundabout. *Well, that makes at least two of them,* Black thought, cruising back up the driveway, past the security hut, and making a right onto the road. He drove the length of the warehouse building, getting a lay of the land. Near the back corner of the building, inside the barbed wire fence, there was another armed guard. This guard turned the corner and walked the side of the building towards the front. "'We process and package seafood.' Yeah right," Black whispered to himself, making a left into a parking lot before turning around and veering on the road in the direction he came.

He made a left at the Administration Building, followed by another left, entering the side parking lot. He found a spot and exited the car. The smell of freshly baked bread struck his nose. There was a sandwich shop attached to the Administration Building. Making note of the restaurant, he walked across the parking lot towards the marina. The scent of bread slowly disappeared as the smell of the ocean overtook the area. Black could hear splashing water, thumping on the deck, and screams of excitement and recreation. Docked at the marina were Jet Skis, small boats, and a few kayaks. On the deck were a couple of mounted binoculars for viewing the bay and a few people standing in swimwear and strapped in life vests. A sign that read *Jet Ski and Kayak Rides and Rentals* was nailed to one of the deck posts. There was a middle-aged man with a head full of brown hair on deck. He was wearing sunglasses, a white button-up, and red shorts. Fuzzy brown hair ran up his arms and legs. The man had a confident smile on his face as he handed out life vests and directed people to the Jet Skis and kayaks.

Black saw the warehouse with barbed wire fencing about one hundred yards out to his left. He creaked across the wooden deck towards one of the mounted binoculars, sliding through a crowd and feeling the dampness of their skin brush against his clothes as he stepped to the binoculars. He hunched over, looking into the eyepieces. At first, his view was across the water of Clipper Cove. He carefully adjusted the binoculars in the direction of the warehouse. It gave him a clear view of the side closest to the water. There was a small window and a door on that side of the building. Barbed wire fencing stood between the building and the water. Something interesting caught his attention. Part of the fencing near the bottom appeared to be split. *No one noticed that*, he thought to himself, continuing to watch for a few moments before standing straight and squinting at the building, then stooping down to the binoculars again. He watched for a couple more minutes and didn't see a single guard on that side of the building the whole time. *Hmm… No guards checking that side,* he thought, standing back from the binoculars. He spotted the guy in the red shorts and was about to approach him, but he changed his mind after seeing that three other people had the same idea. Black shrugged and walked across the parking lot to the sandwich shop.

The inside of the restaurant was small and sparse with a few tables scattered around and a few pictures of San Francisco hanging from the walls. Besides Black, there were four other customers. Black made his way to the counter, where a tanned woman greeted him with a smile.

"Hiya, sir. What can I get ya?" she said in a British accent.

"Hi," Black said, looking up at the menu board. "Ah… I'll have your spinach salad with grilled chicken and a side of fruit."

"Healthy eater, I see," the lady said, brushing her blond hair behind her ear and typing at the register.

"For the most part. I may be staying up late tonight, so I don't want anything too heavy."

"Eat in or take away?"

"I'll eat it here."

"Anything to drink?"

"Just water."

"Okay…"

The cashier gave Black his total and he handed her some cash.

"This warehouse behind you," Black said, pointing his thumb to his right. "What is it?"

The woman looked up from the register, eyes partly closed, lips slightly pursed, and head cocked. "I think they're a seafood packaging company or something," she said, extending Black his change.

He waved for her to keep it, asking, "How long have they been there?"

The lady dropped the change into the register. "I don't know, to be honest. Three years, maybe?" she answered. "They don't receive many visitors outside of the shipments that come at night."

"Shipments?"

"Yeah, every now and then they have trucks come in. I'm guessing it's for supplies or the seafood they package."

Yeah, I bet, Black thought. "What day do these trucks usually come?"

"You know what?" the woman said, closing the register and craning over the counter. "I don't know if it's ever on a specific day. Why do you ask?"

"Just wondering. I don't remember seeing the building the last time I was here is all."

"Oh, okay. Well, is there anything else I can help ya with?"

"No, ma'am."

"Alright, take a seat anywhere and I'll bring your grub to you."

"Thank you."

"No bother."

Black found a table in a corner of the restaurant and sat with his back facing the wall, giving him a clear view of the entire restaurant. He relaxed into his thoughts. *Maybe I should just leave town*, he thought, but remembered that it would make him look guilty. Not to mention there were a couple of terrorists fresh out of puberty running around the city. On top of it, he knew someone was looking to pin these bombings on him, and whoever it was had connections with law enforcement, considering his little run-in with Reeves and Guo.

Moments later, the cashier came to the table and presented Black's food. He ate and sat thinking for a little while before leaving the shop. Outside, the sun began to set and the evening darkness gradually coated the sky. Black walked back across the parking lot to the marina. The crowd of people and their screams of excitement had been replaced by seagulls and chirping. Black spotted the man in the red shorts and approached him. The guy was on the deck helping someone off one of the Jet Skis. He locked the Jet Ski to the dock, then faced Black.

"How are you doing?" he asked, smiling.

"I'm doing well. Thinking about renting one of these Jet Skis."

The man looked Black up and down. "Where's your swimwear?" he asked, chuckling.

"Won't need it. I won't be going too far."

"Do you have a reservation?"

"No, I don't."

"Okay, well, I'm locking up the Jet Skis. We don't usually rent them out this close to dusk. You can rent one of those kayaks before I lock them up, though."

Black took a look at the kayaks. "Okay, how much?"

"Twenty an hour. It's getting late, so the longest I can rent it out will be one hour, and you'll need to pay with a credit card since you don't have a reservation. We've had a few things go missing, particularly a couple Jet Skis."

"I see. That way if I don't return the kayak, I get billed the price of it."

"That's right," the guy said, smiling.

"Okay, how much do they run for?"

"Well, it depends," the man said, stepping over to the kayaks. "We have some that're three hundred" —he pointed to a dark grey kayak—"... and we have some that're two thousand," he continued, pointing at a slightly longer blue kayak.

Black pulled out his wallet, removing four crisp one hundred-dollar bills.

"I'll take this grey one and a paddle."

TWENTY MINUTES LATER, Black was in Clipper Clove rocking over the waves in a kayak. It was night, but no lights were on at the warehouse building, yet. Black paddled to the area of the fence where he had seen the split earlier through the binoculars. He carefully rolled the kayak towards the shore, lightly knocking against the riprap stones, sending a trace of water splashing into the kayak.

He stood from the kayak, swaying as he gained his balance, and stepped out. Wedging the paddle between some stones, he tied the line from the kayak around the paddle to anchor it. He climbed up the rocks and to the fence line, looking for the split. It took him a few minutes to find it, but once he found it, he could see how the tear in the fence was easy to miss, even if a person was looking right at it in the daytime. He gently peeled open the fence at the split and squeezed through. The smell of cigarette smoke tickled his nose. Creeping towards the door of the warehouse, he reached inside his pocket for his lock pick, but was surprised when the knob turned easily in his hand. *Hmm,* he breathed, cracking the door open and ducking inside.

The door led into a long, dim hallway. Black entered, looking to his left then his right. He was alone, though the ruffle of plastic and the rasping of cardboard boxes being handled flowed from the room directly in front of him. Its doorway was hung with clear plastic vinyl strip curtains. Through the strips, Black could make out stacks of crates and boxes in the room. He also saw a couple of figures moving around in the distance. Squatting, Black pierced the curtains. A fishy crab aroma swept across his face and his body quivered at the drop in temperature as he took cover behind a tower of boxes. He peeked around the boxes, observing the warehouse floor. The area was bright compared to the rest of the building. There were circular lights draped from the ceiling and in the center was a line of tables. On top of the tables were cardboard boxes and plastic bags. Standing around the tables were two workers. Both were men who wore lightweight jackets, dust masks, and hairnets underneath hats. Black watched as one stuffed fish in a plastic bag, sealed the bag, and used a device to suck the air from the bag before tossing it into a box. Black remained low and out of sight, dodging a few pallets, crates, and bins of iced fish as he crept along the side wall towards the back. He kept his eyes on the men the entire time.

On the back wall was another doorway with vinyl strip curtains. Black moved towards it. The sound of shoes scuffing against the floor echoed from the other side as he approached the doorway, so he quickly padded backwards, taking cover behind a pallet of boxes. A third worker walked through the curtains, toting a box. He was dressed like the other two. Black waited for the man to walk to the center and place the box on the table before easing through the doorway. On the other side of the curtains was a room. In the room were a few cages with boxes stacked inside. To Black's right, a cardboard baler. Further to the right was a door with an exit sign hanging over it. Directly to his left was a small room. The room contained a refrigerator, a microwave, and coffee maker resting on a countertop, and a few tables. Black zipped towards one of the cages, passing the baler and a loading dock door on his way. He gently pushed the cage gate open. Stepping inside, he removed one of the boxes from a stack and unfolded the flaps. Inside the box were plastic bags. He checked four more boxes. All the same. He raced over to another cage and checked some boxes inside of it. Again, all basically empty. Black rubbed his chin, eyebrows squishing together.

At that, the sound of the vinyl curtain strips whipping apart and the babble of conversation drifted across the room. Black closed the gate and crouched behind the boxes inside. Two men entered the room. One was a guard and the other a worker. The worker was carrying a box. The two strolled in Black's direction, continuing their conversation as they passed by.

"Remember, when you finish packaging the products, bring them back here immediately, okay?" the guard instructed, waiting on a confirmation.

The worker nodded in understanding.

"Okay?" the guard repeated.

"Yeah, package the product then bring it back here, got it," the worker confirmed.

"Okay, good. I don't mean to sound like a broken record, but small amounts of product have been disappearing. Not a lot, but the boss is very particular when it comes to numbers. It makes him nervous when they don't add up."

The men continued past Black to a large commercial walk-in freezer. The guard draped his AR-15 to his side, removed a key, and unlocked the freezer door. The two disappeared into the cold fog for a few moments. When they came out, the guard was shivering and the worker was rubbing his gloved hands together.

"It's cold in there," the worker said.

"Yeah, no kidding," the guard replied, closing and locking the freezer door. The pair walked back to the warehouse floor.

Black slipped out of the cage and hurried to the freezer. He gave the door handle a quick jerk just to confirm it was locked before removing his lock pick. He knelt at the door and fiddled with the lock, peering over his shoulder every few seconds. The lock snapped open and he walked inside. The chill instantly reached his bones and the cold smoke momentarily hampered his vision. The freezer was roomy and noisy. A large HVAC unit with three fans roared at the back of the freezer. There were shelves on both side walls of the unit which contained small bins, crates, and boxes. Stacked on the floor were plastic shipping containers, the kind with folding flaps. One of the stacks had a hand truck wedged underneath it. He walked over and lifted the flaps on the top container. Inside were frozen plastic bags of fish—salmon. He dug inside the container until he noticed something strange. There was a single bag of largemouth bass amongst the mess of salmon.

He examined the bag more closely and noticed something wedged into the fish's mouth. It was a slim glass tube. Black rocked the bag back and forth. The tube was far down the fish mouth, but there appeared to be a clear liquid slushing within it. *Water would be frozen at this temperature*, he thought. He placed the bag back into the container, closed the top, and set it on the floor, exposing the second container. He opened it and put his hand inside, reaching towards the bottom. The frozen bags of fish crackled at the heat of his hand. There was something hard and metallic at the bottom. Black pulled his hand from the container, bringing with it a plastic bag holding two largemouth bass. He looked at the bag closely and noticed a gun snugged between the fish. It was a Glock 19, unmarked, just like the others he had seen.

At that moment the faint hum of a large vehicle wafted through the frigid air. Black jabbed the bag back into the container, closed it, and settled the one on the floor back on top, just as he had found it. He opened the freezer door just wide enough to case the room. Clear. He pushed at the door but quickly pulled it shut again at the sight of the armed guard sprinting back into the room. The guard's footsteps paused. Black once again cracked the door and spotted him at the loading dock. The man sat his rifle down and unlocked the roll-up docking door from the bottom before hoisting it open, exposing the rear door of a delivery truck. Ten seconds later, three knocks came from the exit door. The guard opened it. Inside stepped another guard. He was tall and slim and armed with only a sidepiece, no rifle.

"That was quicker than last time," he commented, smiling.

"Yeah, I saw you coming up front, so I hurried back here. Hey… where's Larry?" the other guard said, catching his breath.

"Oh. He's in the truck waiting," the tall guard answered, cocking his head towards the door he had entered.

"Okay, well, let's get the product loaded. Should be quick. Only a few containers."

The tall guard nodded and walked over to the truck door, stuck a key into the padlock, pulled the latch, and rolled the door up. "Okay. Where's the containers?"

"Over in the freezer," the guard said, pointing towards the freezer.

Black swiftly closed the door and retreated back into the freezer. The chatter from the two guards became louder with every step he took backwards. Watching the door, Black contemplated his next move. He had scanned the freezer for places to hide earlier. There weren't many options, but he had already determined the best one. The guards' conversation resonated directly upon the freezer door. *Maybe I should just fight them. No, not a good idea,* he decided, dropping to the floor and rolling underneath the shelf to his left. The floor was cold but bearable. The freezer door clanked open. Black saw a pair of dark boots appear right next to him, bringing the scent of nicotine with them.

"Here it is," the guard said, shaking the hand truck with the stack of containers Black had examined just moments before.

"Okay," the tall slim guard replied.

The first pair of boots disappeared and another took their place. The hand trunk leaned diagonally and was wheeled out of the freezer, squeaking, before the door thumped closed behind it. Black rolled from under the shelf and pushed himself from the floor, walking to the door and once again peeking out. The slim guard was loading the containers into the back of the truck. The other guard was standing near the loading dock, supervising.

The tall guard walked out from inside the truck. "Hey. Do you guys have any coffee?" he asked the other guard.

"Yeah, it's over here in the break room," the guard answered, picking up his rifle, and waving his co-worker towards the small room.

The two men strolled towards the room. Black carefully exited the freezer, shaking, in an attempt to knock the chill off. He stooped low and raced towards the loading dock. He was planning to use the exit door and was microseconds away before he heard the tall guard's voice.

"Ah, wait. I forgot something."

Black's eyebrows wrinkled and a tingling shock rushed through his body as he fled inside the back of the truck, hunkering behind a pile of storage bins. Seconds later, the truck door was slammed shut. The inside was absolutely dark. Black could barely make out his hand in front of his face. "Great," he muttered to himself. Ten minutes later he heard the truck's cabin door open, then close. A minute after that the truck was rocking under the revolutions of the diesel engine.

TEN

THE RIDE WAS uncomfortable. Not only was it dark and reeking of fish, but the size of the vehicle made every bump on the road feel like a crater while the bins and containers squeaked and rattled constantly. Black sat quietly, bringing forth a map of the area in his mind, monitoring every stop and turn the truck made to track his location. It wasn't long before the bumps from the road softened and the noise from the storage containers died down. This didn't come as a surprise to Black because in his mind he had already approximated where the truck would be. *I-80 East.*

The drive was smooth for another twenty-five minutes before the truck slowed down, bouncing and swaying at a right turn. For a few moments the ride once again became bumpy and noisy. Black could hear a faint whirring sound high above. He squinted his eyes and pursed his lips, concentrating on the sound.

Twin turbine engines cutting through the air.

Black smiled. He was sure they were near Oakland International Airport.

The truck continued on its course, humming steadily for another five minutes before jerking to a complete stop. Black felt the vibrations dissolve from his body as the engine was turned off. He heard water gently swishing nearby and the truck's cabin doors opening and shutting shortly after. Chatter and laughter flowed from the front of the truck and down the side, accompanied by footsteps. Black quietly lifted himself to a squat on the balls of his feet, removing one of his knives, and peeked around the pile of bins in the direction of the truck's rear door. The door clicked and dinged before it was railed up. The men's voices boomed clearer and the inside of the truck lit up with a beam of moonlight permeating through to the back.

"You're a real charmer, Larry," the tall guard said, laughing.

The guard called Larry laughed in response. "Hey, what's wrong with the woman paying for the man's dinner on the first date? So what if it was my idea to go out?" he said, hunching his shoulders.

His partner shook his head as both men continued to chuckle.

"Hey, give me a hand with this ramp," the tall guard requested.

"Yeah—yeah, I got it."

Black ducked behind the bins, listening as the ramp was pulled from the truck and dropped, scratching against the pavement. Footsteps knocked towards him and the floor of the truck suddenly sunk under added weight. Black's heart rate increased and he pursed his lips, gripping his knife as he heard steps sliding towards him—close, closer, and closer still. The steps paused and he heard the guard Larry yell back towards the door.

"Which one is it?"

"It's the stack of containers on the hand truck," the tall guard answered.

"I don't see—" Larry fumbled around the containers. "Oh, here it is," he announced, grabbing the hand truck and wheeling it down the ramp. "Should we lock the truck door?" he continued.

"Nah. We won't be long, but let's close it."

The truck door rolled closed and the squeak of the hand truck along with the chitchat of the two guards gradually faded. Black replaced his knife in its holster and crept to the truck door, lifting it open about six inches before lowering to his belly and peering out through the opening. He didn't see or hear anyone nearby. There was only the gleam from the moon and the stars in the sky, the sound of splashing water to his left, the contour of a building to his right, and darkness in the far distance. Black raised the door another two feet and slid underneath, safely landing on the asphalt and letting the door close behind him. He immediately noticed a steel chain link fence to his left. On the other side of the fence was a large body of water, wafting waves and cool air to the shore. Black assumed it was San Francisco Bay.

To the right, about ten yards away, was a five-story concrete parking garage. There was a stairwell on the northwest corner. Black took a step towards the garage, but the glare from the headlights of a vehicle approached. He quickly retreated behind the delivery truck to take cover, looking on as the dark SUV swung into the parking garage. Then he ran across the pavement and towards the garage, slipped inside the dimly lit stairwell, and quietly closed the door behind him. Faint voices seeped through the dense brick walls of the stairwell. Black lurked upstairs and stopped at the door with *L2* written next to it. He carefully cracked the door. The parking level had overhead lights and was large and spacious, but there wasn't a single car parked in any of the countless available spots.

Black eased through the door and made it eight steps across the concrete floor before hearing the squeak of the hand truck approaching. He swiftly took cover behind one of the large columns in the shadows near the door. Glancing around the column, he saw the two guards walking up the drive ramp. They came to a stop in the center of the floor, right in the driving lane.

Larry looked around. "We must be early," he said.

"No, I think we're on time. This meet is supposed to be really quick," the other guard said.

The hum of a motor echoed throughout the level and the tall guard pulled the hand cart out of the approaching car's path. Bright blue LED headlights illuminated the level as the dark SUV bumped over the ramp and onto the parking floor. The driver made a circle, orienting the SUV so that it was facing back down the ramp. Two men exited the front doors, engine still running. The driver had blond hair fixed into a ponytail and a serious look on his face. The passenger had dark skin and a low-fade haircut. Both men were medium height with a bulky build. The driver stood at the vehicle, clasping his hands in front of his waist, and watched the two guards approach the SUV with the hand truck.

The man with the low fade walked to the back passenger's side door and opened it. Another man stepped out. His skin was a cream-white complexion with spots of red. His burgundy hair showed streaks of white and was slicked back on his head. The same color hair covered the lower half of his face.

The slick-haired man met the two guards in front of the SUV. "Is that my product?" he asked, in a noticeable accent.

He's from the Czech Republic, Black figured.

"Ye—yes, sir, Mr. Petrak," the tall guard responded.

Petrak looked to the guy with the ponytail and nodded at the containers stacked on the hand truck.

The man returned a quick nod in acknowledgment and walked over to the containers. The two delivery guards took a couple of steps back. The guy with the ponytail took a few minutes opening and examining the containers. After he was finished, he stacked them back as they were.

"It's all here," he said, turning toward Petrak.

"You two can get out of here," Petrak said to Larry and his partner.

The men pivoted.

"Wait before you go," Petrak called to them. "A small but... significant amount of my inventory is... well, unaccounted for. Do you two know anything about that?"

Both men's eyebrows squished together and they both slightly shook their heads. "No, sir, Mr. Petrak," they both replied, nearly in tandem.

Petrak cast a stern gaze on the two men for a few moments before a smile arched on his face. "Well, if you hear anything, let me know. Now get out of here."

"Yes, sir," the two guards said in sync before walking to the same door Black had entered and disappearing into the stairwell.

"Well, there goes my ride," Black whispered to himself.

"Okay, boys, this should be a quick and easy exchange," Petrak commented at the two men with him as he walked back to the SUV, got in, and closed the door.

The two men stood at the front of the SUV, hands clasped in front at their waists.

A few minutes passed before another vehicle wheeled up the ramp. This one was a large dark blue sedan with standard halogen headlights and a somber tint.

Two men exited from the front of the sedan, engine still running. The driver was clean-shaven, had sand-colored skin, and wore a V-neck. On his wrist looked to be a watch or maybe a Fitbit, Black guessed. His partner carried a suitcase. His face was smooth as well, and his brown hair was styled into a short surfer cut. The two men walked toward the SUV, the guy in the V-neck at the forefront. The man at the SUV who sported the low fade walked to Petrak's window and tapped it. The other guy at the SUV, with the ponytail, stuck out his palm to halt the two men from the sedan and began patting them down. After he finished, he stepped back from them but stood in their path, holding them at bay.

By then Petrak was out of the SUV and walking over to the group. The man with the low fade followed behind him.

Petrak opened his arms. "You guys made it," he welcomed the two men.

The guy in the V-neck, looking around the man with the ponytail, replied, "Of course we made it—now, how about you tell Mr. Ponytail here to get out the way so we can talk business."

Petrak looked at the guy wearing the ponytail and nodded. The man returned a nod before taking a few steps back.

"Okay… now we can get on with it," the guy in the V-neck said.

"Is this the product?" the man with the surfer cut asked, pointing at the stack of containers.

Petrak eyed the suitcase he was carrying. "Is that the payment?" he asked.

The guy smirked and walked over to the man with the ponytail, handing him the suitcase before walking over and inspecting the contents of the containers.

In turn, the man with the ponytail walked over to the SUV, placed the suitcase on the hood, and unlatched it.

"It's all there. Just like we agreed," the guy in the V-neck assured Petrak.

"I'm sure it is—I mean, we've known each other for two years. But business is business, right?"

A couple of moments later, the guy with the ponytail walked to Petrak and whispered something in his ear. The man with the surfer cut did the same thing to his partner.

"So are we good?" Petrak asked.

"It appears so," the man in the V-neck answered.

At the same time, Black noticed him covertly push a button on his watch. *What's up with that?*

"Okay, so I guess that concludes our business," Petrak said, turning and walking towards his ride. He made it to the door before the guy in the V-neck yelled to him.

"You're not going to ask what we're planning to do with it?"

"Excuse me?"

"The product, don't you want to know what it's for?"

"What do you mean? I already know what you're going to do with it."

The guy raised his chin, waiting to hear what Petrak was going to say.

"It's seafood, you eat it," Petrak grinned.

"That was some pretty aggressive seafood in New York, wouldn't you say?"

Petrak walked back to the guy in the V-neck, looking him in the eye. "I don't know what you're talking about," he said, shrugging his shoulders.

"C'mon, Petrak—"

"Look, I told you, I didn't have anything to do with that. You're the first person I dealt this type of… seafood to. Furthermore, I can't be held responsible for what the buyers do with the product."

The guy in the V-neck shook his head.

"That concludes our business. As a matter of fact, I don't want to see you again," Petrak said, walking once again to his vehicle.

Before Petrak reached his door, a loud slap resounded throughout the parking level. The stairwell door was flung open and five men in SWAT gear swarmed inside. Four more marched up the ramp, all with MP510s drawn.

Black quickly dropped to one knee in the shadows behind the column, hidden.

All of the armed men were dressed in dark clothing from head to toe and wore bulletproof vests that read *FBI*, as well as tactical helmets and masks. All except one. This particular man had no helmet or mask. He was in slacks and a dress shirt, covered up by a bulletproof vest with *DIA* written on it. He looked familiar, but Black couldn't quite place him.

"Get on the ground!" one of the FBI agents ordered Petrak and the group as the armed men surrounded them.

Four of the five immediately knelt and crawled to their bellies, placing their hands behind their heads. Petrak remained standing, hands in the air, eyes bulging, mouth gaping.

"Get on the ground!" the agent repeated.

Petrak stepped back, gaze wandering, hands still in the air, mouth still open.

The agent allowed his rifle to drape to his side and grabbed Petrak, pushing him face first into the SUV before removing a white zip tie from the front pouch of his bulletproof vest.

Black slipped out of the shadows and quietly entered the stairwell, unseen. He exited the stairwell the same way he entered, turning at the corner of the parking garage and jogging up the sidewalk a good distance before slowing to a normal walking pace. The street didn't have many lights and there were a few small commercial buildings and offices on either side, most of which appeared to be vacant. Periodically checking over his shoulder to make sure he wasn't being followed, Black made it nearly a block from the parking garage before he saw a figure walking towards him. It was an FBI agent. *Great, I can't run—it'll look suspicious.* The agent had the same tactical gear and the same weapon draped around his shoulder as the rest of his team.

Black's plan was to walk on, keeping his distance and pretending he was a scared citizen concerned for his life, considering the agent had a gun and all, but he didn't have a chance to execute this plan. The agent aimed his MP510 at Black at close range.

"Hey, you, ha—hands in the air!" he instructed Black.

Black immediately did as he was told. "What's going on?! Are you a cop or something?" he faked, turning his body at a slight angle to make himself a smaller target.

"I'm F—FBI, don't you move!"

"FBI? What do you want with me?"

"Quiet!" the agent barked, glancing over his shoulder. "Over here I hav—" he attempted to yell.

Black instantly pulled the gun from his grasp. The rifle was strapped around the agent's body, so the force from the pull tugged him along. Black struck him in the face before hip-tossing him onto the pavement back first, then arching over and putting him to sleep with another punch to the face. Before Black could formulate his next move, the scuff of two distinct footsteps hit his ears. He looked in the direction the agent initially came from and saw two dark silhouettes running toward him. He dashed across the street to an old vacant storefront, pushing the door open as he entered. Dust and a musty odor entered his nose. Coughing, he fanned the dust from his face and continued into the building. He immediately scanned the room and noticed a smashed countertop, shelves thrown on the floor, and a hallway in the back. He could hear footwear skipping over the pavement behind him, growing louder with each step. He hustled into the back, high-stepping the shelves on the floor. In the hallway were three doors: an exit door, a swinging impact door, and close to the exit, a bathroom door. Black rushed to the exit door and flung it wide open before ducking into the bathroom, gently pulling the door shut behind him.

Inside the bathroom was a broken sink, mirror, and toilet bowl. The floor was tiled some ugly shade of blue with mildew growing between the cracks. A crashing sound vibrated against the bathroom wall. Two seconds later, Black heard footsteps shoot through the hall and out the exit door. He zipped out of the bathroom and into the main room again. There was another agent fully clothed in tactical gear lying stunned across one of the shelves on the floor. The man groaned, looking up at Black. The agent's gaze moved to the gun that he himself had dropped. He then looked at Black once more. It was as if he was asking for permission to pick up his own rifle. Black shook his head. The agent attempted to lurch towards his gun, but his face met with the sole of Black's boot. The man rolled over the broken shelf, smacking into the wall. Black darted out of the storefront and up the sidewalk, in the direction he'd been heading before. He made it twelve yards from the storefront. Passing an alley, he heard a man's voice.

"Freeze!" the voice demanded.

Black was certain there was a gun aimed at his back, so he stopped.

"Put your hands up!"

Black inched his hands up. "You know, this is the second time today a gun has been pointed at my back."

"Well, aren't you a special guy? Now, turn around slowly," the man said, his footsteps moving closer.

Black spun around and his gaze dropped. Seeing some dressy shoes and slacks, he continued sliding his eyes upward. The man was wearing a long-sleeved button-up shirt covered by a vest with the logo *DHS*. *What's up with all these different agencies?* he thought, proceeding finally to the man's face. Black's neck extended forward, his eyes narrowed, and his forehead wrinkled. He had seen this man before.

The man had the same look on his face as Black, and his head flinched back softly when their eyes met. "Orlando Black. We've been looking for you."

Black shook his head slightly, processing the man's face before the name came back to him. "Agent Toben," he finally announced.

"How do you know my name?" Toben asked, Smith & Wesson still aimed at Black.

"I did some research on you—well, only a little."

"Well, we've done a lot of research on you."

"*We* who? DHS, FBI, or DIA?"

"All of the above."

"Look, Toben, from what I read, you seem to be on the up and up. I'm not your guy."

"You're not my guy for what? Do you have something you want to tell me?"

"Don't play games. I had nothing to do with those bombings. Someone's trying to cover their tracks."

Toben's eyebrows dropped. "Really? Who?" he asked, wetting his lips.

"If I knew the answer to that, I wouldn't be standing here with you, now would I?" Black said, looking Toben in the eyes. "Wait, you know there's something wrong, don't you?"

"I tell you what, let's talk all about it at headquarters, okay?"

"That's not happening."

"Excuse me?"

"Someone wants me silenced, and whoever it is, they're connected. So until I find out who's after me and why, I'm not allowing any three-letter agency to take me anywhere."

Toben huffed. "You don't have a choice, Black," he said, keeping the gun on Black with one arm and reaching to his side with the other. He lifted a pair of handcuffs. "Cuff yourself," he instructed Black, tossing the handcuffs at him.

The moment before the cuffs left Toben's hand, Black saw an opening. As Toben extended his arm to throw the cuffs, his pistol aim shifted from Black a few degrees. It wasn't much, but it was enough for Black to close the gap between the two of them. Toben swung his shooting arm back on target, but it was far too late. Black chopped his opponent's forearm with one hand and thrust the edge of his palm into his gut with the other hand. Both the Smith & Wesson and the handcuffs fell, clanging on the sidewalk. Toben craned over, moaning and clutching his stomach. Black grabbed the back of his head and rolled him to the pavement on his back.

He picked up Toben's gun and aimed it at him. "Like I said, I'm not going anywhere."

Toben rolled to his side, looking up at Black. "So you're going to assault and kill a federal agent, Black?" he gasped, out of breath.

"I think you know that's not my style."

Toben said nothing.

"Give me your phone," Black said, holding out his hand.

"Why would I do that? You already said you're not going to shoot me."

Black shrugged. "No, I didn't. I said I wouldn't kill you. Now give it here," he said, fanning his fingers.

Toben reached into his pocket and removed his cellphone.

"Make sure it's unlocked," Black added.

Toben tapped at the screen and extended the phone to Black.

Black, keeping the gun trained on him, walked closer, reached down, and snatched the phone. He stepped back and pressed at the phone, holding it in his hand until he felt a vibration in his pocket. He ended the call and chucked the phone at Toben. The phone landed on his leg. Black checked his own phone and saw a missed call from a number with a San Francisco area code. "There, now we have each other's phone number. Don't bother trying to track mine. It'll be a waste of your time."

Toben kept quiet, looking at Black with squinted eyes.

"I'll call you tomorrow with a time and place where we can meet and talk," Black said, ejecting the magazine and clearing the chamber before dropping it all in front of Toben.

Observing Toben's gaze follow the gun and magazine, Black wasted no time. He bolted away up the sidewalk, making a right across the street and into an alley. At the far end of the alley was another street. He raced up that street another six blocks before heading right onto a busy avenue. Cars crowded the road and patrons were going in and out of stores and restaurants. He blended with the other pedestrians, walking half a mile before he found a four-star hotel. It didn't have the amenities of the establishment where he had stayed the night before, but he figured it would do.

CHAPTER
ELEVEN

BLACK SPENT SEVEN hours lying in the bed, though he slept only five of them. The remaining two he used to review all the information he had gathered. He conjured up the faces and names of all the players. He thought about the different locations where he saw them and what their interest in the situation might be. Some things became clear, but there were still many holes that needed to be filled. Black played different scenarios in his head, thought about his next move, and tried to decide how he should proceed.

He sighed, rolled out of the sheets and to the floor on his palms, and performed two hundred push-ups. Next, he rolled to his back and performed the same number of sit-ups, before concluding with some breathing exercises and tai chi forms. The bathroom was his next stop. He undressed and jumped into the shower, putting on the same clothes and heading to the lobby after he had finished. The lobby was quiet with only a few people in it. The aroma of toast and pork hit his nose as he walked into the dining area, where he found a continental breakfast bar. He grabbed a plate and scooped some yellow runny substance that passed as eggs onto it, along with hash browns and a couple of sausage patties. He stopped at the fruit bowl and snagged a banana, then at the small fridge to grab a bottle of water before sitting at one of the open tables.

Just as he began to eat, loud voices and chatter flowed into the dining area. A few teenagers entered, making a beeline to the food bar. A smaller kid, five or six years old, followed, and behind him a young mother. The group paraded around the food bar, stacking their plates, and scampered to a table. The teenagers walked past Black and found a table at the far corner. The small kid stomped through the dining area while his mom followed with plates of food in hand. The kid had his arms folded and his bottom lip poked out.

"Find a place for us to sit, Christopher," the mother said.

"No!" the little boy pouted.

"Let's sit here," his mother instructed, taking a seat at a table. "Christopher, come sit down."

"No! I hate you!" Christopher yelled with his back to his mom.

Everyone in the dining room looked at their table.

The mother gaped and rubbed her forehead. "Why would you say that? I'm sorry, come here."

Did she really just say she was sorry? How did she fix her lips to say that? Black was wondering.

"No!" Christopher said as he approached a random woman's table and snatched one of her sausage patties. The woman gasped.

Christopher's mother raced over and grabbed him. "I'm so sorry!" she apologized, pulling the kicking and hollering kid away from the table.

The woman huffed, shaking her head in disapproval.

I know that couldn't have been my sausage patty, Black was thinking.

The little kid calmed down and once again walked away from his mother, ignoring as she called for him. He romped from table to table until he got to Black.

He reached his hand towards Black's plate and received a

gentle slap on the hand for his efforts. The boy jerked his hand back and rubbed it. The next moment his bottom lip jutted out, eyebrows dropped, eyes squinting.

Black watched him the entire time. "I don't care if you make an ugly face," he said.

The kid hung his head, turned from Black's table, and ran over to his mother, fake crying.

Black shrugged and finished his breakfast.

It was a matter of seconds before the boy's mom stomped over to Black's table, dragging Christopher along. "Excuse me, did you just hit my son?" she asked in a raised voice, approaching him from the side.

Black kept his eyes straight ahead. "I would hardly call that a hit, but yeah, and you're welcome."

"Welcome? For making my son cry?"

"Those are crocodile tears. I know it, he knows it, you know it, and everyone in this dining room knows it."

"Maybe the law should know about you hitting other people's kids."

Black laughed. "Or maybe they should know about you teaching your son to steal food from strangers," he said, shaking his head.

The mother paused for a moment. "Wh—what...? I—I didn't tell him to steal anything."

"But you know taking from others is wrong, right? You can teach by negligence too, you know?" Black said, sipping from his bottled water.

"I'm not negligent. I pulled him away."

"After the fact. After you practically allowed him to do it," Black finished, turning to face her.

The woman was quiet for a moment, eyes dropped. "Well, do you even have kids? Probably not—they wouldn't like you."

"No, I don't have kids, but if I did my main priority

would be raising them right, not trying to get them to like me."

"Well now, my son probably wouldn't want to be around you or anyone who looks like you ever again."

"Yet I'm not the one he said he hated."

The woman gave Black a hard stare but said nothing. She stormed out of the dining room, pulling little Christopher along with her.

Black checked the time and sat at the table another five minutes before checking out of the hotel. Outside, the sun shone in a cloudless sky. The streets were busy with the honking of vehicle traffic and the scuffing of foot traffic. Black walked seven blocks to a bus station and rode the bus to Uptown Oakland, where he entered another bus that took him to the Mission District in San Francisco. He exited the bus and walked to a corner restaurant which was also a bakery and cafe, observing as people flocked in and out before stepping inside the restaurant himself and taking a slap to the face by the aroma of coffee and baked bread. The inside was chatty but roomy. There were a number of tables occupied but still many available. Black lifted a menu from near the register and committed both the name and address to memory before laying it back on the counter and walking outside.

He removed his phone from his pocket, went to his recent calls, and selected the last missed call. He held the phone to his ear. The phone rang four times before Toben's voice jumped on the line.

"This is Agent Toben."

"Good morning, Agent Toben."

"Mr. Black."

"I found a nice little restaurant where we can have a chat over breakfast."

"Did you? Where?"

Black gave him the name and address of the restaurant.

"When would you like to meet there?" Toben asked.

"In one hour—and come alone." Black ended the call.

He strolled across the street to an organic juice bar. Grabbing a menu, he found a seat next to a window with a clear view of the restaurant on the other side of the street. Twenty minutes passed before something interesting happened. A black unmarked car parked close to the front of the restaurant. A woman stood from the driver side, and from the passenger side a man stepped out. Black shook his head, recognizing both. *I thought I told him to come alone.* The two cased the outside of the restaurant for thirty seconds before going inside. Five minutes went by before another black unmarked car pulled up and parked on the side of the restaurant. Toben exited the car, looking around the area before walking inside the restaurant.

Black zipped out of the juice bar and to the restaurant. Easing through the front door, he immediately noticed the man and woman who exited the first unmarked car. The woman was sitting at the bar top and the man was sitting at a table near the front. Toben was at the far end of the restaurant seated at a table, facing the front.

Black threaded through the tables to Toben. "You're here early," he said.

"So are you," Toben replied, looking up from the table.

There were four chairs at the table, two on each side. Black moved one to the end of the table so that he sat perpendicularly to the right of Toben.

"Okay, it was your idea for us to meet, so what do you want to tell me?" Toben said.

"I thought I told you to come alone."

Toben said nothing.

"You can tell your team to join us—it's Agents Chapp and Boyar, right?"

Toben stared at Black before sighing and waving Ashley

and Boyar over to the table. The two walked over and sat in the two chairs across from Toben.

"He made you two," Toben said as they took their seats.

Ashley was in the chair closest to Black. "I bet you think you're a pretty smart guy, huh, Black?" Ashley said without looking at him.

"I've been called that a few times before."

"I can think of some other things to call you if you like."

"Agent Chapp," Toben interrupted.

Ashley looked at him, folded her arms, rolled her eyes, and shook her head, sighing.

"Mr. Black," Toben continued, leaning over the table towards him. "You said you wanted to talk, so start talking."

"Well, I was hoping this could be more of an open dialogue. You know, give and take. A Q-and-A session."

"That's interesting," Boyar said, pushing his glasses up his nose.

Ashley looked at him. "What? No it's not." She turned directly to Black. "We should just take you to headquarters and get the answers we want."

Black eyed her, straight faced. "That's not happening." He pointed at Toben. "Like I told him last night. Someone wants me gone and I'm not allowing myself to be taken into custody for something I didn't do, knowing that person is still out there."

"Like you'd have a choice," Ashley's voice slightly raised.

"That's the same thing he said last night, but here we are."

Ashley looked from Black to Toben. The two fixed on each other's faces for a few seconds.

Black noticed. *Hmm. What was that?* he wondered, then quickly blew it off as nothing.

"Mr. Black, we just want to ask you a few questions," Toben started.

"Just 'Black'."

"Okay, Black, if you cooperate and you're found innocent as you say you are, I'll do everything in my power to clear your name. Including overlooking the fact that you assaulted three federal agents last night. Is that fair?"

Black shrugged. "I guess so."

"Alright, now tell us everything from the beginning," Toben said.

Ashley watched Black intently.

Boyar removed a pen and pad from his pocket.

Black exhaled. "I'll tell you everything since I have nothing to hide, but I need you to answer a question for me first."

Toben nodded.

"Have any of you ever heard the names Nick Reeves or Kevin Guo?"

Everyone at the table paused to think but all shook their heads no. Boyar wrote the two names in his notepad.

"Who are they?" Ashley asked.

"A pair of dirty cops who came after me with an untraceable gun."

"Really?" Ashley said in a sarcastic tone.

"Yes, really. Look into them. I'm sure you'll find something."

"Okay, tell us what happened up until your interaction with those two," Toben said.

Black told them about the bomb at the pier and the kid he chased. He continued on about how he was followed onto the Golden Gate Bridge and his confrontation with Reeves and Guo.

"Wait," Toben requested, "You said they were in a white Honda; do you know what model?"

"It was an Accord."

Toben's eyes slightly widened, lips parted, eyebrows wrinkled.

"Why were they after you?" Ashley asked.

Black reached into his pocket, removing the detonator. "This, I'm guessing. It's the detonator I snagged from the kid."

"Give that here," Toben said, removing a plastic bag from his pocket. "That's evidence." He took the detonator from Black and dropped it into the bag. "Now can you tell us how you ended up at Petrak's meeting?"

"Sure," Black said, telling them about his run-in with the young men in Oakland and how one of them had the same type of gun that Guo had.

Boyar looked up from his notepad. "It was the same type of gun?" he asked.

"Yep. A Glock 19 with filed serial numbers," Black confirmed.

"Where did he get it from?" Toben asked.

"He mentioned he got it from a redhead and told me I could find her at Pier 40, you know, near that Spinning Sails place."

"Hmm… that's interesting," Ashley mocked. "There was an explosion near Pier 40 yesterday and you admitted to being there."

"You were there too," Black said.

Ashley stared at Black, lips parted, eyes narrowed.

"I was on the roof above you," Black continued. "I saw you, Johana, the blond kid, and Toben's son," he said, glancing at Toben before turning his attention back to Ashley. "So does it make you guilty just to have been there, Agent Chapp?"

"If you were on the roof, you would've seen that I left with Matt while the dock was still in one piece."

"You mentioned a Johana. Who's that?" Boyar chimed in.

"The redhead," Black answered.

Toben sighed before asking, "What else did you see there, Black?"

Black told them about the conversation Johana, Matt, and

the blond guy were having and about the things he saw inside the unit at the dock. He concluded with the scuffle he had with Johana and her blowing the dock.

"Hold on," Ashley objected. "You're telling me this little girl beat you and got away? We read your record, Black. You studied martial arts most of your life, Army Ranger, Delta Force member—you were a captain in the military and earned many medals. You expect us to believe this story?"

"I wasn't beat, plus my intention wasn't to hurt anyone. I just wanted answers. And that 'little girl,' as you call her, has had some training."

"I believe him," Toben said.

"A lot of what he's saying does coincide with what we have," Boyar followed up.

Ashley threw her gaze on Boyar. He shrugged his shoulders. She then looked at Toben, and finally Black, before rolling her eyes and shaking her head.

"Okay, Black, finish telling us how you ended up at the exchange with Petrak," Toben said.

Black told them about the warehouse in Treasure Island and what he found inside the freezer. He shared his ride in the back of the delivery truck, how he eavesdropped on Petrak's meeting, and finished with his run-in with Toben.

"This is some good information," Boyar said, jotting in his notepad.

"Agreed," Toben concurred.

Ashley said nothing.

"What do you know about the bombing in New York?" Boyar quickly asked.

"All I know about what happened in New York is what I heard on the news two days ago."

"Well, we have someone who says you seem to know a lot about the mind-set of the bomber," Ashley said.

Black raised an eyebrow. "Oh," he said, "you guys interviewed that bartender. Did he also mention how detached from the news I was?"

"What does that have to do with anything?"

"If I was part of a bombing, I would be very familiar with what's on the news because I'd be watching it all the time looking for any new developments found by law enforcement."

"Why are you so detached from the news?" Toben asked.

"I've been on the road."

"Doing what?"

"Being in the wrong places at the right times, I guess."

"We have to find out who's behind these bombings..." Ashley sighed.

"You just heard who's behind it," Black said. "We just don't know exactly when and where they'll strike next."

"Remind me, Black, who's behind it."

"*Johana and that blond kid,*" Black said slowly with emphasis.

"Ty," Toben said.

"Ty?" Black inquired.

"Yeah, that's the blond kid's name—that's what Matt told me he goes by anyway."

"Ty what? Do you guys have his last name?"

Toben shook his head in the negative.

"What? I know you guys have footage with all the cameras that are set up around Fisherman's Wharf. It didn't take long for you to figure out who I was."

"We have clear footage of you as you entered the restaurant," Boyar started, "but the footage we collected for Ty was distorted. We have a graphic artist working on it."

"Black, you seem to think there'll be another bombing. Any idea where?" Toben asked.

"Yeah, I think I may know where..." Black answered, thinking of a question he felt was more important than the one he had just been asked.

"Well, let us hear it," Toben continued.

"Okay, but before I answer that, I have a question. At Petrak's meet there was a DIA agent there. Any idea who that was?"

"Yeah, Agent Stokes, Karl Stokes," Toben answered with disdain.

"I'm sensing some history there."

"Not much history; I barely know the guy."

"The DHS and FBI I can understand, but I'm a little confused why the DIA was there."

"That makes two of us."

"The DIA mainly gathers military intelligence, but then again these agencies always have their hands in more than they admit. Does he have any special training?"

Toben hunched his shoulders, shaking his head.

"Maybe explosives?" Black asked.

Toben looked up to his left, biting the inside of his cheek.

"So that's it? He's good with explosives?" Black said.

Toben raised his eyebrows but said nothing.

"You did mention he knew about the sauce," Boyar said to Toben.

Both Toben and Ashley looked at Boyar. He hunched his shoulders.

"The sauce?" Black echoed.

Toben moved his sights from Boyar to Black. "Yeah," he sighed. "That glass tube you found in the mouth of the fish in Petrak's warehouse—that's what's known as sauce. Undetectable, clear, scentless, tasteless, and as you saw, it can maintain its form under extreme temperatures."

Black remembered Ty saying something about sauce. "Sounds like the same thing that was used back in Desert Storm," he commented aloud.

Toben smiled. "Exactly. This stuff is so dangerous it can cause an explosion if mixed with a carbonated drink."

"So I take it this sauce was used in the New York bombing?"

"I think we answered enough questions from you already," Ashley cut him off.

"It's okay, Agent Chapp. How would you know that, Black?" Toben said.

"It makes sense. We already know who's behind the bombings. It'd be nothing for them to travel with something undetectable like the sauce," Black said. "What I'm curious about is how Stokes came into all this information. Seems like he's been on this investigation for a while. What do you think, Toben?"

"Look, Black, all I can tell you is he was brought into this investigation from up the chain, okay?"

"Why the fascination with Stokes?" Boyar asked Black.

"Pretty obvious," Toben jumped in. "Black is more concerned about who came after him than he is about catching who's behind the bombings."

Good point, but I know I've seen Stokes somewhere before the Petrak meet, Black thought before saying, "The two may not be mutually exclusive."

"You said you may have an idea where the next bombing will be," Toben continued.

"As I mentioned, in the storage unit at Pier 40 I found a flier for that theme park south of L.A., Fantastic Galaxy."

"Yeah…"

"Remember, I also mentioned that Johana and this Ty were talking about going to Florida. Well—what's in Florida?"

"Of course," Toben said. "Fantastic Universe."

"The sister theme park," Ashley followed up.

"Yep, I'd say both locations are possible targets," Black said.

"But when?" Boyar asked.

"I don't know. That's for the three of you to figure out. The last two bombings were at protests for the law 324. So maybe cross-reference any events for the public law 324 near the theme parks."

Boyar wrote in his notepad. "I don't know why these kids are willing to hurt people who are against this law," he said.

"This new law will make parents more accountable, make them really consider the consequences of their actions," Black started. "These kids obviously feel strongly about their parents, probably parents in general, being held accountable for their actions when it comes to bringing children into this world."

It went quiet at the table. Only the sound of Boyar scratching in his notepad echoed around the table.

Toben dropped his head, exhaling. Ashley looked at him, quickly reaching over and patting his hand with hers.

Black noticed. *Yeah… there's something there. Oh well, that's on them.* "Well, that's all I have. I told you as much as I could think of. I'll be going now," he announced to the table.

"Not so fast," Ashley said.

"Whoa. Hold on, Black," Toben said. "We still need to make sure we're clear on some things."

"That's for you to figure out," Black replied with a shrug.

"Have you forgotten you were at the scene of the bombing?"

"And no one was hurt—unlike the bombing in New York, in which case there was no evidence to place me there and many got hurt. That alone proves I have nothing to do with this."

"You assaulted federal agents."

"I can argue self-defense. I didn't see any proper ID."

"What about assaulting two police officers? You saw their IDs."

"You mean two dirty cops? That'll go over well in a court of law."

"Black, I believe you're innocent. But it's your word against the word of two cops and since you have no proof of them being dirty, who do you think a judge is going to believe?"

"Who said I don't have proof?"

"Do you?"

"The gun Guo had."

"I thought you said you tossed it over the bridge," Ashley chimed in.

"No. I threw their police-issued guns into the water."

"Withholding more evidence," Toben said. "The charges are piling up."

"I don't have time for this," Black said, standing from the table.

"Black, I know you served this country and you're a tough guy," Toben said, "but you're in the civilian world now and there are rules you have to follow. I'm still a symbol of the law, so we're going to do things my way. Don't force me to… persuade you."

"'Symbol of the law,'" Black huffed, sitting down and directing his attention towards Toben. "Let me tell you something, Lead Agent Jake Toben. I've been doing my very best to maintain my cool, but after almost being blown apart, twice, and becoming the target of two crooked cops, I'm feeling the urge to snap on someone. I'm not behind the bombings and have nothing to do with it—you know this. Last night I saw it on your face, and just now you said you believe I'm innocent."

"It would be pr—proper procedure to take you—"

"That's a load of crap, Toben. It would also be proper procedure to take your son in knowing what you now know, right? But we both know you won't even consider that unless there's overwhelming evidence that ties Matt to the bombings. Well, there's more evidence against him than me. So don't even try that."

Toben's gaze briefly dropped to the floor. Ashley and Boyar glanced over at him.

"And you talk about *persuading* me," Black continued. "There's no way I'm letting a man who can't even manage his household persuade me, no matter what threats you throw my way—you're not getting me killed. When it comes to me, we're not doing things your way. We're going to do things my way," Black finished with confidence and boldness, staring hard into Toben's eyes.

CHAPTER
TWELVE

"OKAY, I'LL BITE," Toben said with a slight tremble in his voice. "So tell me, Black, how would you do things?"

"For starters, you're going to stop treating me like a suspect. That means I go and do what I want, where I want, when I want, like any other law-abiding citizen," Black said.

"I'm not sure what my superiors would think of that," Toben replied with a nervous chuckle.

"Are you sure what they'd think of your son associating with terrorists?"

Toben sat quiet for a moment before saying, "You have information, and have witnessed things that can help our case. So we may need you around."

"I plan on sticking around, but for my own reasons. Think of me as a… consultant for the DHS."

"What?" Ashley blurted.

Toben took in a deep breath before exhaling, "Fine."

"I don't think that's going to end well," Ashley muttered.

"Now, Mr. DHS consultant," Toben mocked, "you said you have one of the dirty guns. Let me have it."

"I don't have it on me."

"Where is it?"

"In my car."

"Your car? That's still in Treasure Island?"

"Yep."

"Well then," Toben said, turning his attention to Ashley and Boyar. "Agent Chapp, Agent Boyar, head back to HQ, there's a lot of work to do. Chapp, dig up as much as you can on this Johana. I wanna know everything. Boyar, check on the results of the image you sent to the graphic artist. I wanna get to know Mr. Ty. Also—when you have the information you need on those two—make sure you put out a BOLO on them and check if there are any activities for 324 near Fantastic Galaxy or Fantastic Universe. If they're planning another attack, we need to know exactly where and when. Look into Reeves and Guo and see what you can find out. And run this through forensics." Toben handed Ashley the evidence bag with the detonator in it. "One other thing: check into Stokes. I wanna know more about his past and his current team, but be careful, okay?"

"Sure thing, boss," Ashley said, standing from the table. "Let's go, Boyar."

Boyar finished jotting in his notepad. "What are you going to do, Jake?" he asked, standing and dropping the notepad in his pocket.

"Black and I are taking a ride over to Treasure Island to retrieve the evidence that's in his car."

Black shrugged. I need a ride to my car anyway, he thought.

"Okay, be careful," Ashley said to Toben before looking at Black and adding, "See you around, Black."

Black responded with a half-nod.

Ashley and Boyar walked towards the door, dodging a few people and tables as they exited.

"Okay, Mr. Consultant, let's take a little trip," Toben said.

"Whatever," Black replied, standing up and walking out of the restaurant with Toben following behind a few paces.

The two crossed the street and entered the unmarked car.

Black sat in the front passenger seat and Toben behind the wheel. The first five minutes of the drive were silent. Toben was quiet, focusing on the road, and Black wasn't one for small talk anyway. They had already said everything they needed to say, Black figured. The car coasted half a mile across the Oakland Bay Bridge before Toben broke through the silence.

"Black, I have a question."

"Yep."

"You said you saw Matt exit a car that kid Ty was driving. What kind of car was it?" Toben asked, eyes on the road.

"A blue Impala."

Toben pursed his lips and exhaled sharply.

"So did I get it right?" Black asked.

Toben glanced at Black before facing the windshield again. "What do you mean?"

"Was it the same car you saw?"

Toben laughed.

"C'mon, Toben, I know you're not just asking me. Your son was hanging out with this kid, so I'm almost certain you've seen the car before."

Toben nodded. "You're a smart guy, Black."

Black smiled. "So I did answer right. Good."

"Excuse me?"

"The fact that we saw the same car further corroborates my innocence."

"I've already said I believe you're innocent."

"What about the other car?" Black asked.

"What other car?"

"The white Honda Accord. You were interested in knowing the model of the car, and your expression when I told you it was an Accord was telling. So where did you see that car?"

Toben looked at Black then back at the road before shaking

his head. "I was… out and I noticed a white Honda Accord following me."

Black shook his head, trying to make sense of it. "Any idea why two dirty cops would be following you?" he asked.

Toben's lips moved, but he quickly flattened them and shook his head no, staring straight ahead.

Yeah right, Black thought to himself. "Look Toben, if you know something, you should let me know now. If I find out you're in on this—whatever *this* is—"

"The only thing I can tell you is I think Reeves and Guo are working with Stokes," Toben interrupted.

"The DIA guy?"

"Yep. I saw him talking to a man in a green pickup outside of HQ yesterday. The man had a black eye. The funny thing is, I saw that same man with another guy the night before when I was followed, and he didn't have a black eye then. I assume the two men were Reeves and Guo, and the black eye came from you."

"That's where I saw him, Stokes. Yesterday when I was doing a little research, I ran across Guo's social media profile. On his page was a picture of him with Reeves and Stokes."

"What interest do they have in following us?"

"That's the six-million-dollar question. We know they were after me because of the bombing at Fisherman's Wharf and maybe I witnessed something they didn't want me to. I'm thinking they followed you because of your involvement in the investigation. It all seems to point back to these bombings."

Toben gave Black a quick glance. "I think you're right," he said, "but I still don't understand why Stokes is working with cops."

"Dirty cops," Black corrected. "But Stokes already had a certain amount of intel before coming into this situation. Hopefully we'll have more after Chapp and Boyar do some digging into his background."

Toben nodded, looking out to the road.

"You mentioned Stokes was brought into the investigation from up the chain. Who brought him in?"

"My direct supervisor. I'm guessing she got the order from her immediate supervisor."

"Yeah, maybe."

"I just want to find these two kids before anyone else gets hurt," Toben commented, leaning into the turn for the Treasure Island exit.

"Me too."

Toben jerked his head back slightly in surprise. "You're actually interested in helping catch them," he said, looking at Black.

"It's the best play. I mean, I could go find Stokes, Reeves, and Guo, and make them tell me what's going on, but, although they're dirty, it wouldn't go well considering they're still law enforcement. More than likely I'd have the law after me. On the other hand, going after the bombers will be easier because law enforcement is already after them. Once I find them, it shouldn't be difficult to get info and find out exactly what's going on."

Toben glanced sharply at Black before placing his eyes back on the road.

They drove another three minutes before pulling into the side parking lot of the Administration Building and stopping next to Black's car. The two stepped out of the unmarked car into the mid-morning sun. The sound of seagulls squawking, waves crashing, and wind blowing swept across Black's ears as he walked towards his car. He unlocked the passenger side door, noticing a couple of vans and a few unmarked Crown Vics behind the barbed wire fence which surrounded the warehouse. Black reached into his glove compartment, removed the gun he had taken from Guo, and walked to Toben, who was waiting at his own car with an evidence bag in hand.

Black rested the gun inside the bag. "Your people?" he asked, pointing his thumb in the direction of the warehouse.

"No, that would be the FBI and ATF," Toben said, placing the evidence bag into his car before closing the door and continuing. "Since Petrak was caught with the guns and explosive agent, all of his businesses and homes will more than likely be raided."

"It'd be nice to get in there."

"You were in there last night."

"I wasn't exactly given a tour of the place. There's probably more in there that can help us find these two bombers before they can execute their next attack," Black said, turning towards the warehouse.

"How'd you get in there anyway? You didn't really say."

Black looked over his shoulder. "You think you can get us in there?" he redirected.

"Ah—I'm sure I could."

They both hopped into Toben's car and made the two-minute drive to the warehouse building. They pulled up to the guardhouse at the front of the driveway and a man wearing an FBI vest stepped out.

Toben looked at Black. "I know him," he said, rolling down his window as the man approached.

"Toben," the man greeted him. "What brings you here?"

"Hi, Peterson. Hoping to take a look around for the case I'm working."

"Yeah sure, no problem. Who's this with you?" Peterson asked, looking at his companion.

"Orlando Black—" Black said.

"He's a consultant for the DHS," Toben quickly chimed in.

"Oh, well, you guys can drive down and see if you can find a place to park. You can enter in the front near the round-about. Someone will open the gate for you."

"Thanks, Peterson," Toben said, rolling up the window.

"Sure thing," Peterson acknowledged, walking back towards the guardhouse.

They drove up the driveway and parked off to the side before exiting the car and walking to the warehouse entrance. Toben flashed his ID badge to an agent at the gate, who then slid the gate open.

"Just knock on the door," the agent instructed.

Black and Toben passed through the gate and walked to the front door of the warehouse. Toben struck the door with the back of his knuckles three times. The sound of footsteps approached from the other side before the door clicked unlocked and clanked open, exposing another agent behind it.

Toben showed the agent his badge. "Agent Toben with DH—" he started.

"I know, Peterson radioed me," the agent said, raising his walkie-talkie. "Come on in."

The agent led them through a plastic vinyl strip curtain doorway and onto the floor of the warehouse, where they were met with cold air and the smell of sea life. "Welcome to the party," he said before walking off. There were maybe nine agents on the floor. They all either were looking through boxes, running around, writing something down, or talking, all wearing vest or coats marked either *FBI* or *ATF*.

"What a madhouse," Toben commented.

"Yep, I guess you guys have been after Petrak for some time now," Black replied.

"Yes, we have. Now where should we start?" Toben sighed, looking around the warehouse. "Where did you find the sauce?"

"That's where you want to start?"

"Yep."

"Back there," Black said, pointing to the doorway at the back.

The two strolled across the busy floor and whipped

through the vinyl strip curtain. Three agents were in the back room going through containers.

"I found them in that freezer there," Black said, jabbing his thumb in that direction.

"Okay then," Toben said, walking in the direction of the freezer. Black followed behind him. The freezer door was already slightly open, and Toben pulled it the rest of the way. They stepped inside the noisy, cold, smoky, empty freezer.

Toben hunched his shoulders. "There's nothing here, Black."

"I can see that. These agents probably removed everything for examination," Black said, walking back out of the freezer.

Toben trailed behind before stepping around him and walking over to one of the agents. "Excuse me. Do you know where the content from this freezer is?" he asked.

"Yes, sir," the agent answered, "it's all right here." He pointed at bins, crates, and boxes gathered on the floor.

"Did you guys find anything?" Toben asked.

"A few Glock 19s with no serial number and packaged fish."

"That's it?"

"That's it."

"Okay, thank you," Toben ended the conversation.

By then Black was making his way back to the main floor of the warehouse.

Toben caught up to him. "Where you headed, Black?" he asked.

"To the side of the warehouse I didn't have a chance to check out," Black replied. "We don't have a lot of time to waste."

"I know, I just wanted—"

"You just wanted to confirm my story. Although you believe me, you want to cover all your bases, right?"

Toben didn't answer.

"But anyway, what the agent said was in the freezer

further substantiates my story," Black said, walking through the main area and making a right down a hall. Toben dragged behind. There were restrooms down the hall, one on either side. Further up was an office on the right and a conference room on the left, both with glass windows. Near the end of the hall was a door to a room on the left, and at the very end of the hall another vinyl-curtained doorway. Black and Toben passed through the doorway and into a room with another large commercial walk-in freezer. There was a heavyset agent in the room, standing at a workbench, removing small blocks from a box and placing them on the workbench.

He noticed Black and Toben entering and walked over to them. "Can I help you?" he said.

Toben flashed his badge. "Agent Jake Toben with the DHS," he said, shaking the man's thick hand, "and this is Orlando Black, a… consultant for the DHS."

Black shook the agent's hand.

"We have reason to believe weapons from this facility were used in a case the DHS is currently investigating. Can you tell me what you've found so far here?" Toben asked.

"Sure thing," the heavyset guy said, walking back to the workbench. "We found these blocks of plastic explosives here. There's a couple more boxes over there." He pointed to a stack of boxes near the freezer. "Other than that, we didn't find much else."

"Is that all you found?" Black asked.

The man paused for a second with a look that read, *Don't ask me, I only work here*, before saying, "Oh yeah, there was this." He placed his hand palm down on the workbench for leverage and picked up a bin from the floor. Reaching inside, he removed a device. It was a device that both Black and Toben had seen before—the same type of remote detonator Black had recovered from Ty.

Black and Toben exchanged glances.

"Okay, thank you," Toben said to the agent.

"No problem."

Black and Toben returned through the doorway and into the hall, Toben first. Black stopped at the door on his right. Toben continued six steps down the hall before stopping and peering over his shoulder.

"Black, are you coming?" he asked.

"I'm curious to know what's in here," Black replied, pointing his thumb towards the office door.

"Okay," Toben said, shrugging his shoulders.

Black turned the knob and pushed the door open. Behind the door was an office. To the far right was a desk with binders and folders scattered over it. File cabinets stood at both ends of the desk.

Black crackled across the worn carpeted floor towards the desk. "Doesn't look like this room has been searched yet," he remarked, shifting some folders around on the desk.

"No, it doesn't," Toben added, as he walked to a file cabinet that was in the corner near the desk and slid the top drawer open.

Black opened one of the binders on the desk and found documentation titled *Employee Contact Details*. He flipped through the first page and nothing of interest caught his attention, then the second and third pages—just a bunch of words talking about employee-related policies and confidentiality. It was on the fourth page where things began to interest him. Black looked up at the sound of Toben slamming the top file cabinet drawer.

"You okay?"

"Yeah, I didn't realize how easy these drawers slid, sorry."

Black shook his head and continued reading the content of the binder. He saw a list of names with phone numbers and addresses next to them. It was a short list of about eighteen names. One particular name caught Black's attention: *Johana Howard*. Before he could react to what he had found, the office door opened and the heavyset agent stepped inside.

"Sorry, fellas, but this room hasn't been processed yet. You'll have to wait until after we do our initial search," he said, standing at the door.

Toben had a file drawer cracked open. "Sure thing," he said, pushing the drawer closed and walking towards the door.

Black quickly memorized the phone number and address for Johana Howard. "No problem," he agreed, closing the binder and following Toben into the hall. They walked to the main floor of the warehouse, out the front door, and to Toben's car.

"Well, at least we now know where they got the detonators from. There wasn't too much more to see other than that, though," Toben commented, opening the car door.

"Yeah, maybe," Black responded, reaching for the door handle on his side.

Toben looked at Black over the roof of the car. "What? Did you find something, Black?" he asked. He leaned over and rested his folded hands on the roof, waiting for an answer.

Black considered not telling Toben about the address he had found, but he concluded that it would be a show of good faith and a way to build some trust. "Yeah, I'll tell you in the car."

They ducked in the car and Toben drove up the driveway, passing the security hut before making a left turn onto the road.

"Okay, what did you find, Black?"

"That binder I was looking at had employee contact information."

"Okay?"

"The name Johana Howard was in it."

"What? Really? We have to go back," Toben said, flicking on the right-turn indicator.

"No need. I have it memorized."

"Oh, okay," Toben said, changing the flicker to indicate a

left turn and turning at the Administration Building. "This is a big find, Black."

"We're not even sure it's her."

"C'mon. If everything you've said is correct, it has to be."

"Maybe you're right, Toben," Black replied.

Toben made another left into the parking lot, pulling into a spot next to Black's car. "Okay, so what's the address, Mr. Consultant?"

"It's not too far away, just follow me," Black said, cracking the door open.

"Hold on, that's not how this works. I'll have Boyar run the address and I may need to call it in."

"That's exactly what I don't want you doing. Like I said, follow me," Black said, exiting the car.

Toben sucked his teeth, "Fine, just don't lose me," he said just before Black shut the door.

Black eased under the wheel of the Viper and rolled out of the parking lot onto the road with Toben tailing him. He got on the Oakland Bay Bridge, heading back towards San Francisco. It took them twenty-five minutes to reach Presidio Heights. The area was clean, tidy, but a little dense. There wasn't much to see other than a bunch of cars parked at the curb, decorative trees, and commercial and residential buildings between two and five stories high. Black glanced into his rearview mirror, watching as Toben maintained a two-car-length distance behind. They made two more turns before coasting into the Presidio Terrace community. There was a gate, but it was open. The community consisted of large single-family homes and condos. From the architecture, fresh coat of paint, and landscaped lawns, Black knew these homes came with a very high price tag. Observing the mailbox numbers, he stopped the Viper at a curb next to a small open field—an open community park area, Black guessed. He stepped out of the Viper and into the late morning sun, casually waving to a passing driver who had waved at him first.

Stepping to Toben's car, he entered on the front passenger side.

"Okay, which house is it, Black?" Toben immediately asked, turning off the engine.

"It's that small grey house there," Black said, pointing three houses down.

"Why did you park way back here?"

"I don't like to be seen coming. You never know what you'll run into."

"We have nothing to hide, do we? We're just going to knock on the door and ask some questions."

"It's not always that easy," Black said, peering into his side mirror before turning back to Toben.

Toben's mouth gaped and his eyes squinted as he gazed in the direction of the house. "Is that—?"

Black looked in the same direction. "Stokes," he confirmed, finishing the sentence.

THE TWO MEN watched Stokes walk from the house, cross the street, and enter a dark blue sedan. He was carrying a large white envelope. A minute later the taillights flickered on and the car crawled up the street, disappearing with a right turn.

"What was he doing here?" Toben asked.

"That's a good question. Let's go find out."

Black and Toben left the car, crossed the street, and walked up the sidewalk towards the house, a grey stucco one-story with white trimming, a one-car garage, and a small porch. They strolled up the short driveway.

Clonking up the porch steps, Toben looked around. He narrowed his body and side-stepped to the door, placing the back of his hand against the door to knock—and as he did, the door cracked slightly open. Toben glanced over his shoulder down the steps at Black. *It's open,* his lips motioned as he placed his other hand on his firearm. He drew his gun and shouldered the door open.

Black hiked up the steps and eased in behind him. The front door led right into the living room. Past the living room, near the back of the house, was a hall and to the right was a small dining area.

Toben walked towards the back of the house, gun aimed in that direction. Black walked into the dining room. Scanning the scattered documents on the table, he noticed some mail addressed to Johana Howard. He continued into the kitchen, which looked like it had been recently renovated. Polished brown granite rested on top of the counters and island. A shimmery natural color backsplash popped from the wall, and all of the appliances had a new shine. The cabinets wore a glossy finish and some of them were left open. Black heard doors opening and closing in the hall. He walked back to the living room and heard Toben yell, "Clear."

"Clear," Black echoed.

Toben joined him in the living room, dodging the decorative pillows which lay on the floor. "No one's here," he said, holstering his gun. "It would've been great if she was here and surrendered."

"You know it won't be that easy. This isn't an episode of NCIS."

Toben chuckled. "I wonder what Stokes was looking for," he said.

"I don't know. I'm interested in why he was here looking for anything at all. But whatever it was, I think he found it and left in a hurry. Did you find anything in the rooms down the hall?"

Toben shook his head. "Nothing noteworthy. I don't think we'll find anything here that'll help us locate her any quicker. But I'm going to have a team search this place," he said as he pulled out his phone.

"Hold on," Black requested. "We don't know if or when she's coming back."

"Okay…?"

"And you want to catch her quickly—"

"Right?"

"Well, let's say she does come back here. If she notices a crowd of agents outside her home, she'll know she's been made and be scared away. But if you place a small surveillance team here, your chances of an easy capture increase greatly. That's *if* she comes back though."

Toben nodded, sucking in his lips. "Good point. Let's get out of here."

Black stepped outside the house first. Toben followed, closing the door behind himself and placing a call to Agent Boyar. They walked up the sidewalk and across the road to their cars. Black unlocked the door to the Viper and cracked it open.

"Hey, Black," Toben called to him, ending his phone conversation.

Black looked at Toben, waiting for him to continue.

"Looks like my team found something that'll help us catch these two."

"Good. You should have this wrapped up in no time. You've seen enough to know that I had nothing to do with the bombing, so I think this is a good place for us to part ways."

"I thought you wanted to know who came after you."

"I already know who. Stokes."

"But don't you want to know why?"

It does have me scratching my head, Black thought to himself. "Yeah, I guess I'm curious," he said aloud.

"I thought so. How about you follow me to HQ and we'll see if any of this new information can help us figure it out."

Black looked at him for a long moment. "Sure," he finally agreed, smiling.

"Great. Just follow me," Toben said, dropping into the car and starting the engine. Black did the same in the Viper. Toben pulled off, circling around the neighborhood before exiting the community. Black followed him for twenty minutes before they reached a tall concrete building. They passed through a security gate and entered a parking garage. Toben pulled into a spot labeled for visitors and Black parked next to him. The two exited their cars and Black shadowed Toben into the building. They stepped into a large lobby, entering a line for the metal detectors. They cleared the metal detectors, and on their way to the elevators they stopped at the front desk, where a lively blue-eyed receptionist with sunflower-blond hair welcomed them. She slid Black a clipboard asking for some basic information and handed him a visitor card.

Minutes later, the two were entering the office of Toben's unit.

Boyar was at his desk pointing at something on his computer screen and Ashley was sitting on top of his desk looking at it. They were talking to one another in a soft tone, almost in whispers. It took them a few seconds before they noticed Black and Toben standing near the door.

Boyar stared at the pair, raising an eyebrow.

Ashley sprung to her feet. "Alright… What's going on, Agent Toben?" she asked.

"Black is going to work with us on reviewing your findings. He may be able to shed some light on this case," Toben said.

"Are you sure that's a good idea?" Ashley objected.

"Yes. I trust what he has told us."

"What? Wait a minute. You two spent a few hours together and now you're best friends?"

"It's called the truth," Black jumped in.

"Excuse me?"

"When someone tells the truth, people who are looking for the truth tend to believe and trust them, because they both have the truth in common. On the other hand, people who are more… emotional may overlook the obvious evidence and the truth behind it."

"So what are you saying, Mr. Black? I'm not looking for the truth and I'm emotional?"

Black shrugged. "Or your emotions are stopping you from seeing the truth."

"You men are so—" Ashley started but Toben interrupted.

"Okay, okay, let's go to the back room," he said gently, leading Ashley by her shoulder towards the back of the office.

Black followed them and Boyar stood from his chair and trailed behind Black. The four of them entered the room and each found a seat around the circular table.

"We'll start with you, Agent Boyar," Toben said. "Tell us where you're at with the image."

Boyar sighed. "Well… the graphic artists were finally able to clear up the image and we're searching various databases for any facial matches as we speak. While that was going on, I searched for connections between the theme parks and the new 324 law. I didn't find any protest, but I did learn there will be an open panel with activists who are anti-324, speaking at both theme parks."

"That's good. Where and what time?" Toben asked.

"I'm not sure exactly where in the theme parks, but the panelists will be meeting at Fantastic Galaxy tomorrow and Fantastic Universe the day after."

"Where did you find this information?" Black asked.

"From some of the activists' social media pages. And I've already alerted the local authorities to a possible attack."

"Good, good. Did you put a BOLO out on Ty and Johana?" Toben inquired.

Boyar shook his head. "No, because I don't have all the information just yet."

"Oh yeah, you're still waiting on the facial recognition results. Agent Chapp," Toben said, turning to Ashley. "What do you have for me?"

She had her arms folded, lips flattened, staring sharply at Black.

What's this girl's problem? Black thought to himself.

"Agent Chapp," Toben repeated.

She rolled her eyes to Toben, unfolded her arms, and jolted her head as if she was breaking a trance.

"Sorry. I—ah—I checked into Reeves and Guo, and I tell you it doesn't take too much digging to discover they're shady. They've both worked cases where evidence went missing, both have had issues with alcohol and drugs, both are under investigation with Internal Affairs, and both have one failed relationship after the next."

"Did you find anything that connects them to Stokes?" Black asked.

Ashley paused for a few seconds and exhaled before answering him. "No. Didn't get around to looking into Stokes yet. Had to take some calls from the FBI and ATF about Pier 40. Apparently Petrak owns that old Recreation building and the storage units out there."

Of course. Now it's making sense, Black thought.

"But anyway, I looked into Johana and you won't believe what I found out. Her name is Johana—"

"Howard," Toben cut in.

Ashley shook her head. "Where did you hear that name?"

"Black," Toben said, tilting his head at Black. "He's pretty good at sniffing things out. At Petrak's seafood warehouse he found a binder with employee contact details. Among those employees was the name Johana Howard."

Ashley nodded. "Hm. He may be good," Ashley said with a smile on her face, "but he's not that good, because her name is Johana—"

"Petrak," Black interrupted. "Johana Petrak."

The table went silent. Black looked around and saw everyone had their mouths open and their eyes fixed on him.

"How could you have known that?" Ashley asked.

"At the storage unit I overheard Ty mentioning something about how Johana's dad would get upset if she wasn't working the front. And you just mentioned Petrak owns the building, so I put two and two together. What else did you find out about her? I know you did a preliminary background check."

"Ye—Yeah. She was born in Czechia like her father. When she was younger, her mother got sick and passed away. From what I could find, Petrak was in and out of her life. He kept her in things like martial arts and gymnastics, but eventually he moved to the States to chase this lifestyle he currently lives, leaving her in Czechia with her grandparents. When Johana was older, her grandparents moved here to San Francisco so she could have a chance at a better life. Her grandparents died a couple years back, two months apart. I'm guessing Petrak reentered her life around that time, which is probably the reason she's caught up in this mess," Ashley finished, releasing a deep sigh.

"You didn't find anything linking her to Stokes?" Black asked.

"No, Black. You're really fascinated with Stokes. Does he have you spooked?"

Black chuckled. "I don't spook easily," he said before turning his attention to Toben. "Do you want to tell them, or should I?"

"I'll do it," Toben exhaled. "In that binder was also an address for Johana. Black and I went to the address and we saw Stokes leaving the house."

"The house we talked about on the phone? The one you wanted me to put a surveillance team on?" Boyar put in.

"Yep. Let's keep an eye on Stokes."

"Okay, I'll start looking into him now," Boyar said, standing and exiting the room.

"We need to get down to Fantastic Galaxy before that panel meeting tomorrow. How do you feel about making the trip down there?" Toben asked Ashley.

"Are you coming or am I going alone?" she asked.

Toben and Ashley fixed on each other's faces for a few seconds.

These two, Black thought, looking down at the table.

"I—I have a lot to do here, but I don't want you going alone," Toben said. "If our consultant doesn't mind, I'd like him to accompany you there."

Black glanced at Toben.

"No, I think I can manage on my own," Ashley declined.

"I don't want you going by yourself," Toben repeated before turning towards Black. "So Black, what will it be?"

"Sure, I'll go."

"Okay then it's settled," Toben said, standing from the table.

"Wait," Ashley protested.

"Agent Chapp, we don't have time to wait. There's a lot at stake here. Expense the plane ticket, rooms, food, and whatever else you need, okay?"

Ashley glared at Toben for a moment. "I'm driving there," she said, leaving her seat and walking out of the room.

Toben looked at Black expectantly.

Black shrugged and lifted himself from his seat. "Driving may be a good idea," he said before leaving the room. In the main office area, he saw Boyar sitting at his computer and Ashley craned over her desk writing something on a sticky note. Toben brushed past Black's shoulder, stopping at Boyar's desk.

"Agent Boyar."

Boyar looked up at him.

"Agent Chapp will be heading down to Fantastic Galaxy in a little while. Go ahead and move forward with that BOLO for Johana Howard, or Petrak, or—actually, both."

"Sure thing. Will she be going by herself?" Boyar asked, turning in his seat towards Ashley. "You're going alone?"

"Unfortunately not," Ashley replied, slapping her pen on her desk, walking to Black, handing him a sticky note. "Meet me at this address in an hour, hour and a half. And don't be late, because I will leave without you," she concluded, walking to her desk and stuffing items from the drawer into a tote bag resting in her chair.

"This girl is really starting to try my patience," Black muttered under his breath.

"Black will be accompanying her," Toben finally answered Boyar. "You and I'll be looking for this Ty kid."

"And looking into Stokes," Black interjected.

"Yeah… and looking into Stokes," Toben echoed. "But finding the suspect takes priority."

"He shouldn't be too hard to find. Did you get a look at the license plate of the blue Impala?"

"No. I was so mad at Matt I didn't notice. Did you happen to get it?"

"Nope. I saw the car in The Spinning Sails' parking lot but didn't get a look at the plate because of how the car was angled. How did you guys find Matt?"

"Toben put a tracker on him," Boyar answered.

"Really?" Black laughed. "Where did you put the tracker?"

"In his backpack," Toben said.

Black thought and remembered Matt putting his backpack back into the blue Impala. "He left his backpack in the car," Black said.

"What?"

"Matt left his backpack in the Impala. If you follow the tracker it should lead you to the car and hopefully to Ty."

Toben's eyes brightened, lips parted. "Are you sure?"

"I'm certain."

Toben clapped his hands together. "Great! Finally, a break," he said in a raised tone.

At that, the office door flapped open and Black saw a woman entering whom he had never seen before. She walked straight to Toben, giving no regard to Black or anyone else in the office for that matter.

"Good afternoon, Agent Toben. I haven't seen you all morning," she said.

"Good morning, Director," Toben greeted.

"I heard the bust went smoothly last night. I want to talk to you about some—" she started, then noticed Black. She glared at him. "Who are you?"

Black didn't answer.

"Excuse me, sir. I'm Barbara Hanten, the director, and I asked you a question."

"Oh—you talking to me?" Black mocked.

Hanten continued to glare at him. "Who do—?" she uttered.

Toben quickly jumped in. "Director Hanten, this is Orlando Black."

Hanten's eyebrows raised, her mouth fell open, and her head jerked back. "Who?" she said in a tone of disbelief.

"My name is Orlando Black," Black repeated, sarcastically.

"Oh, I know who you are," Hanten said, taking a step toward him. "What I'm confused about is why you're not in cuffs," she ended, looking back at Toben.

Black shrugged. "Because an innocent person shouldn't be in cuffs."

Hanten moved her sights from Toben, placing them on Black once again. She stared at him coldly for a couple of moments. "Agent Toben. I need to go upstairs and handle something. It shouldn't take more than ten minutes. When I get back, I want to see you in my office," she said, taking her eyes from Black and tramping out of the office.

Toben looked at Black, shaking his head before walking over to his desk.

Boyar, still seated at his own desk, exhaled. "Oh boy."

"What?" Black shrugged.

"Argh… unbelievable, Black," Ashley disapproved. "Why were you acting like a jerk to her? She's the director—you know what? Don't answer. I forgot being a jerk is just in your nature."

"Look, she's not *my* boss. I don't have to answer her questions. Especially when she's insinuating I had something to do with the bombing."

"Good for you, but the rest of us actually have to work for her. Keep that in mind, Black," Ashley said, snatching her tote bag from the chair.

Toben called over to Boyar. "You have the ID number for the tracker I gave you yesterday. Track it and keep an eye on it. I'm going to the restroom. I'll stop back by before going to Hanten's office."

Boyar nodded. "Got it."

Toben headed for the office door. As he opened it and went through it, he turned and spoke to Black and Ashley. "You two should get on the road."

Having gathered her things, Ashley moved to follow Toben out.

"Ash," Boyar called, standing up at his desk. "Be careful."

She turned around, "I'll be okay, Victor," she said, winking before stepping out of the office.

Black was about to pass through the doorway before he heard Boyar's voice sweep over his shoulders.

"Hey, Black," he said. "She's your responsibility now. If anything happens to her—"

Black looked over his shoulder. "I won't allow anything to happen to her. You just focus on finding that kid and digging up what you can on Stokes." *Someone has a crush,* Black thought, leaving the office and catching up with Ashley at the elevator. Inside, Ashley poked the button for the lobby. The elevator thumped closed and rasped downward. The silence inside the elevator was thick, nearly suffocating. Both Black and Ashley were facing the elevator door; neither spoke nor looked at one another. The elevator bumped to a stop and the doors slid apart.

Ashley stepped out and headed straight for the parking garage. Black dropped his visitor card at the front desk before following her. He spotted her waiting for him near a column and walked across the pavement to her. On his way, he noticed a parking spot labeled *Director Hanten*. There was a silver Mercedes-Benz parked in it. Although it was a slightly older model, it gleamed like a brand-new car. Black paused to look the car over and something caught his eye. On the front bumper was a decal plate which featured a picture of an eagle sitting on top of a shield. The word *Quantico* was written next to it, and underneath a date of twenty-one years past. Black continued toward Ashley, keeping his eyes on the car.

"Remember, Black, meet me at that address no later than an hour and a half from now," she warned.

Black pointed his thumb behind him to the silver Benz. "Is that Hanten's car?" he asked.

"It says 'Director Hanten,' does it not? Just don't be late," Ashley said before storming off, in the direction of her own car, Black guessed.

He watched her until she disappeared. He then walked to the visitors' parking, found his car, settled into the driver's seat, and streamed out of the garage.

UPSTAIRS, TOBEN RECEIVED a folder from Boyar and walked into Hanten's office, closing the door behind him. She was waiting for him, leaning against her desk with arms folded.

"Mind telling me what you're thinking, Agent Toben? Your unit is already in the hot seat and you have one of the persons of interest in a high-profile case walking around freely."

Toben raised his palm, chest height, as he moved closer to

her. "Wait, wait. It's not like that," he pled. "Black has nothing to do with these bombings."

"But he's still a person of interest, is he not?"

"No. Not anymore. Black's last address of residence shows North Carolina. I had Boyar check and there's no record of him buying a plane ticket."

"Okay," Hanten said, hunching her shoulders and slightly shaking her head.

"We know that Petrak is the only one dealing the sauce in the entire country. And you said it yourself that the sauce was used in the attack over in New York. To orchestrate an attack in New York then here, Black would have had to have flown. But I can tell you who we did find a plane ticket for," Toben said, handing Hanten the folder. "Johana Petrak. She's on the first picture in the folder."

"Petrak?" Hanten echoed, opening the folder. "Is she—"

"Yep. Petrak's daughter. And she worked for him, but under a different last name. It's clear she had access to the sauce and a lot of other contraband."

"You're saying Petrak and his daughter are behind it?"

"Not necessarily. We don't believe Petrak had anything to do with planning the bombings."

"So his daughter, Johana, acted alone?"

"We believe she's the mastermind, but she wasn't alone. In the folder you'll see another image of a young man in a cap and sunglasses. We believe he's working with her."

Hanten shuffled the documents around in the folder, staring into it for a long moment. There was one document that seemed to hold her attention, but Toben couldn't tell which one from where he was standing.

"Director Hanten," he said to get her attention.

"Huh? Y—yeah," she stuttered, looking up at Toben before adjusting the contents of the folder. She walked around her desk to her chair. "This other guy. Have you ID'd him?" she asked, sitting behind her desk, looking through the folder.

"Not yet, but we're close. All I know is he goes by the name Ty."

"Ty. Who gave you that name?"

Toben was quiet for a second. "An anonymous source," he finally said, shrugging before taking a seat at the desk.

"Hmm. Well, please let me know when you've ID'd him."

"We're actually in the process of tracking him as we speak. We have reason to believe there'll be other attacks at the Fantastic theme parks with his involvement. The local authorities have already been contacted."

Hanten thumbed through the documents in the folder. Toben sat quietly watching her.

"Is there anything else?" she asked, eyes still in the folder.

"There is something, but I'm not sure how to tell you about it."

"What?" Hanten inquired, looking up with furrowed eyebrows.

"It's about… Agent Stokes."

She leaned forward. "Jake, I know you and I don't always see eye to eye, but you have to know I'm on your side. So you can tell me anything."

Toben exhaled, fixing on her eyes for a few seconds. "While following a lead, we went to the home of Johana Petrak—"

"Who's we?"

"Black and myself."

Hanten bobbed her head.

"When we arrived, we saw Agent Stokes leaving the residence."

Hanten reclined in her chair, inhaling a labored breath.

"I know it's thin, but how much do you really know about him?"

"Apparently not as much as I thought."

"Did he mention anything to you about going to the home?"

"Why? Do you think he has something to do with this?"

Toben nodded. "Yes. I think he has something to do with it. Not exactly sure how. Where did you guys meet?"

Hanten leaned forward in her chair. "We met years ago. That bastard… If he has something to do with…" she sighed, shaking her head. "See if you can keep an eye on him. I want to know what angle he's playing."

Toben, a bit surprised, responded, "Sure thing."

"Who's privy to this information?"

"Myself, Boyar, Chapp, you, and Black."

"Okay. No one else needs to know about this. I'll hold on to this," Hanten said, fanning the folder before dropping it into her desk drawer.

"Of course," Toben said. He stood and walked towards the door before thinking of another question. "Director Hanten," he said, pivoting to face her.

"Yes."

"Do the names Reeves or Guo mean anything to you?"

"No. Should they?"

"Probably not," Toben said, turning around and leaving the office. He paced down the hall, removing his phone and placing a call.

"Hi, sweetheart," Kristi's voice jumped on the line.

"Hi, honey. Is everything okay?"

"Yep. Just checked on Matt. He's in his room doing some assignments."

"What about you, how are you feeling?"

"I feel okay, just a little tired. What time are you coming home tonight?"

"Not sure. I'm deep in this case."

"Jake, please be careful."

"I will. Hey—why don't you and Matt take a trip to Sacramento to visit your brother and his wife? I'm going to be busy probably for the next few days and I don't want you two home alone."

"That's a good idea. I think we'll do that. I'm sure they want to see Matt, and being around his cousins will be good for him."

"Yeah I think so. Just let me know when you finish packing, when you take off—"

"I know the drill, Agent Toben. I'll call you back in a little. Love you."

"Love you too, bye."

FOURTEEN

BLACK WAS FINISHING a meal. It was a club sandwich with sides of fruit and fries. He washed it all down with a bottle of water. The sandwich shop was furnished with five small square tables. The place was more or less a hole in the wall, but the sandwich tasted great, seasoned nearly perfectly. He disposed of his trash and used the restroom before exiting the shop.

On the other side of the street was the building Ashley had given him the address of an hour ago. He crossed the street. The building was composed of many units, the number Ashley had given to him being the largest of them. It had two large glass windows on either side of the door and the business name *Combat Krav Maga* was painted above a logo of a fist with two swords crossing behind it. Black looked through the window and observed two lines with five people in each punching, grappling, kneeing, and kicking the person in front of them. He reached for the doorknob but noticed the reflection of a car stopping at the curb behind him. He turned around to see Ashley sitting at the wheel of a teal-colored Toyota Camry. In his periphery, he also noticed a green pickup truck creeping up the street in the same direction from which Ashley had come. It was one of those newer hybrid trucks, really good on gas. The truck backed into an intersecting street three blocks down, parking at the curb.

Ashley rolled down her window and Black walked over. She was wearing blue jeans and a white long-sleeved button-up shirt, sleeves rolled up to her elbows.

"You're early, good. Get in. We have a six-and-a-half-hour drive," she said by way of greeting.

"What am I supposed to do, just leave my car here?" Black asked. He nodded towards his car parked in the small lot beside the sandwich shop.

"Yep."

"You want it to get towed?"

Ashley exhaled in annoyance. "It won't get towed. Here, put this on your dash," she said, poking a rectangular sheet of paper out the window.

Black grabbed the sheet of paper and read it. The paper had a design emblem with an eagle and a shield that read *Citizen Protection Administration*. Next to the emblem was the number *751* and under that the word *OFFICIAL*, and under that, *Vehicle Identification*. "A parking permit?" he said.

"Yes," Ashley responded. "Now hurry up, Black."

"Okay, give me a minute," he requested, before crossing the street back to his car. He placed the permit on his dashboard, opened the trunk, removed a small travel sack, and hiked back to the Camry, opening the front passenger door and relaxing into the seat.

"Are you ready now?" Ashley said.

"Yep."

"Are you sure?" Ashley asked again, sarcasm in her voice.

Black rested his travel sack on the back floorboard and set his attention on Ashley. "Are you sure you weren't tailed here?" he asked just as wryly.

Ashley grinned. "Smart mouth..." she grumbled, throwing the car into drive.

As they pulled onto the mildly crowded road, Black looked into his side mirror and noticed the green truck easing into a subtle pursuit. The truck continued to tail them as Ashley wheeled the car a few blocks, making a right turn, a left, and another left onto I-80 East. As I-80 East eventually became I-580 East, the highway widened to about five lanes in both directions. Ashley carefully found a middle lane, riding it as traffic raced by on both sides. Black noticed the green truck, a couple cars back, move into the same lane. Both he and Ashley were quiet. Neither said a word to one another, only exchanging looks of discontent and disapproval.

A little over an hour into the drive, Black figured him and Ashley not talking wouldn't be good if they ran into trouble. He looked at Ashley and exhaled. "I think Boyar likes you," he said aloud.

She swung her sights from the road to look at him briefly. "Excuse me?"

"I think—"

"Yeah, I heard what you said. Just wondering why you said it."

"Before we left, he seemed concerned about you. I told him, don't worry about it."

"Well, I'm pretty independent—I don't need anyone's protection. Not his and definitely not yours, okay?"

"Not saying you need our help. Just thinking it's nice to have someone who's looking out for you like that."

"I heard you, so let's drop it."

Black shrugged and looked through the windshield at the blue sky blotted with fluffy white clouds before glancing out his window and seeing the trailer of an eighteen-wheeler droning past.

"Plus, he's not my type," Ashley added in a low tone, eyes on the road.

Black looked at her. *I thought she said to drop it... She's complicated.* "Not your type, huh? What's that? Caring, kind, considerate, *single*?" he replied.

"I'm not even going there with you. Wait—what do you mean, single?"

"I don't know. There's a lot of research that suggests that single women are attracted to married men."

Ashley sat quiet, facing the windshield.

"Something about social validation," Black continued.

"Well, I—I don't need society's validation, or a man. Never have."

"Of course you have, we all have. If not for parents, we wouldn't have been born. A *man* and a woman each played a role in bringing us into this world."

"That's about all a man is good for. Most don't stick around after that."

"I take it your mom and dad are not together?" he said, concern in his voice.

She looked at him before placing her sights back on the road. "How about you worry about your... multiple parents and I worry about mine."

Black glared at her.

Ashley locked eyes with him. It was a brief stare, but the tension made it feel like minutes. She timidly settled her eyes back on the road. Black continued to watch her for a minute. All the while, Ashley just peeked at him from the corner of her eye.

The car hummed up the highway for another thirty minutes, the interior silent again. Black shared his attention between his window and the windshield. Ashley was fixed on the road the entire time. She checked her mirrors repeatedly before exiting off the highway and making a left turn onto a road in a commercial area. They drove for a minute before making another right. They followed that road for a few miles, sitting quietly and watching as the commercial buildings rolled by.

Black checked his mirror and noticed the green truck was three cars back.

It wasn't long before open fields started to appear. Ashley slowed down and steered left onto a country road. Farmhouses, cow pastures, worn fences, and leaning power line poles welcomed them. They continued up the narrow, winding road. The green truck kept behind at a safe distance, trying not to be seen, Black figured. After another ten minutes of driving, the scenery changed. The road was still winding, but the cow pastures and farmhouses were replaced by open, hilly, grassy fields with the sun glowing above in a nearly cloudless sky. They passed a field with a community of windmills spinning in the far distance. The views were breathtaking, majestic, and maybe even moving, because Ashley began speaking to Black again.

"I'm sorry," she said, keeping her eyes on the road.

"What?" Black replied, looking at her.

She looked over to him briefly. "I shouldn't have said that about your parents." She slightly shook her head. "I'm sure it wasn't easy being an orphan."

"Don't worry about it," Black said, turning back to the view outside his window.

"And yes."

"Yes what?" Black asked, still turned away.

"My parents are not together."

Black peered over his shoulder at her.

"My father left when I was a little girl," Ashley continued. "I don't remember much about him."

Black shifted in his seat, twisting in her direction.

"I always wonder why he left, you know. And when something triggers that thought, it makes me mad, I guess. I'm working on it, but I've kept it bottled up for so long. I mean... what did I do? What would make a man leave his wife and little daughter?" she asked, glancing at Black and hunching her shoulders as if she expected him to answer.

"Are you asking me?"

She shrugged. "I don't know, sure."

"Your father's the only person who can answer that, maybe."

"Why do you say 'maybe'?"

"Sometimes people do things without knowing why and never put in the work to figure out why. I'm sure you see it all the time in your line of work. Someone makes a choice that hurts those around them, but they themselves don't really know why they made the choice to begin with. It can be an impulsive, emotional, passion-fueled decision. That's an indictment on them, not the people who are innocently standing by."

Ashley inhaled and exhaled quickly. "Well, my mom told me my grandfather—my dad's father—was an alcoholic and cheated on my grandmother a lot. So it may not be entirely his fault."

"Your dad may not be to blame for everything that happened in his life, but he is responsible for how his behavior affects the people around him. Especially his wife and child."

"I know. That's very unusual for a man to leave his wife and kids. I know it's on him, but I feel like I'm the one who is broken. It makes me so mad."

"It may be unusual in your world, but among my community it's very common," Black said, turning once again to his window.

Ashley looked over to him for a moment, then back at the road. The two went silent for a few minutes, snaking down the road and enjoying the view.

"So what about you, Black?"

"What about me?" Black replied, facing her.

"Are there things that trigger anger in you?"

"Yeah, sometimes, but I'm a lot better than what I used to be. I used to get really angry. Almost uncontrollable."

Ashley slowly nodded at the wheel. "Did you get mad because of what happened to your parents?" she asked.

"I think it has something to do with it, but my parents died when I was just in elementary school. I didn't start feeling like that until I was in the military. I guess I had it bottled up."

"What changed?" Ashley asked, glancing at Black and lifting her right palm in a gesture of surprise. "You don't strike me as a man who will fly off the handle."

"I had some help, some training, and I learned to take responsibility for my behavior and everything that comes into my life, even if it's not my fault. Some days are better than others, but I have a handle on it."

Ashley smiled. "Now I see why you're sticking around to help out with this case."

"I want to see this through until the end because I don't want it coming back on me."

"We're pretty certain you had nothing to do with these bombings," Ashley said, shaking her head. "You could've left instead of coming on this trip with me. Maybe you don't want this to blow back on you, but I think you want to see this through because you feel a responsibility to do so. That's an honorable thing."

Black said nothing.

"What about your sister? How did she take your parents' death?"

"Olivia was an infant. She barely remembers and there was no funeral or wake. We never had a chance to properly say goodbye."

"I'm sorry, Black."

"No need to be. My parents put things in place to make sure we were taken care of practically for the rest of our lives, and most of the foster homes were good to us. Our final foster parents really took us in as their own."

"Do you consider them your parents?"

"Well—my sister does more than me."

"So you don't?"

Black shrugged. "They're not, really."

"They took you in as their own, right?"

"Yeah."

"Did they make sure you and your sister had what you needed?"

"Yeah."

"Did they call you their son and her their daughter?"

"Yeah."

"Would you say they loved you two?"

"Yeah. I would say that."

"Then like it or not, they're your parents, Black."

Black took in a deep breath, exhaling as he peered in his mirror and saw the green truck trailing behind them.

"Black, I have a question to ask."

"Go ahead. This has already turned into a shrink session."

Ashley chuckled. "Seriously," she said. "Anyway. Some areas of your file are highly redacted."

"Okay?"

"We have record of you spending time in Asia after the military, but the few years prior to that we can't place where you were. What were you doing those years?"

Black sighed. "I'm not at liberty to say," he said, looking out his window.

Ashley shifted her gaze between him and the road for a few seconds. "Fine. You don't have to tell me."

They continued on the winding road, watching as the grassy hills and power lines rolled in. It was another five minutes before the hills flattened and they found themselves traveling parallel to a train on their right. The train whistled and steamed by, leaving a light stream of smoke behind. It smelled like a charcoal grill being preheated at a barbecue. A couple of minutes later, Ashley was veering right, back onto I-580 E. The conversation ebbed and flowed, with Ashley doing most of the talking. She talked about her upbringing with her mom and how she got started in law enforcement. Black was only half listening and actually dozed off a couple times.

"Are you listening to me, Black?" Ashley asked, smiling.

"Yeah—Yeah. You know, you've been driving for a while. Do you want me to take over?"

"No, I'm totally fine," she answered before continuing to tell him about how she had ended up in San Francisco.

I would've never thought she's such a chatterbox, Black thought.

I-580 East turned into I-5 South and the landscape became flat. Not a single hill or dirt mound for miles. Ashley fell quiet. She must have said all she wanted to say, Black was guessing. He slowly closed his eyes after getting a final peek of Ashley peering into her side mirror. When he opened his eyes, he saw her doing the same thing. The sun was descending below the horizon and darkness began to wrap the sky.

Ashley gave him a quick stare with squinted eyes. "Welcome back, Sleeping Beauty," she said in a chuckle, turning back to the windshield.

"Where are we?" Black asked with a slight yawn in his voice, pushing his arms out in a stretch.

"Near Bakersfield."

"So we've been driving nearly three hours?"

"Yep, and I think someone is following us," Ashley said, glancing up at the rearview mirror.

Black lifted himself upright in his seat. "Green pickup truck?" he asked.

"Yeah. H—how did you know?"

"That truck was following you when you came to pick me up."

Ashley's head jerked in Black's direction. "They've been following us the whole trip and you're just now telling me about it?" she said, neck bending forward, frown on her face.

"I was thinking about it, but you told me you were independent and didn't need anyone's help."

Ashley rolled her eyes and sighed. "Any idea who they are?" she asked, sharing her attention between the road and the mirror.

Black nodded. "Yeah, I have a good idea who it is."

"Who?"

"We need to gas up. Take the next exit."

Ashley flicked on her indicator and eased over to the far right lane. Black saw the green truck perform the same maneuver. After a couple of minutes, they were coasting up the off ramp. They made a left across the overpass, turning into a large gas station and attached restaurant lot. There were about fifty gas pumps and fifteen diesel pumps specifically for eighteen-wheelers. They parked next to one of the available pumps and watched as the green pickup stopped at a pump on the far side of the station.

Ashley exhaled, "Okay, I guess I can get the local authorities here."

"No, no, don't do that yet," Black said, looking out his window at the green truck.

"Okay. So what are we going to do?"

Black looked at Ashley. "This is what we're going to do..." he began with a smile on his face.

CHAPTER
FIFTEEN

"SO THAT'S YOUR plan—to wait? Simple plan," Ashley commented.

"In my experience, keeping it simple keeps you alive," Black said.

Ashley hunched her shoulders. "Okay," she said, opening the door and dropping her feet onto the concrete. She stood from the car, closed the door behind her, and leaned backward in a stretch before ambling into the store.

Black watched her through the store windows as she walked to the cashier. A few minutes later, she waved to him from the window. He stepped out of the car and circled around to the driver side, where the pump was located. He began filling the car while inconspicuously watching the green truck parked on the other side of the station. When the pump handle clicked, Black replaced it and the gas cap and crossed the pavement, passing in front of a couple of vehicles before entering the store. He met Ashley and together they walked into the adjoining restaurant, finding a booth with a window view of the pumps outside.

"Alright. They're still there," Ashley said, peeking out the window.

"Give it a few minutes," Black said.

"Okay, keep an eye on them," Ashley said, sliding out of the booth. "I'm getting something to eat. Want something?"

"Whatever you're having," Black replied, eyes on the green truck.

Ashley walked to the restaurant's front counter. Black continued to watch the truck. Five minutes passed and Ashley walked back over.

"They're still in the truck?" she asked, scooting into the booth.

"Yep," Black replied, tapping his palm against the table.

"Our food should be ready in a little."

Black nodded, fixed on the truck.

"Hey, Black," Ashley said, staring at him with a smile.

He turned to her, keeping an eye on the truck in his peripheral.

"They're not going anywhere. You can relax some."

Black smiled.

Then he saw a thought occur to Ashley. "You said you may know who's in the truck. Who do you think it is?"

As if in answer to her question, the green pickup's passenger door opened and a man stepped out under the glow of the overhead lights.

"Wait, he looks familiar," Ashley said. "That's—um—"

"Guo."

Seconds later, the other door swung open as well, and Reeves stood from the truck. The two men talked for a few seconds before Guo walked over to the pump and Reeves paced toward the store's entrance.

"He's coming in," Ashley said, turning from the window and facing Black.

"Don't make eye contact—just act normal. Remember, he doesn't know for sure that you know who he is."

Black heard the automatic doors zip open five yards behind him.

"That's him," Ashley muttered, quickly moving her sights from the door to the table, and finally Black's face. She smiled and locked eyes with him as if the two were having a deep conversation.

"Remember, be natural," Black said in a low tone, almost a whisper.

"I am," Ashley replied without moving her lips, still smiling. The two continued their act for a few minutes before Ashley informed Black, "He's ringing out."

He smiled at her in a quiet chuckle, amused by her ventriloquist performance.

"Okay, he's walking out now."

Black looked out the window from the corner of his eye and caught sight of Reeves walking back to the truck. He was carrying a plastic bag of what appeared to be snacks and drinks. Once at the vehicle, he said something to Guo, who then began pumping gas in the truck. Reeves threw the bag and himself inside the cab. After Guo finished pumping the gas, he too jumped inside the pickup.

"Now what do you want to do?" Ashley asked.

"We wait."

"More waiting."

"Yep. Keep an eye on them. I'm going to the restroom."

Black walked across the restaurant's ceramic tiled floor, opening a door which led outside. His feet landed on a smooth concrete sidewalk which ran into the blacktop for the gas pumps. A couple yards up on the left were the restrooms. He walked into the men's and was hit by the scent of Pine-Sol. The restroom was much cleaner and more modern than he had expected for a gas station in the middle of Bakersfield. He used the urinal and washed his hands at the sink before walking back inside the restaurant and taking his seat.

"That was quick," Ashley said.

"The restroom's not that far away."

"They're still in the truck. Your turn to watch. I'm going to the restroom now," Ashley said, standing from the booth and walking out.

Black watched the truck for five minutes. There was no activity. Ashley strolled back into the restaurant and headed to the booth but made a detour to the food counter when she saw their order was ready. With one hand, she lightly whisked a tray of burgers and fries across the table before hunkering down in her seat and resting two bottled waters next to the tray.

"Did I miss anything?" she asked.

"Nope," Black answered, facing her.

"Alrighty then—let's eat," Ashley shrugged.

The two ate their burgers and fries, keeping an eye on the truck while casually discussing the food before them and how much further they had to drive.

"That was good," Ashley said afterwards, cradling her stomach.

"It was pretty good for a gas station burger," Black replied. "I'll clean up the mess since you were nice enough to bring the food over."

"Aww, how sweet of you," Ashley joked, smiling.

Black grinned. He stood from the table, placing the leftover trash on the tray, and carried it to the trash bin. On his way back to his seat, Ashley waved at him to speed it up. He hurried to the booth and peered out the window, standing with his head tilted. Guo had exited the truck and was walking in the direction of the restrooms.

"He's on the move," Ashley commented.

"Keep an eye on Reeves," Black said.

"Where are you going?"

"To have a conversation with Guo. Oh yeah—" he added, pausing as he turned away, "call the police."

"I thought you didn't want me to."

"I didn't want you to at the time."

"Okay," Ashley said, reaching into her pocket for her phone.

Black nodded and walked to the door. Cracking it open, he watched Guo enter the men's restroom. Black slipped through the restaurant door and jogged over to the restroom. He leaned against the wall next to the entryway and listened as Guo relieved himself and flushed the urinal. He heard him shuffle to the sink and waited until he heard water running before swiftly racing in.

In the mirror, Guo's facial expression altered to surprise as he saw Black standing behind him. He started to turn, but Black quickly put him in a rear choke hold. Guo began to buck and throw his arms, gasping and fighting to break free.

"Hey, hey, calm down," Black said.

Guo ignored his request and continued to gasp, throwing his hands over his shoulder in an attempt to hit and grab his attacker. Black leaned back to avoid his opponent's flapping hands and lifted him off of his feet before dropping him to the floor on his butt. Guo's movements slowed and his loud breaths turned into wheezes as he fainted.

"I guess I won't be getting any information out of you," Black said, frisking Guo. He found another unmarked Glock 19 tucked in the back of his pants next to a case of handcuffs. Black removed the gun, stuffed it in his own pants, dragged Guo's wasted body to the handicap stall, and heaved him onto the toilet seat, using his own handcuffs to lock him to the handicap bar in the stall. He took one last look at Guo's slouched body before closing the stall door. Then he hid in a corner near the entrance, next to the urinals. Three minutes went by before Reeves opened the restroom door.

"Kevin," he called. "What's taking so lo—"

Black jumped at him. Reeves reached to his waist and gripped the handle of a gun—the same model Glock that had been so popular the past couple days. Reeves yanked the gun out of his belt, but Black was already on him. He had control of Reeves' hand and squeezed, causing him to drop the pistol. Black then locked his assailant's elbow with his free hand while stepping in front of him and tossing him over his leg, all in one smooth motion. Reeves flew into a low somersault before rolling across the floor and crashing shoulder first into the far wall near the handicap stall.

Black picked up Reeves' gun and pointed it at him. Reeves pushed himself up, sitting on the floor with his back against the wall.

"Start talking," Black said.

Reeves chuckled. "Ow… About what?" he said, rubbing his shoulder.

"Start with why you've been following me."

Reeves shook his head and looked away.

Black thrust his boot into the shoulder Reeves was favoring. He wailed in pain, grabbing at his shoulder and falling on his side.

Black squatted and looked him in his eyes. "Let's try this again. Why is Stokes having you follow us?"

"Who?" Reeves panted.

Black exhaled. Standing up, he stamped on Reeves' same shoulder. The injured man once again clutched his shoulder and wormed on the floor, moaning.

"You better start talking. That shoulder may be dislocated," Black mocked. "And if it's not, it will be soon at this rate."

Reeves said nothing. He just leered up at Black.

Black shrugged and raised his boot.

"Wa—wait—wait," Reeves pled. "He said it was for his family."

"His family?"

"Yeah. He said you knew or had something that could harm his family. He wanted to protect his family, so he asked me to arrest you or take you out if it came to it."

"Who's his family?"

"I don't know. I didn't even know he had family in California," Reeves said, sitting up, still holding his shoulder.

"So you're telling me you just did what he asked without knowing why."

"We served together, we're brothers. I didn't ask because I felt he'd do the same for me."

Black shook his head. "I think there's more you're not telling me. Stokes has something on you. Maybe he knows about your terrible drug issue and your Internal Affairs investigation and is using it against you."

"Up yours," Reeves sneered. "You think you're pretty tough, but my brothers will take care of you," he ended with a smirk on his face.

Black grinned at him before flipping the gun and connecting the butt of the pistol with his head. Reeves immediately nodded off to sleep. Black ejected the magazine and cleared the chamber, placing the gun in Reeves' lap and the magazine in his own back pocket. He found handcuffs on Reeves and cuffed the unconscious man's arm—the one with the good shoulder—to the metal grab bar above his head. Opening the stall, he removed the other gun he had taken from Guo, ejecting the magazine and clearing the chamber before flinging the gun in Guo's lap.

As Black closed the stall door, Ashley came into the restroom with her gun drawn.

"Good, you're okay," she said, holstering her gun. "The waitress came to the table and I lost track of Reeves." Her eyes widened as she fixed on Reeves' slumped body. "Is he—"

"No, he's just taking a nap. Let's go," Black said, walking towards the exit.

"We can't just leave him here."

Black turned to her. "You called the police, right?"

"Yeah..."

Black shrugged. "Okay, they'll be fine," he said, stepping

to her, touching her arm, and gently leading her out of the restroom.

Ashley peered over her shoulder twice. "Where's Guo?" she asked as they exited.

The two continued away from the restroom area and over to the car.

Ashley stopped walking and pointed her thumb towards the restroom area. "I can't believe we're going to leave them there," she said.

"They'll be fine," Black told her again.

She hunched her shoulders. "I guess so," she yawned.

"Let me drive," Black said, extending his hand for the keys.

"Nah, I'm okay."

"You look tired and I've already taken a nap."

"I should be fine. We're only about two hours away."

"You'll feel better if you sleep those two hours."

She gently swayed her head from side to side as if she was making a decision. "Okay. You can drive," she finally said, handing Black the keys.

They entered the car. Black adjusted the seat and mirror for his height while Ashley pressed at the navigation system. She entered the address for Fantastic Galaxy.

"We're going straight to the theme park?" Black asked.

"Yep. Local law enforcement should be performing a sweep of the park as we speak."

"Really? That's not a small park."

"A lot of the employees are helping out."

Black shrugged, turned the engine, and wheeled onto the road, jumping back on I-5 South. The highway was dark and nearly empty, with the exception of a few taillights gleaming ahead and a couple headlights illuminating from behind. He noticed Ashley relaxing into her seat. The interior of the car was quiet until her phone rang.

She raised the phone to her ear. "Agent Chapp," she said.

"Yeah, we're okay... A couple hours out... Oh that's good. What did you guys find? ... Ahhh... I see... Uh-huh... Okay, we'll call you then. Bye." She ended the call, turning to Black. "That was Toben. They were able to find Ty's car using the tracker in Matt's backpack."

Black nodded with his eyes on the road.

"It was at the airport. Oh yeah, Toben also said he told Director Hanten about Stokes. She's on board with looking into him."

"That should make things a lot easier," Black replied, staring out the windshield.

"He said to call him back once we settle in at the hotel. And before I forget—were you able to get anything out of Reeves or Guo?"

"Only that Reeves and Stokes served together, and that Stokes told him to come after me because I had or knew something that could harm Stokes' family."

"What could you possibly have or know?"

"That's a mystery to me, considering three days ago I had never heard of Stokes."

"Strange," Ashley said, shaking her head and again relaxing into her seat.

Black cruised down the highway, taking in the sights of the star-filled night sky and the moonlit mountains. He looked over at Ashley, who was sound asleep. She looked comfortable, peaceful, angelic... all of which were completely different from his initial impression of her. Black smiled and shook his head at the thought before settling his attention back on the road. He drove for two hours. Road construction signs welcomed him into downtown L.A. Another thirty miles after that, the GPS was directing him to take an exit onto Fantastic Galaxy Drive. He followed the directions, coasting on the well-maintained and scenic road where many billboards advertised the theme park's rides and events. He glanced at Ashley and saw her open her eyes.

She stretched. "Are we here?" she asked in a yawn.

"Yeah. Welcome to Fantastic G," Black said.

A few minutes later, they approached a line of drive-thru ticket stations. The gates for all of the lanes were closed except one.

"There," Ashley pointed.

Black angled the car in the direction of the open station. He pulled forward, rolling down his window, and was greeted by a man in a security guard uniform.

"Good evening," the man said.

"Good evening," Black and Ashley both replied.

"How can I help you?"

Ashley removed her DHS badge fold and handed it to Black, who handed it to the guard. "I'm Agent Chapp with the DHS and this is Orlando Black, a consultant for the DHS," she said.

The man nodded, looking her credentials over. "Yes. Okay. We've been expecting you," he said, passing the badge back. "They're expecting you at the main office. Just follow the signs."

"Thank you," Ashley waved.

Black saluted the man, rolled up his window, and pulled off, handing Ashley her badge. He followed the signs and was taken through large parking areas named after the different planets in our solar system. The lots were well lit, so following the signs was easy despite the darkness. After traveling through "Lot Earth" they arrived at the main office and were amazed at what they saw—close to ten police squad cars and two SWAT trucks.

Black looked at Ashley, figuring she would have something to say about it.

"Well, it is a big park," she said, shrugging.

"That's true," Black said.

They exited the car, shaking off the two-hour-plus drive before walking into the main office. The pair was immediately confronted by a SWAT officer dressed in full tactical gear.

"Who are you?" the officer demanded.

Ashley whipped out her badge. "Agent Chapp, DHS, and this is Orlando Black, DHS consultant."

"Oh yeah. You're the one who called us here for nothing," the man replied with a chuckle.

I guess that means they didn't find anything, Black thought.

"Excuse me?" Ashley fumed at the SWAT member. "Who's in charge here?"

"Captain Stuart, ma'am."

"Can you go get him, please?"

"Yes, ma'am," the officer said, walking away and making a left at the end of the hall.

"Can you believe him? We're trying to keep people safe and he's thinking it's for nothing," Ashley said.

"Just means they didn't find anything," Black replied.

"I guess not," Ashley sighed.

Black took in the lobby's vivid interior design. The walls were painted with outer space imagery like planets, stars, and spaceships, with cartoon astronauts and aliens scattered in between. There were also many pictures of the park's popular rides and attractions hanging on the walls. Black stepped to his right, passing through a doorway which led into an open lounge area for the park's guests. He was hit by the smell of baked goods and the sound of a happy, light, futuristic jingle playing over the intercom. The lounge was decorated much like the lobby area, but there was plenty of seating, big flat-screen TVs everywhere, a large play area for kids, and a kitchen and dining area at the far end of the room. Standing in the dining room were two police officers and two park employees having coffee and pastries while enjoying a casual conversation. One of the officers noticed Black and waved. Black returned a wave and stepped back into the lobby, where he found Ashley looking down at her phone.

She glanced at him. "Where did you run off to?" she asked before placing her attention back on her phone. "The reception here isn't great."

Black looked down the hall and saw the SWAT officer walking back towards them accompanied by a shorter, bulky man who appeared to be in his late fifties. He wore a SWAT uniform and sported a bald head but had snow-white facial hair.

He walked to Ashley, smiling. "Agent Chapp?" he said, extending his hand.

Ashley smiled and shook his hand. "Yes. You must be Captain Stuart," she said.

"Yes, ma'am, I am. Nice to meet you," he said before turning to Black. "And you are?" he asked, still smiling.

"Orlando Black," Black said, shaking his hand.

"Nice to meet you, young man."

"Same to you."

Stuart turned to Ashley. "We've searched this park top to bottom and didn't find anything," he said. "I was gonna suggest to the manag—"

"Excuse me!" a voice interrupted from down the hall.

A slender, fair-skinned, dark-haired man wearing slacks, a polo shirt, and glasses paced in their direction. Captain Stuart rolled his eyes as the man approached the group.

"So what's happening?" the man asked, folding his arms and continuously shifting his weight from one leg to the other.

"I'm sorry—who are you?" Ashley asked.

The man craned his neck towards Ashley. "I'm the park manager. Who are you?" he said, tilting his head.

Ashley stood quiet for a moment, lips sucked in. "We're DHS, sir," she eventually said, sighing at the end.

"So you're the one responsible for all of this. We wasted manpower and lost a lot of money today for nothing. What were you thinking?"

"We were thinking about keeping people safe."

"Safe from what, fun?"

Ashley filled her cheeks with air, releasing an audible breath.

Black quickly jumped in to break the tension. "Captain Stuart, do you know where the anti-324 event will take place?"

"Yes. It will be on the east side of the park. We checked and double-checked that area."

"Have the panelists been notified of the potential threat?"

"Yes, they have, and they plan to be at their panels at 10 a.m.," the park manager cut in.

Black ignored the manager. He kept his eyes on Stuart and waited for him to answer.

"Yep, we let them know, but they're still adamant about holding the event," Stuart said.

"Hey!" the manager blurted.

Black continued to disregard him, as did everyone else in the group.

"Captain," Ashley spoke to Stuart. "Do you think you could lend a couple of men tomorrow? Just as a precaution."

"We're not lending any of our employees for this," the manager put in.

No one responded or even looked in his direction.

"Yep. I was gonna have a small SWAT unit ready and a few officers at the event. I'll make sure they're all properly briefed and familiar with what the female suspect looks like," the captain answered.

"Thanks, Captain. We'll be back here tomorrow," Ashley said before looking at Black and nodding towards the door.

"See you then."

As Black and Ashley walked off, she stopped.

"Thank you," she said.

A few steps ahead, Black grabbed the door handle and turned to face her. "For what?" he asked.

"Showing me how to deal with difficult people. Sometimes you just have to ignore them."

Black shrugged. "If you focus on people and situations that upset you, you're going to become upset. You have to choose your battles with care. It's something I learned to help keep my anger in check," he said, opening the door for her.

Ashley smiled. "So you can be a gentleman," she said, passing through the doorway.

Black followed her to the Camry. With Ashley at the wheel, they cruised toward the park's exit.

CHAPTER
SIXTEEN

THEIR NEXT STOP was a Hyatt Place hotel. The two rolled into the attached parking garage, grabbed their bags, took the elevator to the lobby, and strolled across the hardwood floor to the check-in counter. Ashley talked to the clerk while Black scanned the area. He was performing his exits, threats, and weapons assessment. It wasn't that he anticipated any warning sign in particular, but rather it was just a habit. Ashley finished checking in with the clerk before she and Black walked to the elevators.

"Which floor?" he asked.

Ashley looked at him with a brief expression of confusion before answering, "Oh—um, three. The third floor."

Black jammed the right button and the doors thumped closed.

"Here," Ashley said, giving him a keycard. "You're in room 308."

When the elevator doors rolled open, Black walked in the direction of room 308, according to the indicator arrow in the hallway. Ashley followed. He found his room and was about to insert his keycard into the door when Ashley's voice floated over his shoulder.

"Black. Remember Toben wants us to call, so I'm going to settle in then I'll come over and we can call from your room."

"Okay," Black shrugged before inserting his card and opening the door. He heard Ashley doing the same at her door, straight across the hall—room 309.

As he stepped inside, a prominent lavender scent swept across his face. The room looked like a business suite for road warriors and executives who spent most of their life living out of a suitcase. There was a bed, a large U-shaped couch with a coffee table in front of it, a desk, and a small kitchen. Black tossed his travel sack on the bed, entered the bathroom, and washed his hands and face. After drying off, he lay on the bed with his hands behind his head, thinking. His eyes became heavy and he dozed off.

He opened his eyes at the sound of a knock at the door. He walked over to it, glancing through the peep hole before tugging the door open and walking to the couch. He sat down while Ashley grabbed the rolling chair from the desk. She faced the chair toward Black before sitting down and removing her phone.

Black yawned.

Ashley smiled. "You look tired," she said, thumbing her phone.

"I'll be fine."

Ashley placed her phone on the table. It rang through the speakers four times before Toben's voice eased on the line.

"Agent Toben," he said.

"Jake. This is Ashley and Black."

"Okay. I'm here with Boyar in the back room."

"Hi, Victor."

"Hey—Hi, Ash," Boyar replied. You could hear him blushing through the phone.

Black rolled his eyes and massaged his forehead, thinking, *Why doesn't that guy just tell her how he feels?*

"So how are you two holding up?" Toben said. "I see you haven't killed each other yet."

Ashley released a slight chuckle. "Why would we kill each other?" she asked.

"Because earlier today you wanted to make the trip on your own."

Ashley glanced at Black. "Well, he has a way of quickly growing on you."

Black grinned, shaking his head.

"I can believe that," Toben said. "But back to business. As you all know, we have been tracking that kid we know as Ty. We have since ID'd him as Tyler Robinson. He was a foster kid, but now he lives on his own. Didn't have anything in his past that was a red flag. His foster parents were good normal people and there weren't any major incidents in the homes he was in."

"There is a red flag," Black refuted.

"What do you mean?"

"Have you found his biological parents?"

"Still working on it. What do you mean, there's a red flag?" Toben asked again.

"I mean the fact that he's in the system at all is the red flag. It can affect kids in negative ways if they feel their real parents didn't love them."

"I'm still looking into who his biological parents are," Boyar chimed in. "It's a little difficult to find them. Seems Tyler was given into foster care anonymously. It's strange because, according to the clerk at Child Welfare, the record was updated three days ago. But I'll keep looking into it."

"Man… finding information on this kid is tough," Ashley expressed.

"Well, I—I do have information on Stokes."

"Do you know where he's at?" Black asked.

"No," Boyar answered, "but I know he lives in Arlington, Virginia. He's originally from upstate New York and served in the military. In the Army—leading a Green Beret unit. Guess who was part of his unit."

"Reeves," Black answered reluctantly.

"That's right, but why the doubt in your voice?"

"I had a couple of run-ins with Reeves—he didn't fight like a Green Beret. But then I thought, excess alcohol and drugs will do that to you."

"Wait, a couple of run-ins? I thought you only ran into Reeves once, Black," Toben contended.

Ashley's mouth gaped, forming an O-shape. "I… um… I forgot to mention we were tailed by Reeves and Guo," she said.

"What?" both Toben and Boyar blurted in tandem.

"What happened?" Toben continued.

"Uhh… um…" Ashley searched for words.

Black saw her struggling to formulate an answer. "Nothing much happened," he said. "We noticed them following us as we left San Francisco. They tailed us all the way to a gas station in Bakersfield and it was there we got the drop on them. Tied them up in the bathroom and called the local law enforcement."

"Okay, but did they say anything?" Toben asked.

"Guo didn't have a chance to say much. But Reeves mentioned Stokes wanted him to come after me because I had something that could hurt Stokes' family. And before you ask —I have no idea what he was talking about."

"I don't get it."

"That makes two of us. Boyar," Black redirected the conversation, "you said Stokes led a unit and Reeves was part of it. Who else was in his unit?"

"There were three other guys," Boyar answered. "And, unlike Reeves, these three are still active. They all either participate in military training programs or head small ops for the government. I'm surprised the government still uses any of them from that unit."

"Why?" Ashley asked.

"The whole team was under investigation for an operation that went wrong in Colombia. Apparently, some money went missing from a drug bust the unit was involved in. I think the investigation is ongoing."

Black nodded. "I take it these other three members of the unit live on the East coast."

"Yep, two have residence in Maryland and one in D.C."

"What did you guys find at Fantastic Galaxy?" Toben asked.

"They didn't find anything," Ashley answered. "But they'll have a small SWAT unit and a few officers at the 324 event tomorrow. We're going to be there too, of course."

"Okay. Boyar and I will see if we can track Stokes and this Tyler down. If Tyler is going to Fantastic Universe, he's probably already in Orlando or on his way there. You two be careful and get some rest."

"Toben," Black said, "before we adjourn, is there any news on Petrak?"

"Oh yeah. Mr. Petrak is denying having anything to do with the bombings. He denies having anything to do with the firearms or the sauce," Toben said.

"So that means he's probably denying having anything to do with his daughter."

"Yep. According to him, she acted all on her own."

"What a pig and coward," Ashley condemned. "He supplies all the unmarked firearms for the Bay Area and denies it, even to the point of betraying his own daughter."

"Don't get worked up. We finally have him and he's going away for a long time. Now you two get some rest and, remember, be careful. I'll call tomorrow," Toben concluded.

"Good night," Ashley said.

"Good night," Boyar echoed.

The call ended. Black stood from the couch and Ashley placed the phone back in her pocket as she stood.

"I guess we should get to bed," she said, walking the chair back to the desk. "I want to make sure we get to the park early. If there's a chance we can catch Johana before she does something to hurt others and completely ruin her life, I don't want to miss it."

"You seem to have a soft spot for her," Black commented.

"No, it's not that."

"Then what is it? Because this girl can be pretty dangerous. She almost blew me to pieces. I don't want you freezing… because she'll exploit the opportunity."

"I don't know… I just see a little of myself in her."

"Attitude, good-looking, and dangerous. I can see that."

Ashley chuckled. "Yeah, but not exactly where I was going. I meant… my father wasn't around, and I often think how different my life could've turned out."

"But you turned out okay because you made okay decisions. I understand where you're coming from, but this girl made her own choices."

Ashley said nothing.

Black stared into her eyes and she looked into his. They stood that way for a long five seconds.

"I should get to my room," Ashley said, walking towards the door.

Black trailed a couple of steps behind.

Ashley pivoted at the door, facing Black. "Oh yeah. Thank you again," she said.

Black moved closer to her. "For what?"

"Covering for me. I didn't know Reeves and Guo were tailing us until we were near Bakersfield."

Black said nothing. Leaning in closer, he could hear Ashley's heart rate increase.

"It was nice working with you today," she said as her breathing became heavier.

Black remained quiet and continued to lean in until he was within kissing distance.

Ashley bit her bottom lip. "It—it was great working with you today, Black, but…"

Black moved in closer. He dodged her face, reached around her, grabbed the door handle, and opened the door. "We have a big day tomorrow. We better get some rest."

Ashley brushed her hair behind her ear. "Oh yeah, o—of course. I'll see you in the morning," she said quickly, clearing her throat and stepping into the hall.

Black watched as she fiddled with the key card reader. She entered her room, turning around with a forced smile and waving before closing the door. Black smiled and waved back as he shut his own door. He chuckled to himself on the way to the bathroom before taking a shower and preparing for bed.

EARLY THE NEXT morning, Black rolled out of the sheets. Within thirty-five minutes, he had performed his push-ups, sit-ups, and stretches, gotten dressed, and packed his travel sack. Exiting his room, he was surprised to see Ashley standing in the hall already dressed and packed.

"I was just about to knock on your door," she said.

"Well, no need to now. Good morning."

"Good morning. The hotel has free breakfast. Let's see what they have."

"Let's go."

They took the elevators down to the lobby, where they found the dining room and had breakfast. Forty minutes later, they were entering Fantastic Galaxy. The sun was just dawning when they reached the ticket stations. This time there were a lot of cars in line. Ashley angled for the ticket station to the far right. She pulled up to the station and flashed her badge. The guy nodded as if he was expecting her and signaled for her to go through. She crawled past, steering in the direction of the main office.

"Didn't have to buy a ticket or anything," she said.

"That's a good sign," Black said.

"What makes you say that?"

"The ticket clerk was expecting you. More than likely that means the park staff has been informed and they're on the lookout for Johana."

They found a space in the parking lot outside the main office. Standing out front was the park manager.

"Aw… I really don't feel like dealing with him," Ashley sighed.

"I know what you mean, but don't let him get to you."

The two stepped out of the car and walked over to the manager.

"Good morning, Agent Chapp," the manager said with a smile on his face.

Ashley squinted her eyes and slightly tilted her head back. "Good… morning," she said with reluctance in her voice.

The man moved his attention to Black. "And you're Mr. Black, right?" he said. "Good morning to you."

Black responded with a single nod.

"I was told to take you to the clubhouse, where the event will be held. Follow me," he said, walking in the direction of a golf cart.

"Why is he acting so nice?" Ashley whispered to Black.

Black shrugged.

The group hopped on the golf cart. Black and Ashley together in the back seat. On their way to the clubhouse, they passed a number of roller coasters, restaurants, theaters, and game booths. There were employees dressed up as various characters, astronauts, aliens, space rangers, and kings and queens of planets all around the park. The place was empty and quiet for the most part, with only the employees running around getting prepared for the park to open, from what Black could tell. The cart stopped in front of a long set of granite steps. At the top of the steps was a concrete structure. The front and the sides of the building were flat like most buildings, but the back was rounded outwards. The roof was made of something that imitated the sparkle of crystal.

"This is the clubhouse," the manager said. "Go in and help yourselves to the drinks and refreshments. I'll be back once I finish up at the main office."

Black and Ashley skipped off the cart, watching the park manager as he waved and wheeled off.

"He was acting strange," Ashley said, looking at Black, gently shaking her head.

"Maybe he had a change of heart," Black commented, before reading two large signs near the steps.

One of the signs read *The Galactic Clubhouse* and had a large arrow pointing to the building up the steps. The other had the number 324 with a circle around it and a line crossing through it, just like Black had seen on the fliers at Fisherman's Wharf three days ago. Under that sign was written, *No child's life should be taxed. For our kids. For our families. For our futures. Come join the conversation!* There was also a large arrow under this sign pointing to the same building.

"They make it easy to find the party," Black said, throwing his head towards the signs.

"Yeah… I guess so," Ashley replied.

The two hiked up the steps, approaching the front entrance. The doors hissed and pulled open with a dramatic swooping sound, providing the impression of entering an actual galactic space station. The inside felt cool and had the scent of newness. It was bright with a lot of different shades of white assaulting the eye—the floors were white, the walls were white, the counters were white, and the ceiling was white. To his right, Black noticed a counter which had dozens of different buttons and lights blinking at the top. On the other side of the counter were a few employees dressed as space cadets standing behind computer screens. To Black's left was a long white hall. There were fake windows along either wall which contained screens playing animated movies of stars and planets moving past, which gave guests the effect of walking down the hall of a real station in outer space.

"This is pretty neat, huh?" Ashley enthused.

"It's interesting," Black replied, taking note of a holographic image of the solar system at a circular terminal located near the center of the lobby.

A couple of seconds later he saw Captain Stuart walking around the hologram terminal towards him and Ashley.

"You two made it," Stuart said. "Good morning."

"Good morning," they replied.

"Okay, so let's get to it. Walk with me," Stuart continued, leading them towards the back of the building. "I'll have two guys outside at the front and two in here during the event. I'll make sure we have a metal detector and security checkpoint in the lobby and, as I mentioned yesterday, I have a small SWAT unit in a nearby parking lot ready to go. The park is on board and the employees have been briefed."

"So how did you get the park manager to change his tune?" Black asked.

"Yeah," Ashley echoed.

Stuart looked over his shoulder. "I just told him I'll charge him with obstruction," he said, shrugging with a smile on his face.

"Good play," Black said.

They dodged the hologram and walked towards the back of the building, where there was a small auditorium with stadium seating and a stage at the far back wall. The platform was decorated with anti-324 posters, and on the back wall of the stage was a large circular window providing a view of one of the popular attractions of the park, a planetary-shaped roller coaster ride. Against the far right wall of the auditorium was a long table heaped with refreshments. The group took the steps down towards the stage.

"We performed another search of this building and park and didn't find anything," Stuart informed the other two. "I guess now we just need to be on the lookout to ensure nothing happens."

"I guess so. Thank you for all the hard work, Captain," Ashley said.

"My pleasure. Now excuse me for a moment. I have to speak to one of my men," Stuart said, walking to an officer on the left side of the auditorium.

Ashley looked at Black. "It's time to do your favorite thing —wait."

"I don't have anywhere to be," Black said, shrugging and following the scent of coffee to the refreshment table.

Ashley paced behind him. He grabbed a cup and filled it with coffee, and she did the same. Then they waited for about two hours while chatting, enjoying coffee and pastries, and watching the employees and local law enforcement set up for the event. Black went to the restroom and on his way back he noticed the park manager in the auditorium talking to a younger man who was dressed in jeans and a blazer. The man had creamy skin, great hair, and a glowing smile—movie star material.

Black walked over to Ashley. "Who's the young Brad Pitt?" he asked.

"That's the star panelist. He's probably the most popular of the activists that'll be here today."

"Well, I guess we better keep a close eye on Mr. Pitt."

After a few minutes, the park manager walked over. "Did you two get any refreshments?" he asked with a smile on his face.

Both Black and Ashley nodded.

"Good. Enjoy the event," he said, walking over to the food table and speaking to a tall girl with dark hair. "Hey, Julie."

The girl turned to face him. "Sir?"

"We need to make sure the refreshments stay filled."

"Yes, sir," she replied.

"Thank you," the park manager said, walking in the direction of the lobby.

ANOTHER HOUR WENT by and the auditorium seats filled with guests. On the stage were three panelists and one person behind a podium facilitating the discussion. The really good-looking guy sat between the other two panelists. Black stood near the refreshments table as people filtered in and out, keeping his eyes on the stage as the panelists continued on and on about problems he felt a little common sense could easily solve. Soon Ashley approached and stood next to him.

"The security checkpoint at the entrance is working well," she said. "Did I miss anything?"

"Not a thing," Black sighed.

"You seem uninterested."

"That's because I am."

"This is an important subject."

"Very important. That's just it. I don't understand why we need a law to tell us how to take care of our kids."

Ashley gestured at the crowd and smiled at Black. "I believe that's why people are here. They don't want any laws telling them how to take care of their children."

"That's one way of looking at it," Black said as he glanced around the auditorium.

"What do you mean?"

"Most people in this auditorium don't look like they have one child, let alone five. And none of them look like they're on welfare. So how is the law impacting them negatively, is what I'm wondering."

Ashley turned to face the auditorium. "I don't disagree with you, but maybe people feel they have rights."

"That's the same thing a young couple at Fisherman's Wharf told me, and guess what—they had no kids."

"You're for the law, Black?"

"No, I'm for doing what's right, considerate, and makes the most sense. If you can support your family and children emotionally, relationally, financially, and parentally, have as many kids as you want. But if you can't or are not willing to, then maybe you need to really give it some thought before having kids or… any more kids. I know everyone's situation is different."

"Sometimes kids just happen, Black," Ashley pointed out with a faint giggle.

Black smiled. "One maybe, but three or five? Not likely," he laughed.

"Like I said, I don't disagree with you."

They both turned their attention to the stage, listening for another fifteen minutes as the panelists discussed humanity and what they felt a family should or shouldn't look like. As Black was listening, something caught his eye. It was one of the park employees—a girl, average height and dark hair—walking towards the stage with a tray of water bottles. It was difficult to determine her shape because her long-sleeved white shirt and dark slacks were a bit loose. Black continued to watch as she placed the waters on the table in front of each panelist and hurried off the stage. At that very moment another employee, a young black man, walked over toward him and Ashley. He seemed to be taking a break and catching what the panelists were talking about. Within a few seconds, the park manager appeared at his side.

"Hey, Reggie," he said to the young man.

"Yes, sir," the young man answered.

"Did you get the waters to the guest speakers?"

"Julie was supposed to bring them out."

Black quickly turned to Reggie. "Julie? The tall girl?" he asked.

"Yeah, that's the only one I know," the young man replied.

"What's wrong?" Ashley asked Black.

"The girl who brought out the water was shorter," he answered, racing towards the stage.

Jerking to a stop in front of the speakers' table, he studied the water bottles and easily found what he was looking for. The untouched bottle in front of the guy at the center was bubbling and beginning to shake. Black grabbed the bottle and tossed it high towards the circular window at the rear. He lifted and flipped the table over and behind the panelists to serve as cover, and diving to the ground, he yelled, "Get down!"

CHAPTER
SEVENTEEN

THE FIRST SOUND Black heard was a deafening pop, followed by glass shattering and a ringing in his ear. A cloud of smog coated the air and the smell of smoke swept across his face. People were screaming and coughing and running about the auditorium. Lying on the stage, Black peered in Ashley's direction. She staggered to her feet, looking over at him. He scanned the room and, through a gap in the fog, he saw the dark-haired woman who was supposed to be Julie. She was near the top of the stairs and leaving the auditorium before she looked back at the stage. She stared into Black's eyes, smiled, and removed her wig, exposing her long red hair.

"Johana," Black grumbled as he looked to Ashley and pointed at Johana. "That's her!" he shouted.

Ashley followed his gesture and raced up the stairs after Johana.

Black crawled to his feet and pushed the table that somehow had ended on top of the good-looking male panelist. "Is everybody okay?" he asked them. No one answered; they all seemed to be in a daze. *They look fine*, Black thought, dashing after Ashley and Johanna. He had to fight through a panicked gaggle of audience members to make it to the entrance. Near the front door, at the security station, he noticed one of the police officers rolling on the floor, cuffing his groin. Black continued through the crowd of frantic people, pushing his way out the door. On his exit, he coughed and brushed the debris from the explosion off his face and clothes. Outside it was bright and quiet. The rest of the park was operating as if there had been no explosion at all.

Immediately Black spotted Ashley at the bottom of the stairs hounding after Johana. He took four long hops and was at the bottom of the stairs, about six yards behind Ashley. Another five yards ahead of her was Johana. The group sprinted through the park, passing rides, souvenir stores, booths, dodging pedestrians and food carts. The sound of laugher, fun, and happiness permeated the air, along with the smell of popcorn, hot dogs, cotton candy, and funnel cakes. Johana glanced over her shoulder as Ashley slowly gained on her and Black on Ashley. Suddenly the sounds of a barrel organ, flute, and percussion triangle permeated the air. The group rapidly approached a carousel loaded with kids sitting inside spacecrafts and rockets which circled a planet.

Johana jumped on the carousel. Ashley grabbed the back of her shirt mid-flight but fell to the ground when Johana shrugged her hand off. Black increased his stride, circling around to meet Johana as she sprang from the carousel. He stuck out his foot and watched as she did her best to avoid catching her foot on his boot. She did anyway and stumbled a few paces before tumbling onto the pavement. She jumped to her feet, brushed her hair from her face, and raised her fist.

"You again. Ready for round two?" she panted.

"It's over. You don't want to do this," Black said.

"You don't know what I want. You know nothing about me."

"I know enough, Johana Petrak."

Johana winced. "Don't call me that," she demanded. "My name is Johana Howard."

"We both know that's not your real name. You're the daughter of Milo Petrak."

"No," Johana denied.

"You even work for him," Black continued.

"No," she shook her head. "Just because I work for him doesn't make him my father. I don't have a father, never had one."

"You do, but he abandoned you. This whole thing is about getting back at him."

"Shut up!" Johana screamed as she rushed towards Black, throwing a jab at his face.

Relaxed, Black waited for her fist to get two inches from his face before he swung his leg behind him while grabbing her wrist with one hand and pushing the back of her shoulder with the other. He spun his opponent three hundred sixty degrees before rolling her to the asphalt. She bounced to her feet, lobbing two more jabs in quick succession, followed by a kick. Black parried both shots and blocked the kick with his shin. His attacker ended her combination with a right cross. Black was able to slip by the punch and hip-toss her, sending her sliding on her back across the blacktop.

She rolled to her stomach and crawled to her feet while removing a remote device from her pocket. "You thought I wouldn't have a backup plan," she jeered.

Black exhaled sharply as the sound of dashing footsteps approached.

"DHS, freeze!" Ashley ordered, gun drawn.

Black looked back and pushed his palm towards her. "Wait!" he yelled, turning his attention back to Johana, who had a grin on her face. He froze, staring, and she pressed her remote. She dashed off just as a loud blast resounded from fifty feet to his right. There was a concrete structure suspending a replica of the planet Mars in the air. The supporting structure tore into pieces instantly and the Mars replica collapsed to the walkway and started rolling his way. Black estimated the sphere was about eighteen feet in diameter, not too big, but large enough to possibly hurt someone. A mass of people was running, yelping, hollering, and leaping out of the path of the large ball.

"I got her," Ashley said, jetting after Johana.

Black went to follow her but something his subconscious felt was urgent drew his eye again to his right. At that very moment a little girl tripped and sprawled in the path of the giant sphere.

Get up, kid!

The girl lay on the ground and began to cry.

Great. Black sprinted to the kid, quickly heaving her under his arms and darting out of the path of the huge globe with only seconds to spare. It rolled and bounced until it crashed into the carousel.

Black sat the crying kid down. He knelt and leaned in close. "You're okay now," he said gently.

The girl whimpered, drying her eyes with her forearm.

"Are you hurt?"

She shook her head.

"Where are your parents?"

"I don't know," she answered, tearing up again.

At that moment a woman brushed past Black and scooped the little girl up. "Ah—thank goodness," she said, embracing and kissing the child.

"That answers that," Black muttered, bolting in the direction he had seen Ashley chasing Johana. He ran for ten seconds before spotting them through a crowd. Ashley had her gun aimed at Johana, who had her back pressed against a chain link fence. He dashed over and stopped ten feet behind Ashley.

"Johana," Ashley said. "It's important you understand I don't want to hurt you. I know you've been through a lot.

What I need is for you to turn around and put your hands behind your back, slowly."

Johana stood still, glaring at her.

"I need you to do as I say."

"And if I don't?"

"I won't hesitate to shoot you. I really don't want to, but I will."

Johana's gaze dropped for a couple of seconds before she looked up with pursed lips and dull eyes. "Okay," she said in a flat voice.

"Okay," Ashley said. "Okay. Turn around slowly and put your hands behind your back," she ordered, moving closer.

Johana did as she was told.

Ashley kept the gun trained on her with one hand and used the other to remove the handcuffs from her belt. Holstering her gun, she stepped closer, reaching for Johana's wrist.

She's being too compliant, Black was thinking. "Ashley, watch out," he warned aloud.

Before he could get the last word out, Johana pivoted and grabbed Ashley's wrist with one hand and pushed the back of her shoulder with the other. The cuffs fell to the ground as the force sent Ashley staggering into the fence. Black stepped forward to help, but she had already recovered, hurling a spinning back fist to Johana's jaw. Black stood at bay, watching as the two circled each other.

Johana held her jaw as she scowled at Ashley with bulging eyes and flared nostrils.

Ashley stared back at her with tightness in her eyes and curled lips. "If this is how you want it. Let's do it," she said, raising her hands, fists open.

Johana pitched a quick jab, connecting with Ashley's shoulder. The DHS agent absorbed the attack and countered with a front kick to her opponent's gut. Johana ignored the pain, returning a kick to Ashley's ribcage, grabbing her throat and pushing her against the fence.

Black noticed Ashley was in trouble and moved closer to help, but she gave him a nasty look.

"Don't you dare, Black," she strained under the pressure of Johana's choke hold. "This tramp is mine," she finished, breaking the grip her adversary had on her. She struck Johana in the throat with the curve between her index finger and thumb.

Johana immediately clutched her own throat, gasping. Ashley continued the assault with a knee to her opponent's stomach before grabbing a hand full of red hair and slamming her head to the pavement. She picked up the handcuffs and stooped to restrain the unconscious Johana.

Black walked over to her. "I guess that Krav Maga is paying off," he joked.

Ashley quickly looked up, giving him a stern eye through a slit in her messy hair before chuckling and shaking her head.

Within the next few seconds loud voices drew nearer.

"Police!"

"Stand back!"

"Out of the way!"

Captain Stuart approached with three SWAT members in full tactical gear. Stuart stopped near Black while the small unit surrounded Ashley and Johana.

"I guess it paid off to stick around after all," Stuart said.

"We'll see," Black replied.

FORTY-FIVE MINUTES LATER, Black was in the Fantastic Galaxy's parking lot with Ashley and Stuart, all standing in the midst of emergency responder vehicles and workers.

"This is what we found on her," Stuart said, handing Ashley an evidence bag.

She examined the bag for a few seconds before passing it to Black. Inside the bag were keys, some cash, a key card, and a pack of Alka-Seltzer with one tablet. He took note and swung the bag back to Stuart.

"We'll get it all processed," the captain said.

"Sounds good. Where is she?" Ashley asked.

Stuart pointed to a police cruiser. "Over there."

"Thanks."

Black and Ashley walked to the car. Johana was sitting in the back of the cruiser staring towards the front of the car, lips turned up. She glared at the pair as they approached.

Ashley opened the door. "How's your head?" she asked, sincerity in her voice.

Johana rubbed the bandage on her own forehead. "How's your ribs?" she sneered.

Ashley sighed. "I don't think you realize just how much trouble you're in."

"I don't think you realize how little I care."

"Tell us what you know about Tyler Robinson and I'll see how I can help you."

Johana shrugged. "Who's Tyler Robinson?" she withheld.

Black, standing behind Ashley, released a deep audible breath. *This girl is working my last nerve.*

"What's wrong with him?" Johana said, eyeballing Black. "Is he out of breath?"

Black nudged Ashley to the side. "No, he's out of patience," he hissed. "The guy at the pier, the one whose face you aimed your gun at. What do you know about him?"

Johana pursed her lips, widened her eyes, and raised her eyebrows. "Could it be you got the wrong person?" she asked, hunching her shoulders.

Black was quiet for a moment, thinking. "Well, Tyler sure knows who you are," he said.

"What's that supposed to mean?"

"He's been telling us a lot about you."

Johana huffed and shook her head. "He wouldn't do that. You're messing with me."

"What makes you so sure?"

"Because he knows better."

"He knows better," Black echoed. "Hmm. Does that mean you have something on him?"

"Maybe."

"What you have on him wouldn't happen to be in a large white envelope at your place in Presidio Heights, would it?"

Johana eyes narrowed. "You been to my house? Who do you think you are?"

"Someone who'd rather be somewhere else, but instead is here because a little girl who feels the world did her wrong threw a temper tantrum."

"You think you know everything, huh?" Johana said before looking away.

"Not everything, just enough. For instance, I know you've been sneaking into your father's warehouse and stealing some of his contraband. Using some of it to supply your little vendetta and selling the rest to street thugs and corrupt cops."

Johana turned back around. "Corrupt cops," she said, squinting her eyes. "I don't know anything about any corrupt cops. So keep that to yourself. I'm not going down for something I didn't do."

"Honey, there's plenty you're going down for," Ashley chimed in. "You used a deadly explosive multiple times in places you knew would be greatly populated."

"Deadly explosive?" Johana played dumb.

"Yes. The one you nearly blew a guy's head off with earlier."

"Oh… I thought that was water. Unless you can prove it was something more," Johana grinned.

Ashley stepped closer to the door, but Black extended his arm to block her.

"Oh, it won't be hard to prove," he said. "That liquid explosive, sauce, needs carbonic acid to combust. Water by itself wouldn't have been enough. A chemical agent that could excite carboxylation would've had to been introduced to the water. So I'm thinking when the crime lab examines the contents from the explosion debris, they'll find compounds that match the synthetic makeup of that Alka-Seltzer tablet found in your pocket. It's not a question of *if* you're going down, it's a matter of how fast and far down you'll be going, and that's up to you."

Johana shifted in her seat and bit her lip but said nothing.

"Tyler Robinson," Black pressed. "What's his part?"

The detained woman dropped her gaze briefly before looking up with parted lips. "His part is… I—I'm sorry, I can't remember. I bumped my head pretty hard," she diverted, smiling.

Ashley's phone rang. "Good. I'm done with her," she said, taking the phone out of her pocket and walking away.

"Have it your way," Black said to Johana, easing the car door closed. Noticing a smirk on her face, he quickly pulled at the door again. "One more thing I think you should know. Your father is in custody and has been protecting himself."

The sly grin on her face pulled straight.

"That's right. He denies any involvement with the bombings, the firearms, the explosives—or you."

"You smug bastard!" Johana snapped. "You don't know me!"

Black continued to speak from where he left off, perfectly calm, unmoved, unshaken by her. "Your own father is saying you acted all by yourself and he has no clue about your motives or where you got your supplies."

Johana looked straight ahead, glaring towards the front of the police cruiser, blowing heavy breaths.

Black exhaled. "I'm telling you this because I thought you might want to start helping yourself. Your father is protecting his own skin. So being angry at him and taking it out on innocent people is not doing you any favors. It's only showing the rest of the world just how much you hate yourself."

She glanced up at Black.

"Look, there's a young man who is about to ruin his life and possibly the lives of many other even younger kids. I decided I'm not going to let that happen. If you have any information that can help resolve this quickly before anyone else gets hurt, now is the time to share."

Johana faced the front, quiet.

Black shrugged and began to close the door.

"Tonight," she said, still looking straight ahead.

"Tonight what?"

"He's going to hide in the park and set up for the event tomorrow. Tonight when the park closes."

"At the Fantastic Universe theme park in Florida," Black confirmed.

Johana nodded yes before hanging her head.

He shut the door completely and walked to Ashley, who had her back turned and was finishing up a call.

She spun around. "That was Toben. He said he had something urgent to talk to us about."

Wrinkles crossed Black's forehead. "What, he wants to do another conference call?"

"No… he actually said he'll be here in thirty minutes."

CHAPTER
EIGHTEEN

TWENTY OF THOSE minutes passed and they were in the main office waiting on Toben. Black was busy in the kitchen area while Ashley was seated on a couch in the lounge, resting. He walked to her with two cups of coffee in his hands, one black, no sugar and the other with cream and sugar.

"Here you go," he said, handing her the latter cup.

Ashley adjusted in her seat. "Ow. Thank you," she said, favoring her ribcage and reaching for the cup.

"You might want to have that looked at," he said.

"It's okay. I'm fine. Trust me."

Black shrugged, sitting in a chair next to her. He took a sip from his cup and placed it on the coffee table in front of them. Ashley did the same with hers.

"Did Toben give any clue as to what was urgent?" he asked.

"Nope. And he got off the phone so fast I didn't get a chance to give him the details of what took place here. All he knows is we caught Johana."

Black nodded.

"This has been a rough morning. It's pandemonium outside," Ashley said.

"At least it's quiet in here."

"Yeah, we have the whole place to ourselves," she smiled, glancing around the silent lounge before lifting her cup and taking another sip. She fixed on the cup for a moment. "Black, how did you know all that stuff about the sauce needing carbon combustion and all?" she asked, circling her finger around the brim of her cup.

"Oh, that. I made most of it up. I remember Toben saying how it can cause an explosion just being mixed with a carbonated drink. All I did was draw off of the bit I know about the carbonation process and the role the Alka-Seltzer plays in it. Will the crime lab figure it out? I'm not sure."

"Well, it made you sound very smart, Mr. Black," she said, biting her lips and batting her eyes.

"Why, thank you."

They heard the front door creak open and a pair of footsteps knock against the hardwood floor. The park manager appeared in the lounge and walked over to them. He stood with a smile on his face, waiting for an acknowledgment, but didn't receive one.

"Excuse me, Agent Chapp, Mr. Black. I wanted to see if you two needed anything," he said, still smiling.

"No, I think we're okay," Ashley said.

"Good. I also wanted to thank you for what you've done today. If it wasn't for you two, someone could've gotten hurt. Especially those guest speakers."

"It was a team effort. Credit should go to the police and you and your staff too. Thank you for getting onboard."

The manager nodded. "Just so you know, I've already informed my boss and my counterpart at Fantastic Universe. They're taking the necessary precautions."

"Necessary precautions," Black echoed. "I guess that means the 324 event is still happening tomorrow?"

"Yep… the panelists were already adamant about it, but after this they're even more pumped."

Black and Ashley exchanged a glance.

"But I have to get back to it. Don't hesitate to let me know if you need anything," the manager said before disappearing into the foyer area.

"So these activists are still going through with it," Ashley sighed.

"To them, it makes sense," Black started. "They believe the whole thing is a big government conspiracy and the government is behind the bombings. They won't allow the government to beat them when it comes to human rights. But if they knew the truth about who's behind the bombings, they might give it a second thought."

The front door opened once again. This time multiple footsteps scuffed across the floor. Black and Ashley both turned their heads toward the doorway into the foyer, and a second later Toben came through it. Stuart and a uniformed officer were behind him, but they stopped in the foyer. Black stood first and Ashley followed suit as Toben paced over to them.

"I'm sorry I got off the phone so fast. I was trying to hurry off the plane—I didn't realize there was an explosion. Are you okay?" He posed the question to both of them before placing his hand on Ashley's shoulder and repeating the question in a lower tone to her only. "Are you okay?" The two looked at each other for three or four seconds before she answered.

"Yeah... Yeah, we're fine. No one got hurt."

Here they go again, Black thought. "Did you say you got off a plane?" he asked.

Toben nodded, finally removing his hand from Ashley's shoulder. "That's what I wanted to talk to you guys about. As you know, we were able to locate Tyler's car using the tracker in Matt's backpack. We searched through the airport's surveillance and records and discovered Tyler got on a flight to Orlando, Florida, last night. Guess who else we saw boarding a flight to Orlando, two hours later?"

"Stokes."

"Exactly. So I'm on my way to Florida now."

"You're flying out from LAX?" Ashley asked.

"No. I have one of Homeland's private jets."

"What? How?"

"I wanted to get to Florida as fast as I could. Hanten approved all of it."

"The director," Black said, "she approved it?"

"Yep. That's the one. Look, I figured you guys can come with me. The plane is at a private airstrip about ten miles northeast of here. I'm thinking we fly there today to be at Fantastic Universe bright and early tomorrow morning."

Ashley fluttered her hand. "Wait. Do we have any idea why Stokes would be following Tyler? I'm sure it's not to bring him to justice."

Black said nothing. He was in his thoughts, trying to make sense of everything.

"That's the question I plan to ask when we find him," Toben replied.

I wonder if— Black was thinking before he said aloud, "Toben, if you want to make sure you catch this kid, we should leave now."

"Why?"

"Johana mentioned Tyler would be hiding in the park tonight to set up for his attack tomorrow. Florida's time is three hours ahead, plus it's about a four-, four-and-a-half-hour flight. If we're going, we should go now."

Toben hunched his shoulders. "Okay."

The three started for the front door. After a few steps, Ashley rubbed her side.

"Oww," she exhaled.

"What's wrong?" Toben inquired.

"She took a hit to the ribs," Black answered. "Ashley, I think you should stay here and rest a little."

"Black, no, it's nothing," she said.

"Yeah, but we don't want the injury to get any worse."

"I agree with Black," Toben said. "Stay here and rest, Agent Chapp."

"What am I supposed to do? Sit here and watch TV while you two go after these guys?"

"Exactly," Black encouraged. "Take a load off. We can handle this."

Ashley paused for a moment. "Okay, okay. I'll rest here for another hour or two, then head back home," she agreed.

They said their goodbyes, then Black and Toben headed to the foyer, where Stuart and the other officer were standing. Toben talked to the captain about hitching a ride to the airstrip, and five minutes later the group was in an SUV, exiting the theme park and steering onto the main road. Black was in the back seat with Toben. Stuart was in the front passenger seat and the officer was behind the wheel. The vehicle's interior smelled like takeout and gym clothes, as if it belonged to a bachelor. Black rolled down his window to about halfway. The breeze infused with the warm rays from the afternoon sun created a tranquil experience. He wanted to doze off but figured he would have time to do that on the flight.

AFTER TWELVE MINUTES of driving, the car hung a right onto a long, deserted road. Another mile on the road and the sight of a hangar appeared in the distance. They stopped at a security booth, where the officer at the wheel and Toben presented their badges to the guard. The guard nodded as if he recognized Toben. He raised the barrier gate and waved them through. They drove across the tarmac before veering a half circle and stopping in front of the hangar. Black opened his door and slapped his feet on the blacktop. Toben did the same. The two walked to Stuart's window, which he rolled down.

"Thanks, Stuart." Toben shook his hand.

"Thank you, Captain," Black said, also shaking his hand.

"Anytime. You two have a safe flight."

Toben pivoted and started walking in the direction of the hangar. Black turned his back to the car but paused at his name being called.

"Mr. Black," Stuart beckoned.

Black turned to face him.

"Do me a favor and catch this kid. This whole mess has caused too much uproar."

"You got it, Captain." Black smiled and rotated in the direction of the hangar. He listened as the SUV tires sped against the asphalt of the airstrip. The hum of the vehicle had completely disappeared by the time he caught up with Toben. The two stopped near the double-door entrance of the hangar where the private jet was parked. It was a *Dassault Falcon 10*, a small, lightweight jet. The top half of the aircraft was painted dark blue and the belly white. Two turbine engines were to be seen near the back, below the stabilizers but above the wings. It appeared to be a well-maintained bird. The exterior door was already open and provided a steep staircase into the plane. Standing next to it were two men in similar attire—a white shirt with a tie, dark slacks, and pistols. Black was certain they were the pilots. The men were chatting and laughing. One of them noticed as Black and Toben approached.

"Agent Toben. You're ready to go?" he asked.

"Yes, we're ready."

"Okay, how many passengers are we expecting, sir?"

"Only two. Myself and Mr. Black here."

"Alright then. Let's get you two onboard."

They followed the other pilot into the plane. He pointed them to the cabin area as he slid into the cockpit. Black ducked into one of the chairs close to the back on the right side of the plane. Toben took a seat across from him. They sat quietly and watched as the first pilot closed and latched the cabin door before easing into the cockpit.

"So, Mr. Consultant," Toben said. "What's your current prognosis of the situation?"

Black looked at him and opened his mouth to answer.

"Hold that thought," Toben said, standing from his chair.

He walked to a cubby attached to the wall of the cockpit. From a small crate, he lifted two wrapped sub sandwiches in one hand and two bottled waters laced through his fingers on the other. The subs were ham and cheese. Black could smell it as Toben handed him one and a bottle of water.

"I thought you might be hungry," Toben said, sitting in his chair.

"Thanks."

"What's your situation appraisal?" he asked again over the ruffling of the sandwich wrappers.

"I think we have at least two forces at play, two motivations," Black answered.

"Which are?"

"The first is Johana. She's broken because of her childhood and wants someone to pay for it. Specifically, parents who are not taking responsibility for the kids they bring into this world. She wants them and all who support them to suffer like she did. That's why we had the bombings."

"Yeah, I get that. Both she and Tyler are cut from the same cloth. How do these kids get like that?" The question was expressed as rhetorical.

"Don't be so quick to judge. I do remember seeing your son, Matt, with the two of them. All of them are hurt. Just in different stages of the process."

"I don't think my son is like them—but wow, Black. Tell me how you really feel."

"Speaking of which, how long have you and Agent Chapp been having an affair?" Black asked, finally taking a bite of his sandwich.

Toben adjusted in his chair. "What? What are you talking about?" he asked in a higher octave than normal.

Black looked at him with a mouth full. "Don't play with me."

The pilot entered the cabin. "We'll be up in the air in about eight minutes. You can buckle up for takeoff." He nodded, then disappeared back into the cockpit, closing the door behind himself.

Black found his seatbelt and clicked it over his lap. Toben did the same. The cabin was quiet while Black swallowed his first bite.

"So how long?" he asked again, taking a second bite of his sub.

"Months."

"Has Stokes seen you two together?"

"No. At least not directly, but he knows about it."

"What do you mean, not directly?" Black asked.

"The night of the bombing at Fisherman's Wharf, Reeves and Guo followed me to Agent Chapp's house. I'm sure that's how Stokes found out."

Black said nothing, just chewed his food.

"But don't worry about him using that against me. I broke things off with Ashley."

"Plan on telling your wife?"

Toben paused before answering. "I don't know."

The jet engines kicked on. Faint vibrations waved through the cabin.

"I'm sure she already knows," Black said.

"What makes you say that?"

"If anyone has spent any time around you two, they know something's up. Maybe except Boyar. He's so high on Agent Chapp he can't see her doing any wrong. But it's up to you if you tell your wife or not. I just want to know what Stokes can use against us."

Toben's eyebrows wrinkled. He was quiet for a few

seconds. "So what's the other force? You mentioned there were at least two at play."

"Stokes, of course."

"And what's his motivation, you think?"

"Not sure."

"So you have no idea?"

"No, I have an idea."

"Okay, tell me."

"No," Black said, taking another bite.

"Why?"

"Because it's only a hunch. It's a little thin. I'll let you know when it fattens up," Black mumbled.

The jet began to taxi forward and Toben finished unwrapping his sandwich.

"Has Boyar come across anything new with Tyler's adoption records?" Black asked.

"No, not yet."

"Let's check with him once we land."

"Sure," Toben hunched his shoulders before taking the first bite of his own sandwich.

Ten minutes passed and they were up in the air. The little plane hummed along—smoothly, to Black's surprise. He took his and Toben's trash to the garbage then wavered back to his seat. He noticed Toben reclined. He wasn't sleeping but seemed to be in a trance. Maybe rehearsing that conversation he'd have with his wife, Black guessed, as he reclined his chair and closed his eyes.

WHEN HE NEXT opened his eyes, he was soaring across the Gulf of Mexico towards Florida. Turbulence shook the plane. He sat upright and glanced at Toben, who was sitting tensely and holding the armrests of his chair as the craft quaked under the turbulence.

"We ran into a thunderstorm," Toben said. "I forgot

there'd be scattered storms in Florida tonight and throughout tomorrow."

Black shrugged. The plane hit a large pocket of air, bouncing from a brief drop.

"Whoa. Good thing we have two pilots," Toben continued.

"I guess," Black replied.

"Let something happen to the pilots. Then you'll start worrying."

"If something happened to the pilots, I'd just fly the plane myself."

"Yeah, that's right—you have the Air Medal."

The intercom system popped and one of the pilot's voices crackled on the line. "We hit a storm but should be through it shortly. There're scattered storms across the state, so we won't be landing in Orlando, and Tampa is a little backed up because of the weather. We have the okay to land in Lakeland." The intercom line scratched closed.

"Lakeland?" Toben winced. "That's a small, ratty city. You ever been?"

"Yeah, actually I have. But I didn't have much time for sightseeing. It was a quick *hit-in, hit-out* deal," Black said with a grin on his face.

Twenty minutes passed and they started their initial descent. Ten minutes after that, the wheels of the jet touched down on the airstrip at Lakeland Linder International Airport. The aircraft took a few moments taxiing to a hangar before it stopped and the engine switched off. The pilot slid from the cockpit and stepped to the cabin.

"We made it," he said with a smile, raising his hands palms up. "Sorry about the bumps towards the end, but like I mentioned, we ran into a storm. I told the airport you're in a hurry so they're getting a loaner car ready for you. We'll run some checks on the aircraft then probably grab a bite and get some rest. You have our numbers. Just let us know when you're on your way back."

"Sounds like a plan. Thanks," Toben said.

The man nodded before sidestepping to the cabin door and unlatching it. He pushed the door open and the hydraulics did the work of lowering the steps. Toben ducked out of the plane first, with Black a few paces behind him. Both pilots stayed inside. Outside the sky was dark, covered by clouds crying drizzles of cool rain. The rev of an engine sliced through the moist air. Black saw a dark-colored car streaming across the slick tarmac towards them. The car stopped a few yards in front of them and a young lady with a yellow hooded poncho exited from behind the wheel and jogged over.

"Mr. Jake Toben?" she asked, shifting her glance between Black and Toben.

Toben raised his hand. She walked over and handed him the key to the car.

"Thank you," Toben said.

"You're welcome, sir."

Black and Toben waved to the pilot, who was standing at the cabin door. He waved back as he knelt, grabbed a lever, and pulled to close the door. Toben reached in his pocket and handed the young lady some cash. She smiled her thanks, then walked off in the direction she had driven from. A guy on a go-cart met her, she hopped on, and they took off. Meanwhile Black had already started walking to the passenger side of the car. He eased into the front passenger seat while Toben made a call. A couple of minutes later, Toben opened the door and settled in under the wheel.

"That was Boyar," he said. "He still hasn't had much luck with Tyler's adoption records."

Black said nothing. Toben placed another call. He talked for less than thirty seconds before ending the call.

"Sorry. Had to confirm the manager is still at the park. He and a couple of uniforms will be meeting us there."

Black nodded. Toben pressed the ignition button and the

engine purred over. He peered around the small-scale airport, looking for an indication of the way out. Soon they were cruising out of the airport and onto a local road westward, which led them to a tolled parkway, which took them even farther west. At the end of the highway were two exits, one for Tampa and the other for Orlando. Toben veered right, taking the Orlando exit onto I-4 East. The drive was quiet and the roads were mostly empty. The sound of the engine humming, the intermittent swiping of the wiper blades, the slush of the tires treading the wet road, and the occasional pair of headlights from other traffic kept their senses occupied for most of the ride. The car droned on for another hour before Toben exited onto Fantastic Universe Drive.

"You know exactly where you're going," Black commented.

Toben kept his eyes on the road. "Yeah, I brought Kristi and Matt here a couple years back," he said. There was a tone of sorrow in is voice.

The drive into the theme park was nearly identical to the drive into Fantastic Galaxy. There were similar billboard advertisements and the ticket booths were oriented the same way. Toben rolled the car to the only open booth, where he flashed his badge to a security guard and received directions to the main office. They traveled through a couple of parking lots before making it there. A police squad car and a white Chevy Blazer with the Fantastic Universe logo were parked near the office. Black and Toben exited the car and headed to the front door. Toben knocked twice. Footsteps raced towards the door from the other side, and the next moment the door swung open and a husky middle-aged Hispanic man stood before them.

"Agent Toben?" he asked.

Toben nodded yes, flashing his badge. "You're the park manager?"

"Yes, sir," the man answered, shaking Toben's hand. "Come in."

They stepped inside, entering the foyer. The layout and décor of the building mimicked that of the main office at the sister location. As two uniformed officers walked in from the lounge area, the park manager threw his index finger in the air.

"One minute, gentlemen," he said, leaving the group and racing towards the hall in the back.

The two uniformed officers approached Toben and Black. One was young with messy brown hair. He looked fresh out of the academy. The other was clearly older and wore a buzz cut, a chevron mustache, and a gruff expression. He spoke first.

"Good evening, gentlemen. Who are you with?" he asked.

Toben flashed his badge. "DHS," he said.

The man nodded, walking over to the front door and peering out the window. "That's your Ford Fusion outside?" he asked.

"Yep."

"Okay."

"Have you guys searched the park yet?"

"No, sir, not yet. We have orders to wait for a few more units before we start our search. Politics. I guess they want a captain onsite before we start. They'll probably be late getting here though, due to the weather and all, but the two of us will be here just in case."

Toben thanked the officers and they strolled back into the lounge area.

The manager came back. "Sorry about that. I had my boss on the line. Everyone is on edge after what happened at Fantastic Galaxy. So this guy we're looking for—is he planning on making his move tomorrow?"

"Yes and no," Black jumped in, not wanting to waste any

more time. "We expect him to make a move during the 324 event, but we think he may already be in the park."

"Really? Where?"

"Where's the event being held tomorrow?"

"At the Meeting Hall."

"Can you take us there?"

"Sure. It's within walking distance."

The manager led them outside. The light sprinkle of rain had become large drops while they were inside.

"It's raining hard and there are no guests in the park, so let's actually take the truck," the manager said, pointing at the white Blazer.

The three of them entered the vehicle. The manager got behind the wheel and pushed the start button and the engine whirred, but it was quickly drowned out by the echo of the rain hitting the roof. With headlights flicked on, they drove southwest. The car coasted maybe fifty yards before a large building appeared on the right. Black took a long look at it. Through the rearview mirror the manager noticed his gaze.

"That's the Intergalactic Food Court. It has a food court, arcades, and some souvenir shops inside," he said before taking a swig from a soda bottle in his cup holder.

"Uh-huh. I see," Black replied. He looked to his left and saw a large canopy with a bumper car arena underneath, and then a tilt-a-whirl ride and some game booths.

The Blazer continued for another minute as the rain intensified. The manager parked directly in front of the Meeting Hall to avoid having to walk far. The three of them dashed from the car, taking cover under the shelter at the entrance. The manager unlocked the door and they ducked inside, flapping the water from their clothes. It was dark and silent inside, but dry and warm. The manager found a switch and clicked it. Light immediately chased away the darkness. Black walked to the center of the lobby, noting to his right a counter with three computer screens and to his left a hall with a couple of doors on either side. Directly in front of him were dark orange-colored double doors with planets and stars painted on them.

"I'll check down the hall," Toben said in a low tone.

"I'll go with you," the manager whispered, "just in case you need me to open a door."

While the two walked down the hall, Black opened the double doors and found an auditorium behind them. It had standard seating with maybe one hundred chairs and had a stage at the very back. The middle aisle was lit with neon lights. Black walked down the aisle towards the stage, swiveling his head and inspecting the rows of seats on both sides. He made it to the stage without finding anything except three more doors along the walls. Three more places Tyler could be hiding. Two of the doors were smaller and on either side of the stage, while a larger door was located at the north wall, to his right. Black started with the door next to the stage, on his right. He grabbed the knob and, hearing foot-steps behind him, peeked over his shoulder to see Toben and the park manager making their way down the aisle.

"Find anything?" Toben asked.

Black shook his head. He then opened the door and found a broom, a mop and a bucket, and shelving full of cleaning supplies. As he closed the door, a boisterous clang drifted from the larger door. Everyone turned in that direction.

"You heard that?" the manager whispered.

"What's behind that door?" Black asked him.

"The—um—the kitchen."

"Okay, let's go check it out," Toben said, unholstering his gun.

They walked to the door. Black pulled the door open and Toben slipped through, gun raised. The manager hung back. Inside, there was a large rectangular table at the center surrounded by a couple of commercial stoves and a few commercial refrigerators. Beyond the far end of the table

Black saw scattered pots, pans, silverware, and pooled water on the floor. Behind the mess was a pair of shoes sticking out from behind the corner, with feet nervously tapping up and down, up and down. Black gestured, *I see something* to Toben who nodded and gestured, *I see it too*. Black lurked noiselessly towards the tapping feet. Toben circled around the table and tiptoed in the same direction from the opposite side, gun aimed. With each step, the tapping grew louder. The person's breathing became heavier and heavier. Black made the corner and saw the person they had come for: Tyler Robinson.

CHAPTER
NINETEEN

HE WAS SITTING on the floor hugging his legs and rocking back and forth. His hands and arms were wet. He looked up at Black with a mix of fear and confusion in his eyes. Toben had his gun trained on the young man.

"Tyler Robinson. I need you to get up, turn around, and slowly place your hands on the table," he instructed.

Tyler kept his eyes on Black. "I—I can't do this anymore. The kids. There's too many children here," he mumbled with watery eyes.

Black said nothing, just stared at Tyler.

"Get up, turn around, and place your hands on the table," Toben repeated.

Tyler peered at Toben and did as he was told. Toben frisked him and found a wallet, a pack of Alka-Seltzer, two granola bars, and a small glass tube of the sauce. After cuffing Tyler's hands behind his back, he removed an evidence bag and placed everything on the table inside it. The young man didn't put up a fight nor utter a word of protest.

"Let's go," Toben said, leading his suspect out of the kitchen by his upper arm.

The manager was waiting outside the door as the three exited. "That's him?"

"Yep," Toben answered.

The manager's eyebrows crunched together and his lips parted. "My—he—he's just a kid," he stuttered.

"A very confused kid," Black commented, brushing past the group.

Everyone walked out of the auditorium and exited the Meeting Hall. Outside, the rain had eased up to a drizzle but there was a bit of thunder and lightning roaring and flashing through the murky sky. The manager locked the door and everyone sprang into the Chevy. Black and Toben sat in the back with Tyler between them. The manager steered them in the direction of the main office.

They drove for a minute in silence before the manager lifted his arm in a gesture of, *I almost forgot.*

"Oh yeah. I received a call while you were in the kitchen. My security guy up front let someone else in from the government. I figured he was one of you guys," he said, looking at them through the mirror.

"Who was it?" Toben asked.

"I don't remember his name. But he was with one of those three-letter agencies. DA—DH—DI—something."

"The DIA?" Black asked.

"Yeah, that's it."

"Where is he now?" Black asked, urgency in his voice.

"He should be at the main office by now. Why, what's wrong?"

The moment the manager uttered the last syllable of his question, four blasts resounded in quick succession. The noise flushed out the hum of the engine and the roar of the thunder. Black heard four small projectiles impact the grill of the SUV and strike the engine block. He knew it was gunfire. The manager lost control of the vehicle, hollering as he swerved to a stop near the entrance of the Intergalactic Food Court. The shots, which had come from the passenger side, stopped firing as everyone crawled out on the driver side of the Blazer.

Tyler dropped to his butt near the back door, panting. The park manager fell to his backside near the front of the SUV.

"Who are they?" he cried with shock and fear in his voice. "They're trying to kill us."

"Everybody calm down," Toben ordered, out of breath, squatting with his gun in hand.

In contrast, Black was calm. His breathing was normal. His face was expressionless. He crouched, peeking around the back of the vehicle. There were four dark shadows approaching from nearly thirty yards away. The figures slowly shaped into the silhouettes of four men as they drew closer. Three of the men had rifles aimed in the direction of the Blazer and the fourth was holding a pistol down by his side. Because of the distance, rain, and darkness, it was difficult to make out any specific features, but Black knew exactly who they were.

"Here's the situation," he said, looking at Toben. "Four armed men. Three equipped with assault rifles and more than likely a sidearm and combat knife. The other one only has a pistol from what I can tell."

"That—that's a lot more than we have," the manager panted.

Black looked at Tyler and then Toben. "Uncuff him," he said.

"What—why?" Toben protested.

"Because he may be the reason we're still alive."

"What are you talking about?" Toben asked but reached for his keys to free the young man.

Black didn't answer. He peeked around the SUV a second time, noticing the men were now about twenty yards away.

"How much ammo do you have?" he asked Toben.

Toben removed the cuffs from Tyler. "A full mag and two spare," he answered, placing the cuffs in their pouch.

"Okay, we have a fighting chance."

"How so?" the manager asked, panic in his voice.

"By using our heads and controlling our emotions," Black answered. "Pull yourself together. Do you have a key to this building?" he asked, pointing to the front door of the Intergalactic Food Court.

"Yes."

"I need you to have that key handy."

The manager nodded and started fiddling with his key chain.

"Toben," Black continued. "Where's the evidence bag?"

"I left it in the back seat."

Stooping, Black quickly searched the back seat, finding the evidence bag on the floorboard. He grabbed it and the bottle of soda from the cup holder in the front. On his way out, he glanced through the back passenger side window. It was spotted with rain droplets, but he could see the men fifteen yards away. He crouched back towards the tail of the SUV before placing the soda bottle and evidence bag on the ground slightly under the Blazer. The footsteps of the men were now audible. Black removed the sauce and Alka-Seltzer from the bag before peeking around the back of the vehicle once more. The four men had stopped, still ten yards away. Three of them were dressed similarly in boots, dark pants, dark shirts covered by a tactical vest with a couple of slots for extra rifle magazines, and a handgun strapped to their right thigh. The fourth guy he identified as Stokes. He stood second from the left in the group, pistol in hand. Black ducked back behind the Blazer.

"They stopped," he announced.

"Agent Toben!" one of the four men shouted, "You back there?"

"Stokes! What do you think you're doing?" Toben yelled back.

"Send out the kid and we'll be on our way."

Tyler looked up at Black. His eyes were wide and his lips trembled. "What—wh—why do they want me?" he asked with tremors in his voice.

"What do you want with the kid, Stokes?" Toben asked.

"Just hand him over and we'll let you go."

"That's not happening," Black shouted. "The moment you have him you'll try to kill us."

"That must be Black. I've really been looking forward to meeting you."

"You'll change your mind when I have my hands around your throat."

"Don't be foolish, Black. You're surrounded by trained ex-Special Forces members. So just do the right thing and hand the young man over."

"Do the right thing," Black repeated. "Is that what you guys did in Colombia when you stole money from the drug bust?"

There was faint conversation between the four men. After a few seconds Stokes began to chuckle.

"You've now managed to give these men more of an incentive to kill you. Look, no one's coming to your rescue. We tied those two cops in the office up. And now my team wants you, and they have very itchy trigger fingers."

"They better want me more than your little crony Reeves did!" Black yelled.

"Reeves is washed up. You know that. Enough talking. In ten seconds, we start to shoot."

"You're not going to do that."

"And why not?"

"You won't risk shooting your *son*."

Both Toben's and Tyler's mouth gaped opened. Things went silent on Stokes' side for a few moments.

"Smart," he finally said. "How did you find out?"

"Reeves said I was in possession of something that could harm your family. It didn't make sense at first, because I didn't know anyone in your family. I had to think about what I was in possession of, and the only thing that came to mind was the detonator I picked off your son, Tyler. And then there was Petrak's daughter admitting she had leverage on Tyler. That's why you were at her house, to make sure she didn't have anything that could incriminate your son. But you found something in that white envelope Toben and I saw you take from her house—didn't you? But even knowing all of this, I was only ninety percent certain he was your son. When you shot at the SUV, you aimed at the engine. You only wanted to stop us because you weren't sure where Tyler was in the car. After that, I was ninety-five percent certain he was your son."

Stokes chuckled. "So when were you one hundred percent certain?" he inquired.

"When you asked me how I found out," Black answered, peeking around the back of the Blazer.

One of the guys in Stokes' group, the one on the far right, fired a round. The bullet hit the back taillight, barely missing Black's head as he ducked back behind the vehicle. Rage started to bubble in Black's gut. *Just for that I'll make sure I take care of you first.*

"That was a final warning shot. Toss your weapons to us and send him out. You have till the count of ten before we start shooting," Stokes demanded.

Tyler held his forehead in his palms.

Black looked at the park manager. "Do you have the key for the building ready?" he asked.

The manager nodded, using the front tire to pull himself into a crouch.

"What are you thinking, Black? You think he'll shoot?" Toben asked.

"I'm thinking I don't want to take the chance."

Stokes began to count. Black opened the soda bottle and ripped open the Alka-Seltzer packet, dropping a tablet in with the soda.

"When this explodes, everyone run for the front door of the building," Black instructed.

Stokes reached seven.

"Okay, okay," Black shouted.

Stokes stopped counting and the rain became heavier.

"Toben, you'll have to provide cover for everyone," Black said.

Tyler was still holding his forehead.

"Kid, you ready?" Black asked, pouring the sauce in the bottle.

Tyler nodded, lifting himself into a squatting position.

"We're going to slide you Toben's gun, then we'll send your son out," Black yelled, fastening the top on the bottle.

The bottle immediately began to fizz and bubble. Black crawled to the pavement and rolled the bottle under the SUV, aiming slightly left. As the bottle rolled, Black hurried to his feet and glanced around the back of the Blazer. He saw all four of the men direct their guns at the bottle as it rolled towards them. It came to a halt near the guy directly to Stokes' left. The four stared at the bottle, stiff. It was as if they were frozen in time for that brief moment. Even the downpour around them seemed to pause. The sight was similar to a still portrait. That short time in space was serene, even hypnotic. And then it wasn't. Stokes, realizing what was happening, waved his arms in the air and pivoted in the opposite direction. The men on his right and left sides, out of reflex, did the same. The guy on the far right shuffled farther to the right, almost stumbling in his haste.

"Bomb!" Stokes screamed as he sprinted off.

He and his men were able to create some distance before the bottle erupted into an explosive flash of light. Stokes and the two men directly next to him were flung in the air. The sound from the blast rang out, knocking against the Chevy Blazer. Black ducked behind the SUV just in time, then quickly faced those who were back there with him.

"GO!" he yelled.

The manager was the first to race towards the door. Following him was Tyler, and Toben trailed last, pointing his Smith & Wesson in the direction of Stokes' team. As they did so, Black dashed from behind the vehicle. In his peripheral, he could see Stokes and the two men squirming on the pavement. Directly in front of him was the guy who was furthest to the right—the one who had nearly shot him in the head—standing with his arms raised over his face, a natural reflex to create a barrier between himself and the blast. Dazed and exposed, he didn't see Black rushing towards him. Black grabbed him in a tackle, blitzing him through PVC fencing and under a canopy before slamming him, back first, into the seat of a bumper car. The man's rifle fell to the floor and he leaned forward, attempting to rock back to his feet, but the underside of his chin met with Black's fist. Black delivered a devastating uppercut, snapping the man's head backward and laying him flat in the bumper car, sound asleep. Wasting no time, Black quickly removed the man's sidearm, stuffed it in the back of his own pants, and peered in the direction of Stokes and the other two men. All three were lifting themselves from the concrete with heads turned in the direction of the Intergalactic Food Court entrance.

Black wasn't able to see Toben, the manager, or Tyler from his vantage point, but he knew they needed more time. Taking into account the nerves of the park manager, he calculated it would take him twice as long as it would normally to unlock the door. *They need more time,* he was thinking as he slid to the floor towards the assault rifle his unconscious opponent had dropped during their scuffle. The weapon was a BREN 805. Black was on one knee as he picked the gun up. He used his forearm to wipe the rainwater from his face before pressing the gun's stock against his shoulder, peering through the sights, and targeting Stokes' team, who were moving into shooting positions, eyes on the front door of the food court. Stokes was on bended knee, lifting his pistol. The guy to his right was on his feet, aiming his assault rifle. The guy to his left was still staggering to his feet. The sound of two booms stuffed the air. Black knew the shots came from Toben, so he didn't allow it to interrupt his aim. The canopy provided him cover from the rain. There were no distractions as he flipped the fire mode and pulled the trigger, sending the rifle into a full mag dump. Hot spent shells clacked out onto the floor of the bumper car arena and multiple brazen claps popped ferociously in his ears.

Half of the magazine emptied before Stokes' crew knew what hit them. Most of the rounds struck the man on the far left, the one closest to Black, hitting the back of his vest, legs, and neck. The man's body shielded Stokes before falling on top of him. The other guy was able to drop to the ground unscathed as the remaining bullets zipped past. He shifted on his belly, aiming his gun at Black, and unloaded. Black saw the bright flame from the muzzle flash. He pitched the empty rifle and hustled to his left out of the trajectory of the rounds. The rapid fire was steady. He heard bullets buzz through the air as he dove to his stomach for cover behind a game booth. He heard the crash of .223 Remington ammunition ripping through bumper cars and the game booth. Pieces of stuffed animals, toys, and broken wood floated around him. Debris and drops of rain whisked across his back.

The shooting stopped. Black peeked around what was left of the game booth and saw the man, now on one knee, reaching for a spare magazine for his rifle. Stokes was crawling from under the fallen body of the other guy. *Only two more left.* Black sprinted from behind the booth. He hopped over the short fencing and removed the pistol he had tucked in the back of his pants, aiming at the man with the rifle. The man loaded the rifle and started to aim, but Black had already fired off two rounds. The first round hit the man in his vest, near his chest. The second round caught him in his lower neck, above his collarbone. He dropped his rifle and clutched his neck before tipping over to the pavement. Stokes wobbled to his feet, jumped some fencing, and made a sharp left, turning at the northeast corner of the food court building. Black kicked the rifle away from the body of the man he had just shot. He heard footsteps shuffle behind him and turned to see Toben exiting the building, pistol in hand.

"Where's Stokes?" Toben asked.

Black pointed to the northeast corner of the building.

Toben nodded.

Side by side, they raced after him.

The rain began to pour and electric pressure built in the sky. Lightning flickered through the clouds with thunder clamoring seconds later. They saw Stokes scurrying into a large spaceship-like structure through a front door that mimicked the cargo bay door of a spacecraft. The construction was not complete—there were cones and caution tape all around the area. Half of the building was painted in a shiny pearl white and the other half was an ugly cream base color. Black and Toben dashed inside, guns leveled in front of them. The inside was dry and dark. There were small holes and slits in the structure providing strips and spots of light from the outside. It was quiet with the exception of the rain thumping on the roof and the thunder roaring above. Crates, plywood, drywall, tools, and concrete pillars were scattered about, and the smells of sawdust and paint wafted through the air. There were a few windows, but no interior walls or doors, only the skeletons and frames for them. A spark flashed from the darkness about twelve or fifteen yards away. Black heard the bullet whiz past, cutting between him and Toben. A sonorous boom followed as Black and Toben dropped behind a hefty wooden crate for cover. Broken wood and debris rattled as they pressed their backs against the crate.

"That was too close. He's a good shot," Toben commented.

"He is a former Green Beret," Black replied.

"Please tell me I hit one of you," Stokes voice hovered from the shadows.

"Stokes, why don't you just give up? Your team is down, it's over," Toben said.

There was silence for a moment, only the rain tapping upon the roof. Then a lightning strike filled the space with a brief blue glow. Black glanced around the crate, scanning the area for Stokes' location. It was hard to make out, but he saw two pillars right next to each other with a crack of maybe two inches between them. He figured that was where Stokes was. It made sense. He could shoot while standing and be shielded by the pillars. An easy spot for him to see and hit his target, but difficult for his target to locate and hit him.

"I should've kidnapped your wife and son, Toben," Stokes fumed. "I'd have leverage right now. Argh... this was supposed to be quick and clean. Find Tyler and get him out of the country, but you two had to get in the way. I told her this boy was more trouble than he's worth. When I get out of here, I may put a bullet in his head myself."

"What—who?" Toben shouted, still squatting with back against the crate. "You told who—?"

Another round fired. Wooden fragments from the edge of the crate on Toben's side splintered and bounced in the air. Toben was quiet. His eyes widened. His eyebrows rose. His mouth fell open. Black had seen this look before. *He's shot.*

TWENTY

TOBEN CLOSED HIS eyes tightly, flattened his lips, and leaned forward, gripping his shoulder and slightly rocking back and forth. Black looked over his back and examined the injury. A smiled crossed his face.

"It's a flesh wound. The bullet grazed you," he whispered.

"Feels a lot worse than that," Toben replied in a low tone.

"Trust me. The worst you'll have is a scar," Black whispered, peeping over the crate. "I think I know where he is. I'll need you to distract him."

"How?"

Next to Black was a small pile with hunks of chopped wood. He picked up a piece.

"You two are quiet!" Stokes hollered. "Did I hit one of you?" he followed with a laugh.

Black moved the index finger of the hand he was using to hold the piece of wood to his lips, signaling for Toben to remain quiet. Then he shouted, "You're going to pay for that!"

Stokes chuckled. "So I must have hit Toben," he said. "Is he still with us, Black?"

Black said nothing and continued to gesture for Toben to remain silent.

"Black?" Stokes continued.

Black remained quiet.

"Good. Because I was hoping to save you for last. I'm going to enjoy it. You've been a thorn in my side ever since you stuck your nose into my business."

Black flung the chunk of wood to his left. It came to rest after a few clunks and dings. Stokes fired two rounds at the noise. Then Black picked up another piece of wood and handed it to Toben. Black nodded. Toben nodded back to let him know he understood the plan and hurled the block towards the left again. It knocked and thumped, and two more shots were fired in its direction. Black hustled to the right, swiftly but quietly. He knelt behind a stack of plywood and peered around the corner in the direction of the two pillars. Lightning flashed, illuminating the open room. Black caught a glimpse of Stokes' shadow behind the pillars. *Now I know exactly where you are.*

He kept an eye on him, waiting. The anticipation made the next minute that passed feel like ten. Another noise echoed from the opposite side of the area. Black darted towards the pillars. Stokes was able to fire one round towards the sound before Black was on him. He turned to face Black and attempted to aim the gun, but his hand was stuck between the pillars. Black hit him with a jab and the DIA agent dropped his gun between the pillars and faltered backward. Black skipped forward, planting the sole of his boot on Stokes' chest and rolling him backward, smashing into some tools and buckets. Stokes crawled to his feet with a two-by-four in hand and thrust it into Black's stomach. The force from the blow caused Black to shuffle back a few steps. His gut turned with rage as he glared at Stokes, who swung the piece of lumber at his head. Black ducked and punched him in the ribs with one hand then used the other to punch his stomach, allowing the jab to flow into an uppercut to the chin. Stokes wobbled backward and dropped the piece of wood, clawing at anything that would break his fall. Black continued after him with a fierce sidekick to the chest, sending him crashing through a wall and splashing onto the puddled walkway outside. Black climbed through the break in the wall, stepping outside where the rain once again poured on his head and ran down his face.

Stokes lifted himself to his knees, coughing as the rain slapped the back of his sport coat. Black towered over him from behind.

"It's over, Stokes," he said. "There are only two ways this can go, the easy way or the hard way. You give up and turn yourself in with no fighting, no problems. Or I'll knock you out and drag you in."

Stokes flung water towards Black's face. The water was inches from his face before he waved it away. By that time Stokes was on his feet, hooking Black in a tackle and scurrying him backward. Black planted his feet, sliding to a stop across the wet pavement before delivering a knee to Stokes' jaw, grabbing a fist full of his shirt, and tossing him to the ground. The shirt ripped as Stokes hit the concrete, flat on his back, gasping. Black put him to sleep with a boot to the face.

"I guess some people just like the hard way," he said to himself, sighing.

"Black!" Toben called, "You got him?" Holding his shoulder, he craned through the hole in the wall.

Black nodded and Toben smiled, pumping a victory fist.

The rain eased up and Black gazed into the cloud-filled night sky. Drops of rain hit his face as he exhaled, then smiled. *A theme park and bad weather. Two things I'm not fond of.*

AN HOUR LATER, he was in the main office lounge, enjoying two things he was very fond of—coffee and pastries. His clothes were still a little damp so he had two cups of coffee, figuring it would help him keep warm. He finished up and stepped outside. The rain had stopped completely but it was very wet out. The parking lot was swarming with cop cars, other emergency responder vehicles, and workers. He spotted Toben sitting in the back of an ambulance, watching as an EMR patched a bandage to his shoulder. Black walked over as Toben stood and thanked the EMR.

"How's the shoulder?" Black asked.

"Like you said. It's nothing—just a few stitches," Toben answered, looking over at a police officer who was escorting a handcuffed Tyler. "Hold up," he hollered, waving down the officer and jogging over.

Black followed him.

"Where are you taking him?" Toben asked the officer.

"He'll be going to FBI HQ for questioning. After that I don't know," the officer answered.

Tyler kept his head down but raised his eyes at Toben. The two stared at each other in silence for a moment before Toben sighed.

"Lucky for you, no one was hurt by your direct involvement. You may be able to get off easy if you cooperate," he said.

Tyler lifted his head. His cheeks hollowed and his lips parted.

Toben elevated his hand towards him. "Don't say anything," he said. "This officer is going to take you to the FBI for questioning. Tell them everything. The truth, okay?"

Tyler slowly nodded as Toben's phone rang.

"I have to take this," he said, turning away from the group.

"C'mon. Let's go, kid," the officer said, tugging at Tyler's arm.

"One minute," Tyler requested. "Sir," he called to Black with a crackle in his voice.

Black raised his index finger to the officer, gesturing it was okay.

"Was that man really my father?" Tyler continued. "I want to know. He may know my mom, my family."

Black looked away and took in a breath, carefully considering his words before exhaling. "How many foster parents have you had?"

"Three."

"When they took you in, did they make you feel welcome?"

"Yes."

"Did they make sure you had what you needed?"

"Yeah."

"Did they call you their son?"

Tyler paused for a moment. "Yes," he answered in a low tone, clearing his throat.

"Would you say they loved you?"

Tyler dropped his head and nodded. "Yes…"

"Then they're your parents. That's your family," Black finished.

Tyler looked at him with watering eyes before dropping his head.

"Okay, kid, let's go," the officer said.

Black watched as the officer guided Tyler to a squad car. He kept his eyes on them until Toben walked back over.

"Okay… Just had a conference call with Chapp, Boyar, and Hanten. They've been at the office working all night. They're going home to get some food and rest up to be back in a few hours," he said.

"It'll be early in the morning there," Black commented.

"Yep. But Homeland's work here is done. The FBI will take it from here. I'm so happy this is over."

Black said nothing.

The two made their way over to the Ford Fusion, which was surprisingly unblocked by any vehicles. On the way, they crossed paths with Stokes. His hands were cuffed behind his back and he was flanked on either side by two officers who were carrying him by his arms. His face was filthy and tired, his hair was wet and messy, and his clothes were ripped. He gave Toben a hard stare and Black an even harder glare as he hobbled by.

"I'm still not satisfied," Black said, stopping and turning to Toben. "We're missing something."

"What do you mean?" Toben asked.

"I mean, Stokes didn't seem too interested in helping Tyler."

"Okay. So he's a jerk."

Black sighed, shaking his head. "But why would he even —?" He paused, staring at Stokes and catching a glimpse of an image he had seen before.

One of the officers with Stokes was opening the back door to an unmarked car. Black walked towards them. Toben followed.

"Wait a second!" Black called to the officer.

The officer looked over his shoulder. "Sir," he said.

Black walked past him and stepped in front of Stokes. He moved a shred from Stokes' torn shirt, exposing his chest and an ink tattoo of a symbol familiar to Black.

"Nice tat," Black remarked.

Stokes looked at him and scoffed.

"If that's it, sir, we have a long drive," the officer said, opening the car door and guiding Stokes into the back seat.

"What was that about?" Toben asked.

"I think I know what we're missing."

"What?"

"I'll tell you on the way back, let's go."

THE DRIVE BACK to the airstrip felt quicker than the drive to the theme park. They drove forty-five minutes on I-4 West before taking the exit for Lakeland Linder International Airport.

"Are you sure about that, Black?" Toben asked as they entered the airport.

"Yep," Black answered.

"You sure this isn't just one of your hunches that needs to be fattened up?"

"Positive."

"I have to admit it does make sense… but you know what this means?"

"Yep. Everyone will be at the office early so it shouldn't be an issue."

Toben nodded at the wheel. They stopped outside near the familiar jet, where they met the pilots and an airport employee. The employee took the key for the Ford Fusion from Toben and drove off. Everyone else hustled inside the jet and were in the air twenty minutes later. Black slept most of the flight. When he opened his eyes, the sky was still coated with darkness and the plane was descending towards San Francisco International Airport. Minutes later, the aircraft bumped across the runway. It taxied to a private hangar and parked inside. Black and Toben thanked the pilots and exited the jet, then ducked into a dark-colored sedan. Toben fired up the engine and drove out of the airport and onto the main road. It was a little under an hour before they arrived at the DHS headquarters. It was still dark outside. The grass and parked cars were covered with the morning dew. They eased up to the security gate, where two armed guards waved them through. Toben wheeled the car into the parking garage and found a spot close to the entrance. They entered the lobby and walked towards the elevators, stopping at the receptionist desk, where another armed guard was sitting.

"You're here early, Agent Toben," the guard commented. "Whoa. Looks like you've had a rough night."

"Yeah, it was a doozy," Toben replied. "Has my team made it in yet?"

"Yes, sir. Chapp, Boyar, and the director are all upstairs."

"Okay, thanks. Can you send a couple of your guys up?"

The guard's face wrinkled. "Send them to your office?"

"Just have them find me."

The guard shrugged. "Okay."

Black was the first to the elevator. He pressed the up arrow and the doors immediately split open. He stepped inside with Toben sliding in after him. The elevator traveled up a few floors and thumped open. They walked to the unit's office area. Toben opened the door, entering first. Ashley and Boyar both stood from their desks. The bags under their eyes made it evident that they hadn't gotten much sleep.

"You two look like you've come out of a war zone," Ashley said.

"Where's Hanten?" Toben asked.

"In her office."

Toben nodded, then started catching Ashley and Boyar up to speed. Black didn't hear all that was said because he had already left the room on his way to Hanten's office. Her door was closed, but he opened it and walked in without knocking. She jumped from her desk as he entered. Dark circles had formed around her eyes and her face was puffy, as if she hadn't slept a wink since Black last saw her.

"Mr. Black," she said in a dry tone, "happy to see you made it back. Where's Toben?"

"He's on his way in here," Black answered.

"Have a seat, tell me how everything went."

"I'll stand. We caught Karl Stokes—"

"H—how's the kid?"

Black smiled. "Tyler?"

"Yeah, that's his name, right?"

"Right. He's not as good as he could be."

"What do you mean?"

Black ignored her question. "Remind me again how you know Stokes?"

"Huh?" Hanten winced. "From around the organization."

"You normally assign people from around the organization to work with your team? No. I think you know him more intimately than just 'around the organization'."

Hanten said nothing. Just stared at Black.

"The silver Mercedes-Benz parked in the garage," Black continued, "it's yours, right?"

"Yes, it is."

"On the front was a Quantico graduation decal."

Hanten sighed. "Is this going somewhere?" she said, sitting in her chair.

"I saw that same symbol tattooed on Stokes' chest. We know you're Tyler's mother."

TWENTY-ONE

HANTEN DROPPED HER head. She took in a breath and exhaled before looking up at Black. "You found out?"

"It wasn't too hard after we discovered Stokes was the father," Black said. "It didn't add up. He was the father, but he wasn't too concerned about Tyler. Got me thinking, why would he try to clean up the mess for a kid he gave up for adoption and didn't care about? Then it hit me—the mother. A mother in her right mind would do anything to keep her child safe. Including getting the cold-hearted father to protect the child. Even if he said he wanted to kill the kid."

"What! That bastard… I knew it was a mistake—"

The doorknob for the office door turned and the door swung open. Toben stepped inside, staring at Black and Hanten as the door shut behind him.

"You're just in time, Agent Toben," Black said. "The director here was about to confess to everything. You may continue." The last sentence he directed to Hanten.

She frowned and closed her eyes before sighing and opening them again. "About twenty years ago I was at Quantico training for the FBI. Karl was training in the same class. He was in a special unit of the military that required the training. We were both fairly young and inexperienced in life. We spent a lot of time together and took a liking to one another. One thing led to the next and I ended up pregnant. I was able to hide the pregnancy until we completed the training, but it wasn't good. It was something I knew the Bureau would frown upon—and then there were our families. I came from a home where… it was not okay for us to have kids out of wedlock. Didn't want to disappoint my family, particularly my mom and dad. And Karl came from a household where there wasn't much love. He was always seeking his family's love, so he didn't want to be a disappointment to them. So after I had Tyler, we gave him up for adoption. I didn't want to do it, but we had our futures to consider. I thought about Tyler for years and we even kept tabs on him as he got older. But as time went on, I felt less and less like his mother. I thought he was better off with a family that never gave him up to begin with." She paused and sniffled, wiping the rolling tears from her cheeks. "Then about a week ago I was in a meeting with the Secretary of Homeland Security and staff. It was there I learned Tyler was a person of interest in the New York bombing. They had pictures of him and Petrak's daughter here in San Francisco. I immediately contacted Karl. At first, he wasn't interested, but he didn't know I had evidence tying him and his old team to stolen drug money in Colombia. So I gave Karl an ultimatum: either help our son or I'd expose them. He was on board after that, and obviously his old team was too. But I felt guilty about Tyler and wasn't going to let him go through that alone." Hanten shook her head, weeping. "The plan was simple: Find Tyler and get him out of the country until the whole thing blew over. But he attempted a bombing at Fisherman's Wharf before we could get to him. Then footage of him was bouncing around every government agency. We did our best to block his identity from being discovered. Even tried manipulating his adoption records. Anything to keep law enforcement off his trail. It was supposed to be simple, but it turned out to be a big mess that got away from us. My own team started working the case," she said, flinging her hand in Toben's direction. "Then we tried to frame you for the bombing at Fisherman's Wharf," she said, looking at Black. "It was nothing personal. You were just in the wrong place at the wrong time."

"Or the wrong place at the right time—depending on what side you're on," Black replied.

Hanten wiped the sniffle from her nose. "Yeah..." She nodded. "We didn't realize you would be such a problem at the time. We underestimated you, and now I see that was a mistake."

There were three brisk knocks at the door.

"Come in," Toben called.

Two guards stepped into the office. One of them glanced at everyone in the room before fixing his sights on Toben.

"You wanted to see us, sir?" he said.

Toben held his index finger to the guard. "One second," he said.

"I was just trying to protect my son," Hanten pled, shaking her head in a slow, broken motion. She cupped her mouth and sobbed.

Toben faced the two guards. "Gentlemen, I need you to cuff Director Hanten and take her to a cell downstairs."

Both men stared at him for a moment. After a couple of seconds, they realized he was serious and walked over to Hanten. She stood from her desk and placed her hands behind her back. The guards cuffed her and walked her to the door. She focused on Black as the guards escorted her out of the office. Black and Toben followed and watched as the guards walked her to the elevator and the doors closed behind them. Ashley and Boyar were in the hallway outside their office, watching the entire thing. They looked over at Black and Toben before going back into the office.

Toben released a heavy sigh. "This has been a rough few days," he said.

"Tell me about it," Black agreed.

"I'm going to tell her."

"Excuse me?"

"I'm going to tell Kristi. I'm going to tell her about my affair with Ashley."

Black said nothing.

"Even if she already knows. She deserves to hear it from me," Toben continued, dropping his gaze. "I don't want there to be any secrets between us. It'll only tear my family apart," he concluded, pursing his lips and softly bobbing his head.

Black nodded but remained quiet.

They walked into the office and found Ashley and Boyar standing in the center of the room, conversing. Black found an empty seat near Ashley's desk and sat down, relaxing back with his arms folded. He exhaled and briefly closed his eyes.

"Agents Chapp and Boyar," Toben called. "I know these last few days have been busy and have taken a physical and emotional toll on us all. But I'll need you for another few hours. After that, you can go home and have tomorrow off too."

Ashley shrugged.

Boyar paced towards his desk. "Sounds good to me."

"Good," Toben said, clapping his hands together. "I have to contact the Secretary of Homeland Security about Director Hanten. And breakfast. Somebody order us breakfast."

Black's eyes became heavy. He dozed off as Toben was giving orders and assigning tasks to Ashley and Boyar. Just when the sleep was pulling him under, he was snapped out of it by a thump against the floor, near his foot. He opened one eye to see his travel sack lying there. Ashley was standing over him with a hand on her hip and a smile on her face.

"You sleeping on the job?" she giggled. "He's still a consultant, right?" She addressed the question to Toben.

Toben looked over. "Black, would you like to join the DHS?" he asked, grinning.

Black looked in his direction with tired eyes. "Not a chance," he chuckled.

"Have it your way then. You're fired," Toben joked.

Black slightly shook his head, turning his attention back to Ashley. She continued to smile down at him.

"You left this in my car," she said, pointing to his travel sack. "We're about to order breakfast. What would you like to have?"

"I'll have whatever you're having," Black answered, closing his eyes.

"Okay," he heard Ashley say as he stared into darkness.

The sound of footsteps and voices traveled by him. Back and forth. Slow and fast. He heard it all and knew who was doing the talking or walking based on the sound of their voice or the weight of their steps. His eyes opened at Ashley nudging him. She stood in front of him holding a Styrofoam takeout container, a Styrofoam cup, and a smile.

"Breakfast," she said, placing the container and cup on the desk next to him.

He pulled himself upright in the chair and opened the container. Warm steam rose to his face, bringing with it the aroma of a country-style breakfast. The contents were hash browns, sausages, scrambled eggs, fruit, a biscuit, and a couple of packs of jam. Inside the Styrofoam cup was coffee. He looked over at Ashley, who was sitting at her desk, and gave her a smile of thanks. She returned the smile before opening her own container and turning to face her computer screen. Fifteen minutes later the only thing left of Black's breakfast was a morsel of the biscuit and a few drops of coffee. The three DHS agents were still working away, typing at their computers, talking on the phone, and opening and reading paper documents. Black felt a vibration in his pocket and realized it was the phone he had mostly ignored the past few days. There were a few missed calls and a voice message. He played the message and heard his sister's voice expressing her concern for him and wanting to see if he was okay. After listening to the message, he dropped the phone in his pocket, picked up his travel sack, and walked towards the office door. Toben happened to be walking by him.

"You're leaving, Black?" he asked.

Black lifted his travel sack to eye level. "I'm going to clean up. I thought I saw a restroom in the hall."

"Yep. Out the door, down the hall to your left."

The restroom had a pine scent and the floor and countertop shone. He walked to the paper towel dispenser, grabbed a few towels, and doused them with water and soap. He then entered a stall, stripped, wiped down, changed into some spare clothes from the travel sack, and walked back to the office door and opened it a crack. Toben's voice wafted through. He was explaining to Ashley and Boyar how he wanted to walk through an event timeline. Boyar suggested using the whiteboard located in the back room. Footsteps knocked against the floor and faded in the distance. Black opened the door wider, just in time to see the backs of the three agents as they drifted into the back room and the door closed behind them. He stepped into the office, grabbed his Styrofoam trash, tossed it in the garbage can, and strolled back into the hallway. He figured it was best not to say goodbye. They no longer needed his help, his name was cleared, and they were busy. He rode the elevator down to the main lobby and took the front entrance outside, where he saw the sun rising behind the buildings. Beaming strips of light illuminated the city streets. The moist, cool air breezed over his body as he jogged across the street and walked nearly a quarter of a mile to a bus stop. It took two bus rides and three blocks of walking before he arrived at the sandwich shop where his car was parked. He circled around the Viper, tossing his travel sack in the trunk and easing in behind the steering wheel. The car was just as he had left it. He removed his phone, jabbed at it, and held it to his ear. It rang three times before Olivia's voice jumped on the line.

"Hi, I've been trying to reach you," she said.

"I know. That's why I'm calling you," Black said.

"Are you okay?"

"Yeah. Why?"

"I flew to New York for a job after I got off the phone with you the other day. We were running a security detail while repairs were being made on account of that bombing out there. When I got back to Chicago, I heard there was another bombing attempt at Fisherman's Wharf, where you were. And then another bombing attempt at Fantastic Galaxy. Did you hear about them?"

"Yeah, I might've heard something in passing."

"Anyhow, I knew you were at Fisherman's Wharf and wanted to check on you."

"As you can see, I'm fine. Now how about you?"

"Things are going good. I think I might stay with this company for a little while."

Black said nothing.

"Hey, did you go see Mom and Dad?" Olivia continued.

"Not yet."

"That's what you said like five days ago. What have you been doing?"

"Sightseeing."

"Look… I know they're not our biolog—"

"I really want to go see them," Black interrupted.

"Really?"

"Yes, really. I'm not sure when I'll have a chance to see them next—so I'm going to go."

"Okay… well, good," she said. "I have to go, but let's try to do a better job of staying in touch, okay?"

Black nodded at the phone. "Yes, I'd really like that."

"Bye, big bro. Talk to you soon."

"Bye."

The call ended and Black dropped the phone on the passenger seat, silently looking out his windshield for a moment. He reflected on the last few days and how his life, and his sister's, could have turned out much differently. He removed the parking permit from his dashboard and placed it in the passenger seat with his phone. Starting up the car, he rolled onto the empty street, heading east for a bit. Then he turned south on US-101. It was a little over a two-hour drive which took him through the mountains and forestland before he arrived at a town near Del Monte Forest. He cruised through the small downtown and drove a couple more miles until he reached a large gated home. The gate was open and a truck hauling a riding lawn mower and other yard tools was pulling into the driveway. Black turned into the driveway behind the truck and approached the house, a two-story red brick home with white trimming. It had a three-car garage and sat on a large plot of land with thick green grass. The yard was encompassed by thick but sightly brush with a couple of small trees growing in the front. He followed the truck around the circular driveway. The truck stopped at the bottom arc of the circle closest to the gate entrance, while Black parked directly in front of the main door. He looked through the passenger side window and watched as an older couple ambled down the steps. The woman wore loose white pants and a white shirt covered by a grey button-up heather top. The colors helped accentuate her beautiful brown skin. The man behind her had the same skin complexion. He was clothed with a plaid shirt tucked into a pair of navy-colored slacks. As they both stared at Black's car, some wrinkles around their eyebrows joined the permanent wrinkles already on their faces. Black stepped out of the car and rested his arms on top of the roof, lowering his chin to his hands and smiling widely at them. The woman stepped closer, her mouth gaping. She looked back at the man, whose mouth had fallen open also. Her eyes brightened and a smile grew on her face as if she had come to a realization. Black continued to smile. He knew he hadn't seen them in a while. He knew they weren't his biological parents. He knew he wouldn't stay long. But he didn't care about any of that, because he knew he was looking at his mom and dad.

MORE ORLANDO BLACK

YOUR NEXT EXCITING READ IS A PAGE TURN AWAY!

If you enjoyed Bayside Boom, read on for a preview of the next action-packed, thrilling Orlando Black novel by Alex Cage.

BET ON BLACK

BOOK PREVIEW

CHAPTER
ONE

THERE I STOOD, in the corner of a square ring, under the night sky, in the middle of a valley, and in the middle of another fine mess. A crowd of nearly a hundred surrounded the ring. All yelling and cheering. In the opposite corner stood a muscular man wearing a mohawk and red shorts. Wearing MMA gloves, he pounded his hairy chest before gritting his teeth and narrowing his sights on me. Another man, wearing dark pants and a white shirt, stood at the center of the ring.

The man in the white shirt pointed at me. "Ready, black?" he said. Not because of my name or my skin complexion, but because I wore black trousers and a black tank top.

I nodded.

He then pointed to the guy in the shorts. "Ready, red?"

The hairy-chested man nodded.

"Fight!" the guy at the center of the ring shouted before stepping back.

A bell dinged, and I walked toward the ring's center while the guy in the red shorts raced toward me with his fist drawn back. He swung at my jaw. I bobbed under the punch, then quickly pivoted to face his back with my hands at guard. My opponent spun toward me while hurling a back fist at my head. I ducked beneath the attack and shuffled backward. The crowd's cheers grew louder.

The man's nostrils flared and his teeth gritted as he charged. He threw a kick, but I parried it. As I back-stepped, my attacker shuffled toward me and continued his assault with the combination I was waiting on. He jabbed at me with his left. I parried it. Then his right. I slipped inside the punch, and just as I expected, the man hesitated. In that split second of hesitation, I raised my left arm and exposed my ribcage. My opponent took the bait and launched a kick. Before he could connect, I darted to him and delivered a hard elbow to the side of his face. The man stumbled back and doubled over. I closed the gap between us and kneed his face. As he groaned and flopped backward, I skipped-step toward him and planted my heel into his solar plexus. He landed on the ropes, then flipped over and out of the ring. I followed the referee to the ring's edge and saw my opponent sprawled on the floor.

The referee ducked between the ropes, then knelt and lifted the man's head from the ground before saying something to him and moving the fingers of his free hand in the fighter's face. After a few seconds, the ref stood, crossed his arms, then slung them apart. The bell dinged, and the referee crawled back into the ring and raised my arm. Cheers and applause came from the crowd as I snatched my arm away from the ref and turned toward my corner. The person I was looking for wasn't there, so I scanned the other three corners, but still couldn't find him.

As I hopped from the ring, two men hoisted the guy in the red shorts to his feet. I walked past and threaded through the crowd with my head on a swivel, searching for the missing DEA agent. The pats on my back and shouts from the crowd followed me all the way to a passageway for the locker room. I walked through the passage alone and to a dirt field illuminated by large construction flood lights. A pair of mobile homes flanked me on either side. A third home sat on the far end with a flagpole out front. That was where the lockers were. As I made my way across the field toward it, a guard armed with an MP5 approached me.

"Good fight, Ghost," he said with a smile. "You're so quick, the fight didn't even last that long. I bet on you, so I made some money tonight."

"That's great," I said. "The guy I was with earlier, have you seen 'em?"

The guard pursed his lips and shook his head. "Not since he was with you."

"Alright. Thanks," I said before continuing toward the portable home.

"See you around, champ," the guard said to my back.

The portable home was empty inside. I hustled to the locker room, opened my locker, then changed into my jeans and t-shirt. Before slipping into my boots, I made sure my dual knife holsters were secure around my ankles. Once fully dressed, I checked my phone, but found no missed calls or messages. I exited the portable and walked back to the ring area, where the crowd roared in encouragement for an ongoing match. Weaving through the mob, I kept an eye out for my missing DEA agent, but there was still no sign of him. I continued through the crowd, then into a passageway which led out of the valley.

As I exited the passageway, two men in black suits armed with MP5s stood on either side of the entrance. One of them nodded at me as I dodged a line of people and walked onto an enormous field full of parked cars. And not just any cars. Bentleys, Ferraris, and Lamborghinis were all present, but the car I was looking for wasn't as extravagant. It was a dented, silver Ford Focus in need of new tires and a new paint job. When I located the car, I peeked through the window hoping to find the DEA agent who also happened to be my chauffeur but was disappointed when he wasn't there and wondered how I'd get back to my motel room since he had the car's key.

At that thought, I heard a fuss coming from the passageway entrance. When I glanced over my shoulder, I saw the missing agent exiting, but he wasn't alone. Two men trailed behind him. Both were fit, both had ivory skin, both wore a suit with no tie, but one had spiky blond hair while the other had short brown hair. A short man with a gray suit and a ponytail followed close behind them, carrying a brief-case. While keeping my eyes on the group of men, I ducked and circled the Ford's trunk to the passenger side. They all entered a black Porsche Cayenne before cruising out of the parking area and up the dirt road. I removed a knife from my ankle holster, then raced to the front driver's side door of the Focus. With my face turned from the door, I smashed the butt of the knife into the window. The glass shattered, and I used my knife to rake away the loose shards before reaching my arm through and unlocking the door. Using the knife, I poked the steering column and pried it open, then spend the next few minutes relearning how to hot wire a car. When I connected the correct wires, the Focus revved to life. I swept the glass from the seat and slid in behind the wheel. I backed from the parking area, flicked on the headlights, then sped down the road. The road was dim and the Cayenne was nowhere in sight. Not a glint from a taillight, not even a silhouette of the vehicle, just darkness.

Lost them. Not good.

After a minute of driving, I approached two SUVs parked perpendicular on either side of the road. Neither one was the Cayenne. At each SUV, there was the shadow of a man holding a gun. I slowed down and one of them recognized me and nodded. After returning the nod, I rode past. I monitored them in my rear-view mirror until they completely disap-peared into the darkness of the night. The Focus droned up the rough, dirt road for another twenty minutes before smooth pavement caressed its tires. I removed my phone, flipped it open, pressed at it, and held it to my ear. It rang and rang, but no one answered.

"Another missing agent," I muttered to myself. "Not good."

I drove another hour before trying the number again. And like before, no answer.

Where are you?

After stopping for gas and driving another forty minutes, I arrived at my motel, but I didn't pull into the parking lot because something caught my attention. The Porsche Cayenne sat parked a few spaces from my room. I made a note of the license plate number, then continued a quarter of a mile up the road before turning into a local diner's parking lot. Inside the diner, the smell of burgers and fries and customer chit chat filled the space, and as I made my way to the counter eyes from unknown faces followed me. I grabbed a napkin and a to-go menu off the countertop before hearing a voice.

"Hi," the voice said.

I turned to see a slim woman with silky dirty-blonde hair approaching me.

She smiled. "Gonna have dinner with us, Mr. White?"

It took me a split second to process everything before saying, "I sure am, but I'm going to take it to go."

"Ahh, you're not staying here with me tonight?"

"Nope. I'm sorry," I said with a smile.

She smiled again. "So, what are you having?"

"I'll have what I had last night."

"Grilled chicken, brown rice, and steamed broccoli, right?"

"You remembered," I said with my eyebrows raised.

"Of course. Most people around here don't eat like that. I'll get this in for you," she said as she pivoted away from me.

"Thanks—hey."

The waitress turned to face me.

"Do you have a pen?" I asked.

"Sure. Plenty of 'em," she said while handing me a pen from her apron pocket.

"Thanks."

She smiled, then made her way toward the kitchen.

On the napkin I wrote, *After the fight, Vargas left with Long, Snyder, and a short man with a ponytail. Black Porsche Cayenne LPN MXC-F144*, then finished with, *It's parked in front of my motel room*. At the top, I wrote the date and time, then used the menu to create an envelope before placing the napkin inside and folding it shut. I exited the diner, crossed the street, and walked twenty yards in the motel's direction before reaching a slightly worn mail drop box. I placed the folded menu inside, then made my way back to the diner where I sat at the counter for five minutes before the waitress brought me my food.

"Here you go," she said while placing my bag and ticket on the table.

The bill was eighteen dollars. I gave her thirty.

"That's all yours," I said.

"Thanks. Will I see you for dinner tomorrow?"

"Possibly. And maybe the next few days after."

"Well, I'll be here tomorrow night, but the next few nights after, I'll be working late at the mall. There's a large shipment coming in, and we're rearranging the store. Just in case you come and I'm not here."

"I'll keep that in mind," I said on my way to the door.

"See you around, Anthony."

I entered the Focus and placed my food on the passenger seat and removed my flip phone. I tried the number I called earlier and again got no answer.

Something's off.

I backed the car out and veered onto the road toward the motel. The Cayenne was no longer there. I parked, grabbed my food, then walked to my motel room. Before opening the door, I placed my ear to it and listened, but heard nothing. Multiple scenarios played in my mind. They could've really left, or were lurking around waiting to ambush me, but for what? I was sure they didn't want to physically harm me, so I unlocked my door and opened it. And when I saw inside, suddenly I wasn't so sure anymore.

THANK YOU FOR READING

I have a favor to ask. If you have a moment, I would really appreciate it if you could leave a short review on the page where you purchased this book. I'm thankful for you sharing your feedback about this book. It really helps new readers find this series.

Sign up for notifications of new books by Alex Cage and exclusive giveaways

www.AlexCage.com/signup

ALSO BY ALEX CAGE

More books by Alex Cage. Have you read them all? Grab your next adventure today!

Orlando Black Series

Carolina Dance

Bayside Boom

Family Famous (Novella)

Bet on Black

Leroy Silver Series

Contracts & Bullets

Aloha & Bullets

Politics Thieves & Bullets

Get the latest releases and exclusive giveaways, sign up to the Alex Cage Reader List.

www.AlexCage.com/signup

JOIN THE READER'S LIST

Get the latest releases and exclusive giveaways - sign up to the Alex Cage Reader List:

www.AlexCage.com/signup

ABOUT THE AUTHOR

Alex Cage is a thriller author and passionate wordsmith who loves to blend his fascination with martial arts and travel with high-octane action and explosive adventures. He enjoys nothing more than entertaining his readers with death-defying missions, larger-than-life characters, and suspenseful stories that always find a way to keep you on your toes.

As the author of nearly a dozen titles, including the Orlando Black series and the Leroy Silver series, Alex combines his obsession for thrillers with a sprinkling of fantasy and sci-fi, so that readers will always find something to capture their imagination. He currently resides in North Carolina. When not writing his next novel, you can find him reading and practicing martial arts.

Find out more about Alex Cage (and get a free read):

www.alexcage.com
connect@alexcage.com

ALEX CAGE
CLEAN FAST-PACED ACTION THRILLERS

www.ingramcontent.com/pod-product-compliance
Lightning Source LLC
Chambersburg PA
CBHW032112180726

48284CB00002B/546